T0078142

Sleep Sweet

C.R. IMBERY

authorHOUSE®

AuthorHouse™
1663 Liberty Drive
Bloomington, IN 47403
www.authorhouse.com
Phone: 1 (800) 839-8640

Published by AuthorHouse   11/24/2015

ISBN: 978-1-5049-6323-7 (sc)
ISBN: 978-1-5049-6322-0 (e)

Library of Congress Control Number: 2015919427

Print information available on the last page.

Prologue

$\mathcal{D}$ominic Montgomery stood off to the side, close enough to the road to make a quick getaway, as the crowd amassed around their beloved's eternal resting place. He had been to his fair share of funerals, but this one, this one was harder than any he'd ever experienced before. Too young and innocent to be gone so soon. Then again, wasn't that what lay under this cold frozen ground? A life not lived and a road not traveled.

The priest wore a purple robe that broke up the monotony of black surrounding him. He sprinkled holy water around the grave and on the rosewood coffin, his prayer bellowing over the rain.

"O God, by Your mercy, rest is given to the souls of the faithful, to bless this grave. Appoint Your holy angels to guard it and set free from all the chains of sin and the soul..."

The priest went on as mourners choked back their sobs.

"Amen," Dominic muttered, looking down at the frozen grass that crunched beneath his feet and kicking the blocks of ice away in aggravation.

The process gave life, or lack thereof, a finality that made Dominic shiver. It made him think of his own death someday. Should he be buried and eventually forgotten? Or be cremated and scattered among the places he use to roam and love, finding a resting place with the wind? The thought of being put in a box and left behind didn't sit well with him. It was the circle of life that ultimately led to the unknown. That was how it was. He didn't question the process. He would put on a brave face and go forth contentedly, wherever life might take him.

A shiver ran through him. The cold was starting to seep into his skin. He glanced down at his shaking hands and noticed the imprint of the ring that once laid claim to his heart but was now gone, like ashes in the wind. He gripped the silver necklace under his coat. Today it didn't hold the ardent luster it once had, and the thoughts he struggled to keep at bay were once again pushed back so that he could focus on the life he was there to remember.

He resumed observing the funeral proceedings. A wind picked up, and the aroma of lilies drifted on the breeze, reminding him of Eden. The garden was cold and barren now, but the blossom would soon be as luscious as it once was in life. Dominic closed his eyes and breathed deeply. A smile spread across his face at the thought of it. Yes, when Eden returned to normal, everything would resume. The sensation that swept through him brought him to tears. It would take time for the wounds to heal, but everything would be okay. It had to be.

Before Dominic knew what was happening, his fingers gripped the steering wheel. He wasn't aware he had even entered the car. Sometimes, it felt as if he was standing in a room filled with fog, his fingers searching the walls for the door, but he could never find the handle to escape.

The car started, and Dominic drove. His inner autopilot clicked on, and before he knew it, he had arrived at his destination. What frightened Dominic most about death was what it meant—loneliness. If there was one thing that kept him awake at night, it was the fear of loneliness. It was a fear that had reared its ugly head frequently in the past few months. Now was the time to face the loneliness.

Dominic walked back into the hospital, his home for the past five months. Nurses milled about, watching him as he made his way down the hall. Caretakers cleared inhabited rooms of the remnants of their last patients and readied them for other unfortunate souls.

"Hello, Dominic," Mary, the day nurse, said. "They're down at the NICU."

"Thank you," he said solemnly.

"I'm sorry for your loss," she said, lightly squeezing his forearm.

A few nurses glanced at him, the pity unmistakable in their eyes, and today he wondered what they thought of him. Their looks spoke volumes. What was he still doing here? Why was he putting himself through this nightmare? Was he crazy? The same questions he posed to himself when he sat in the hospital room alone with only his thoughts. Even though he wanted to say yes, he knew he wasn't crazy, just hopeful.

To go from a funeral to a hospital room that was completely quiet except for the machines that were helping to keep the human body alive, reflected that exact loneliness that Dominic feared most. There was no room for such thoughts. He had to be upbeat, strong and positive. Soon, this would be a distant memory, and they'd laugh at his fears, having been reassured that he'd never be alone ever again.

Standing in the doorway, Dominic listened to the sounds of the heart monitor and ventilator. The room was scented by roses, carnations, and lilies. Lilies should be reserved for funerals, but they were a favorite. Even with the strong scent of the flowers, that distinct odor of a hospital room permeated the air, and he hated it. He wanted it to be a comfortable atmosphere, one that resembled home and familiar surroundings. In actuality, he knew he'd never be able to make it feel like anything other than a sterile room. He was doing everything he could, but it never felt like enough. Nothing was ever enough.

This was the foggy room that he couldn't escape. Wiping the previous hours of grief and pain from his face, he put on a reassuring smile, one he hoped would strengthen his resolve. Then maybe, just maybe, those blue eyes would open to the world.

"Hey. Sorry I was gone so long. Miss me?" He walked into the room, closing the door behind him, trying to keep the loneliness at bay.

Chapter One

The gurney felt cold and sterile, exactly the way Caleb Montgomery thought a surgical table would feel under his bare skin, but that was not what scared him. It was the deafening sound echoing throughout the room that made him tremble in terror. The rhythmic beep of the heart monitor had suddenly died to a flat line, while all alone, Caleb lay helpless in his own darkness.

EEEEEEEEEEEEEEEEEEEEEEEEEEEEEEEEEEEEEEEEEEEE EEEE!

The shrill scream of the alarm clock finally jolted Caleb's mind and body into the present and far away from his death dream. Clammy sweat slicked across his body, making his pale skin glisten in the morning sunshine that crept through the blinds. Caleb put his hand over his heart and exhaled with relief. After taking in his normal surroundings, he quieted the alarm clock and listened—silence.

That was until Arnold, his energetic three-legged Labrador, bounded into the room and leaped on the bed as if he owned it. Arnie licked Caleb's face leaving granules of dry dog food all over his cheek.

"Arnie! Do you need to kiss me after you eat?" Arnie sat back, contemplating the question, and barked in response. "All right, all right, get it over with before I wash my face." Caleb's playful companion barked once more in excitement, slobber and foul morning breath doing their best to choke the life from his owner. "Go get Mr. Puff and we'll go for a walk," Caleb laughed, playfully pushing Arnie away. In his excitement, Arnie's tail came to life, whisking back and forth as he jumped from the bed and smacking his companion across the face. Caleb, wide awake now, saw the room spin before his eyes.

Wiping the four hours of sleep from his eyes, Caleb willed his mind out of bed, but his body resisted. Most mornings felt like a chore. What had once been the easy task of starting his day now required art and ritual. He began by rubbing his legs to wake them up. The cold hardwood floor that greeted him was enough to spring him to life. Slowly, he put weight on his legs and carefully hobbled his way into the bathroom onto the safety of his yellow smiley face rug—a housewarming gift from his brother. He smirked at it, remembering he had once thought the hideous thing would never reside in his house, but when he'd put it down, he'd never picked it up. Now he couldn't call his house a home without it.

In the mirror, he came face-to-face with the man known as Caleb and his smile faded instantly. Looking in the mirror every day was enough to make him question who it was staring back at him. He had realized in the past few months that he never looked the same in the mornings as he did when he went to bed. Every day, he saw a few more wrinkles, his blue eyes not as luminous. He even believed his 6'3" frame had shrunk, but until he was on Arnie's level, he wouldn't worry.

Recently, his body had undergone a total transformation. Looking at all the photographs displayed in his house, it was hard to believe they depicted Caleb and not a stranger. Brown hair had started to thin and gray. Skin, once kissed by the sun, was now pale, and the lean, two-hundred-ten-pound body that had helped him become a cross country state champion had shrunk to one-hundred-sixty pounds. He supposed all that shouldn't matter. He still possessed a sound mind and his fingers still flowed gracefully along the eighty-eight black-and-white keys of the piano, his livelihood, but sometimes it just wasn't enough to keep him going.

Behind the mirror, which held no lies about his failing health, sat the bottles that were meant to help him. He opened the cabinet and stared at them. He had come to do this every morning. Another routine was embedded into his mind, and he couldn't go through his day without starting it off with his unnatural ritual. He grabbed the Tetrabenazine and poured the remaining pills into the palm of his hand.

"So what will it be today?" he asked his reflection in the mirror.

The pills felt heavy, like the weight of the world resting in his palm, and if he just swallowed, everything would be fine. The world would end peacefully, in a deep slumber. He filled a glass with water and held it in his right hand which shook ever so slightly. Could he do it? He wondered, contemplating how he had come to this peculiar thought process in the first place.

Every day it was the same. Empty the bottle into the palm of his hand, fill a glass with water, stare at his unfamiliar reflection, wondering if today would be the day everything became too much and Caleb swallowed. He knew why he would do it. It wasn't a cry for help. It was justice. People wouldn't understand, but they didn't need to. The choice was Caleb's and it was between him and God. God understood. It was He who beckoned Caleb forth. The only choice left: take the short or the long route to peace.

As he lifted his hand, it jerked in a sudden motion that disturbed some of the pills. Taking no notice, he continued to goad his reflection into making a decision. Everyone had the opportunity to opt out. Today just wasn't his day. He concentrated, slowly turning his quaking palm sideways, spilling the pills into the sink. He expelled a breath he wasn't aware he'd been holding and leaned against the sink, his forehead on the mirror.

"Thank you," he whispered.

Arnie trotted into the bathroom and jumped on the toilet next to the sink. Sniffing its contents, he tilted his head at Caleb and barked. Arnie wasn't stupid. Every time he did this Caleb understood his disapproval, and perhaps that was why he always dumped the pills.

He grabbed the glass of water and downed it in seconds. The remaining pills were scooped up and now safely in their bottle behind the mirror, but not before taking one as prescribed.

"You shouldn't come in here when I'm going through my routine. I don't want you to see me if…you know…something should happen." He rubbed Arnie behind the ears, the dog's second favorite spot behind the patented belly rub. Arnie tentatively licked Caleb's arm and picked up Mr. Puff, his purple dragon, with a gentle grasp of his mouth.

A look of knowing passed between them before Arnie jumped off the toilet and trotted out of the room. Caleb took one last look in the mirror and turned away, leaving the image of his sickness behind him.

The wind was brisk and the morning sun blinding as Caleb walked along his man-made beach on Lake Geneva spanning the five acres of landscaped property. He always enjoyed seeing his footsteps in the sand, the feel of the grain under his feet and between his toes, like he was a settler proclaiming the land as his own.

He held Mr. Puff while lofting a tennis ball into the lake for Arnie to fetch. The water was autumn-chilled and void of ripples, except for Arnie's fervid attempt to get his tennis ball and a few early risers fishing in the middle of the lake. Caleb had never become a fan of fishing, but he loved the water. He needed to be near it.

A small pile of rocks had washed up on the beach, and he picked up a few to skip on the lake. In his peripheral vision, he saw Arnie padding down the beach toward him, ready for the next fetch of the tennis ball. Normally, he would run down the beach with Arnie in an attempt to maintain his endurance, but it was becoming increasingly difficult as of late. His breathing became labored and his body uncooperative, stability a thing of the past. Arnie's collar clinked as he raced to his owner who absently reached for the tennis ball.

"What the hell?" Caleb cried, throwing his hands in the air and dropping the dead fish Arnie was carrying instead of the tennis ball. "Arnie, that's not your ball!" he exclaimed, but Arnie didn't care. Tongue lolling around his mouth, Arnie wagged his tail, tasting the mixture of lake water and decaying fish. Caleb scanned the water for the fuzzy yellow ball now drifting in the opposite direction and out of reach for Arnie to retrieve safely. "There goes another one," he sighed. "Alright, let's go in. I have to get into the city," he said just as his head erupted in massive pain. His hands flew to his pounding temple, pressing against his ears to drown out the noise, but as always, to no avail. A buzzing sound infiltrated his mind, making it annoyingly difficult to function, but beyond the buzzing he could hear their voices again, bits of conversation that always left him confused.

"Why?"

"We have time. There's no need for a hasty decision."

"It's been too long."

"Something could change. Be positive."

"Do you not see what I see? How can I be positive when nothing has changed?"

"Give it till term. Don't you want to –"

"Don't try and tell me what I want. I pray every day, but these are not the instructions left to us."

"You're being too literal. Another life is at stake."

"It's viable now. We shouldn't prolong this. I'm trying to be merciful."

"It's not your call."

"Please, let's not fight. Not here."

"Look, I want things to change just as much as you, but the outlook isn't good. I only want there to be peace."

"Then we agree on one thing."

Chapter Two

Too many decisions. That was the problem. Lately, Dominic had too many decisions on his plate, and now another was heaped on top. The answer seemed easy, right in front of him, like anything obvious was, but he didn't want to make the wrong choice. There had been a period when his most important decisions caused heartbreak, but he couldn't turn his back on family. Even though he was positive he had made the right choice, he couldn't help but wonder.

Staring at both colors splattered on the wall, it was now or never. Green. He was going with green. Yellow was ugly. He had picked both colors knowing he'd ultimately choose green. Yellow was one of his least favorite colors. Green was perfect, and before he could change his mind entirely, he picked up a roller and jumped into the task at hand. Painting wasn't his strong suit. Then again, he didn't have many strong suits. His necklace was a reminder of one of his many failures.

After his conversation with the family the night before, there was no way he could put it off any longer. The room needed to be painted, furniture picked out, supplies bought, and arrangements made. His predicament was one very few could imagine, but that was life. It threw you a curve whenever things were going great. One minute, you're basking in the sun, and the next, you're being thrashed against the rocks. This was one of those thrashing moments that had lasted for months. If only he could get the sun to peek back over the clouds again. Oh, the jubilation he would feel, the ease with which life would resume. Perhaps a smile wouldn't be so hard to muster.

Painting was therapeutic, giving him a much deserved break. The job would be horrid, but his mind would be a little less cluttered. To have a clear mind again...Hell, what did that feel like? He couldn't remember the last time he wasn't plagued with doubts, fears, or life-changing decisions. He supposed that was what the elderly called being a grownup, a position he didn't take to early on, but at a certain point every man is forced into it.

The doorbell rang, slicing into his thoughts. It was a welcome reprieve from his laborious task and the ulcer expanding in his stomach.

"Hello." He welcomed the mailman who was holding a box and envelopes.

"Hi, package couldn't fix into the box. Have a nice day!" the mailman replied cheerfully before heading back to his van.

"You too," Dominic murmured, closing the door to riffle through the mail. A thick envelope stuck out among the rest. A law firm's many partner names scrolled across the top, giving reason for the girth of the envelope. His name was on it. He couldn't imagine why he was getting legal documents— at least that's what he told himself. Still, in the back of his mind he had been waiting for them. He was surprised they had taken this long.

Dominic leaned his head against the back of the couch and stared into the questioning eyes of his companion. "I feel bad leaving you like this all the time," Dominic said. Suddenly, everything had become real, and he couldn't manage to quiet the tears. Painting had been forgotten along with everything except the troubles that plagued him. His own hands, barely recognizable, covered his face, hiding the despair and anguish from the quiet onlooker in the room, but it was obvious to both of them that neither could hide the sorrow or grief roiling in their minds.

This was not the way to handle the situation he faced. "I never imagined it happening this way, you know?" he said trying to smile. There were several attempts to sound reassuring, but the quiver in Dominic's voice and the redness of his eyes did nothing to calm their nerves.

Dominic glanced down, and hastily away, from the paperwork spread out on the coffee table. He knew what all of it meant but never imagined it ever coming to this point. Dominic looked at his coffee mug, cold from sitting for the past hour. He had stared long at the paperwork, going through every last bit to avoid the eventual outcome.

I do. I do. I do. I do. The words replayed in his head over and over until he hated the promise they held.

People were going to blame him for giving up so easily, throwing it all away. The fireplace crackled, making Dominic contemplate tossing all into the flame, losing any trace of responsibility for their crumbling union. Defeat wasn't something he liked to admit. He was aggressive and always got what he wanted, but he needed to figure this out, give it time. The one thing he was in short supply of—time. She would call, leaving subtle reminders that things needed to be finalized so they could move on. They were the only ones that knew about the paperwork. He wasn't going to confide in his family or friends, and since he was keeping it all a secret, he was pushing the limit, waiting for a miracle.

He tried not to feel guilty, but he was heartsick. So much had happened so quickly that all was a blur. "Would you blame me?" he asked, looking over at the corner of the room where Dominic's current roommate silently sat, watching as Dominic fought between judgment, heartache, and responsibility. "Do you think, with time, I could forget?" Still nothing. If Dominic had learned anything in life it was that people could bury the most painful memories, if given enough time and distraction.

The pen was in hand and the signature tabs in sight, leading him to what he considered his biggest failure to date. Without looking, he signed and shoved the papers back in their envelope. Again, he yearned for peace, but in the wake of everything that was happening and the decisions that weighed on his conscience, Dominic had strayed away from the peaceful path. These past few months had been the worst of his life, and in his heart, he knew it wasn't going to get any better. He wasn't entirely responsible, but he was haunted by what he could have done to make things better. Could he have prevented any of this? Unfortunately, he was confronted with a resounding no.

He needed some air. Going for the door, he grabbed his keys and patted his leg not needing to give instruction.

⁓

Dominic showed up at her apartment with his dog in tow. He hadn't expected to go there. He anticipated he'd have to see her eventually, but now he wasn't sure he could hand the papers to her. They represented failure. Failure to work things out, to even try to make the life they had imagined pan out. Failure was never an option, but Dominic had to make a choice between the two people he loved most in the world. Either way, someone would be left behind, but he chose the one in essence, he could live with. Unfortunately, it was more difficult than that.

He tentatively knocked on the door, almost hoping she wouldn't answer. "Am I being stupid?" he asked his four-legged friend. "Yeah, I'm confused too." He lifted his hand to knock a second time but put it back down. What was he doing? He could have simply retained a lawyer and had him do the exchange. There was no point being there. Seeing her would hurt too much. He didn't want to compound the grief he was feeling, but it's what she wanted, and for once, he was going to give it to her.

"Let's go play. You need some exercise. You're getting fat." The dog beside him barked making Dominic laugh. "I'm just playing with ya, buddy." He ruffled his pet's hair, tugging on the leash to get them going. He was halfway to the elevator when he heard the creak of the door open behind him.

"Dominic," she called, poking her head just barely out into the hallway, making it difficult to be entirely sure it was her, but he knew the voice. It was a voice he had awakened to many times. It was a voice that always made his heart skip a beat and put a smile on his face. Only this time, it was a voice that pierced his heart like a dagger.

He spun around, a fake smile plastered on his face to hide from her the truth—that his world was falling apart.

"Hey, Ashley." He walked back toward her but stood to the side, afraid to see what she was hiding behind the door. Maybe it was another man. Dominic scowled, thinking he'd rip the guy's heart out. Ashley was a married woman, at least for the time being.

He shifted from foot to foot trying to do what he'd come there to do; yet when he looked at her face, all he could remember were the good times that outweighed the bad. They shouldn't have come to this place in their lives. She looked as he remembered. Her blonde hair was longer, but her eyes and her face were unchanged. Her eyes were green, but they didn't sparkle like they use to when she saw him, and he felt sad that the happiness they had once brought each other was gone.

"I just wanted to stop by to give you these." He pulled the envelope out from his back pocket. Staring down at it for a moment, their wedding day flashed through his mind. Those were happier times. Now, he stood before her with their divorce papers, the dissolution of a marriage; the dissolution of their love. But he still loved her. It just wasn't reciprocated like before.

"Oh," she held out her hand to take the envelope. "You could have mailed them, but thanks. I'll give them to my lawyer."

He pulled the envelope back. "That simple is it?" his voice turned hard. How easily she was willing to throw away five years of their life together. It made him wonder how he had fallen for someone so cold.

"Look, I know this is -" Ashley began to explain.

"Hard? Maybe for me, but you don't seem to give a damn." He wanted to shove the papers at her, to turn around and run away never to set eyes on her again. He searched her eyes for any semblance of a spark, some feeling that he could pounce on and talk some sense into her. They weren't finished. They just needed to start a new chapter.

"Don't be like that. You know this wasn't easy, and it sure as hell didn't just suddenly happen. I'm not the only one to blame," she countered.

The dog whined, seeing the conversation wasn't going smoothly. He left Dominic's side and advanced toward Ashley's door, making her take a step back. Dominic tugged the leash seeing how uneasy she was, but the pup would not be deterred. He stuck his head in the doorway making Ashley yelp as his cold nose touched her legs.

"He can't be in here." She anxiously pushed Arnie away with her foot trying to close the door on him, but he was relentless.

"He's just getting to know you, Ashley. He's harmless." Dominic pulled his leash. "Come on, Arnie."

"Dominic," she yelled.

Dominic was startled by her demeanor. She was never afraid of dogs before. Why all of a sudden would she care if Arnie smelled her? He was a good dog. Arnie pushed against the door with his front paw, making Ashley step back in retreat. The door flew back, and with it, Arnie crammed into the room dragging Dominic.

"Are you kidding me, Arnie?" Dominic growled.

When Dominic walked through the threshold, he was hit with the smell of cinnamon. The apartment looked just like the one they had shared, the furniture arranged just so, the same artwork on the walls. The only thing missing—them. There were no pictures of them together, just her family and friends. Dominic couldn't help but look around to see what she had been hiding, but nothing seemed out of place. At least, no rendezvous was taking place.

The only odd thing about the room was Ashley standing with her back to him and Arnie sitting diligently by her feet. Her shoulders were hunched, and he thought he heard a muffled cry, making him feel all the worse for showing up with no notice.

"Why're you being so silly?" he asked, directing his soothing voice and question to Arnie. "See, Ashley, he's harmless. What's the problem?" She didn't turn or answer him. Maybe things had changed. "I'm going to put these on your table and leave. I'm sorry for bothering you." It was time to let go, move on. She certainly had. Dominic was now just a name on a piece of paper that said they were no longer married, destined to be strangers. The ring around his throat seared into his skin. He'd keep it. A symbol of how hard he needed to work the next time, if there ever was a next time.

He set the envelope down on the coffee table and glanced at the selection of reading materials heaped in a pile with various notes bookmarking every-other page. He was confused at the array of books she had selected to read. They weren't her typical romance or mystery novels.

Dominic whirled around sharply to Ashley. She was looking at him over her shoulder, her face pale and her eyes wide in fear as she tried to formulate an explanation.

"What to Expect When Your Expecting," he said, more to himself than to Ashley. "The Pregnancy Guide," he sputtered, confusion furrowing his brow. "Are you…what is this?" He flapped the book out in front of him.

"It's a book."

"I can see it's a damn book, why do you have it?" his voice cracked from the anger. He wasn't sure if he should be mad or happy for her. She didn't answer. His head was spinning. Ashley was pregnant with another man's baby, a baby they had talked about, the family they had wanted to build together. He was an outsider looking in on what he had always yearned for, a family of his own.

Before he knew it, he had dropped the book and was standing in front of her, inspecting every inch of her with his own eyes. Exposing Ashley for what she really was—pregnant.

When he saw her pregnant belly he stumbled backward, falling hard onto the coffee table. They had been separated for a little over five months. He thought she hadn't filed for divorce because she was still considering getting back together, but little did he know, she was really shacking up with someone else, building a life before she destroyed his.

"You're pregnant," he whispered.

Ashley stood still, afraid to move. There was no reason to be afraid, what was he going to do? He signed the papers; they were unofficially divorced until the papers were processed. She shouldn't be able to hurt him like this, cause so much pain, but that's what happened when you were still in love with someone and they walked away to lead a happier life without you. He couldn't contain it any longer. It bubbled up inside until it hurt to keep it in. He laughed and laughed until his sides ached, forcing him to fall to his knees and wrap his arms around his body. The situation wasn't funny, but he couldn't stop. After the laughing came the tears. Folding his hands over his face he wept. He wept for himself. He wept for the dream.

Ashley forced herself to move, kneeling beside him and pulling him into her arms. He put his arms around her, remembering the feel of her, but she wasn't who he remembered, and the belly only made him realize that even more, protruding toward him, the roundness pushing against his chest as he cried on her shoulder.

"Dominic, we have to talk," she said into his ear, rubbing his back like a child.

He pulled back from her, wiping his tear stained cheeks. "No," he shook his head, "I don't need an explanation. I'm not a part of your life anymore." He stood up, grabbing Arnie's leash in one swift motion and headed for the door leaving her on the ground, her shirt wet from his tears.

"That's where you're wrong, Dominic. You'll always be a part of it." He paused with his back to her. His breath hitched in his throat. "Is that too vague?" she asked. He turned around to look at her. She was now standing, facing him. He knew what she was saying, but he couldn't believe it. He wanted to hear her say the words, but her expression said all he needed to hear. Maybe the dream wasn't dead after all.

Chapter Three

*I*t was just a piano, but it felt like home and hell at the same time—a conflict brought on by a sacrifice for which his mother had paid dearly. And, like a superstitious hockey player that throws up in his helmet before every game, Caleb ran his fingers over the keys, counting them. There were always eighty-eight, but it soothed and calmed him knowing they were all there to help him perform. Beginning without hesitation or any sheet music, his mind an organized filing cabinet of compositions, Caleb jumped right into playing Chopin's Nocturne #20 in C Minor.

To Caleb, playing was the ultimate artistry—painting a picture, telling a story and weaving a song all at once. Vibrant colors filled the air with every stroke of the keys. With his fingers on the heart of the piano, nothing could touch him. He was safe from the strangling claws of the darkness that had chosen him so long ago. The piano was a haven that held its share of emotional baggage. Sometimes, it felt as though the instrument was a living, breathing person, a martyr, mocking Caleb at every opportunity.

The doors opened, and his concentration broke when he heard footfalls coming toward the stage. The music ended, and Caleb glanced up at Dominic. "Did you have fun last night?" he asked.

"I always enjoy myself," Dominic said, climbing up on stage, leaning his built and agile body against the piano, smirking down at Caleb.

"And did your lady friend?"

"Do you really need to ask that?"

"Went home alone, huh?"

"It happens," Dominic laughed.

Caleb was quite aware that Dominic, always the flirt, could get anyone he wanted. His jet-black hair was always in perfect order, each strand doing its job to hold up to the Chicago heat, wind, or snow. His hazel eyes stood out, always zeroing in on his next unsuspecting victim. He had a quizzical mouth, like Shakespeare, and a chiseled body like that of the statue, David. Caleb played Montgomery Clift to Dominic's Marlon Brando.

After a brief moment of silence, Dominic slipped a manila folder from his bag and pulled out a contract. "I have the contract for Germany. Are you okay with the first two weeks in September?" He arched his eyebrows, already knowing Caleb was open. After all, he kept the schedule.

"Can we ever just talk about something that doesn't involve work?" Caleb sighed.

"I thought we just did," Dominic laughed. "Besides, you always say this 'isn't work,'" he air quoted. "So who's talking work? I'm just doing what you pay me to do. We can stop and go on hiatus, if you only agree to -"

"No," Caleb interrupted, knowing full well where Dominic's train of thought was going.

Dominic slid the contract and a pen across the piano. Staring at it, Caleb knew he really had no choice. An artist wasn't relevant if he didn't perform. Besides, he needed to work. It kept him sane and his mind in working order.

"First two weeks in September it is." Caleb went to grab for the pen, but his hand ceased movement. It could have been dismissed as Caleb taking his time to think over the contract, but Dominic knew better. The errant hand finally jerked to life and, with a loosened grip on the pen, Caleb marked the dotted line with a few messy waves and dropped the pen. With his hands starting to be uncooperative, Caleb worried incessantly that they would one day just stop while he was performing. Though, if there was one thing he was able to conquer, it was the immense weakness that overtook him. He must constantly concentrate, never giving his hands a moment to hesitate. Allowing them to falter was of concern. The highest priority was keeping them moving, mapping out a composition. It was all he could do and, still, never enough.

Dominic snatched the papers up and put them away before he reluctantly brought up the elephant that was starting to crowd the room. "Your, ah – your appointment is in 20 minutes. Maybe you should rethink joining rehearsal tonight."

Caleb rolled his eyes. "It's the first rehearsal. I'm going. I don't care what I have to do, but I'm going to be here." Caleb tapped his finger down on the middle C key and held it. A sign Dominic knew meant Caleb was annoyed. "Think you can give me five minutes alone?" Caleb asked.

"Yeah, I'll just go fax this, and we'll be on our way."

"Thank you."

"By the way," Dominic turned. "You look all kinds of sexy in that Thunder Cats t-shirt," he laughed at Caleb's ridiculous attire, which reminded him of their youth.

"I hate you."

"Never skimpy on the love are you, Caleb?"

"Never," he grinned, waiting for Dominic to walk off stage. "Alright, I love you, too," he said, prompting Dominic to smile in victory before taking his leave.

Dominic slowly walked off stage and watched Caleb as he lowered his head, took a deep breath, and began pounding away, playing Liszt's Piano Concerto No. 1 – ½. Caleb was upset. He only ever played their mother's favorite composer when he was upset.

~

"Are you cold?" Dominic asked. "I can get you a jacket."

The Tetrabenazine was running through Caleb's system to help reduce his jerky and involuntary movements, though it rarely helped. The side effects usually didn't kick in until a few hours after the drug was in his system, increasing the amount of dopamine available in his brain. The chills, nausea, and restlessness were his worst experiences. He tried taking it in the middle of the day or right before bed, but it always led to insomnia. He'd stare up at the ceiling all night, his eyes locked on one particular spot, and before he knew it, the sun was coming up. Taking the pills when he woke up was a better schedule for him. As the day went on the pills eventually made him tired, but it was better than watching a fly sit on his ceiling every night for eight hours.

Dominic watched Caleb and saw the first signs of nausea. "Are you going to be sick?" he asked. Caleb shook his head. "Don't lie to me, Caleb."

"Just take me to rehearsal. I'm fine," Caleb pouted, straightening his posture, which was starting to slouch, rounding his shoulders and back.

They were like fraternal twins, one could always tell what was affecting the other by his tell signs. Unfortunately, Caleb never really mastered the art of the poker face.

"Watch out," Caleb mumbled turning toward the toilet. Dominic and Caleb were crammed into the backstage restroom. Caleb sat on the floor, his arms cradling the toilet and his legs folded under him. If only this were from a long night of drinking, but this wasn't just a careless night of debauchery. It was weeks of physical therapy, lack of sleep and drugs that were taking a toll on his fragile body. Pain was necessary. In Caleb's mind, he deserved it.

Dominic beseeched his brother, "You don't have to rehearse tonight. You're supposed to be resting and in a place that isn't filled with germs. You know your immune system can't -"

Caleb threw his head back from the toilet, wiping spittle from his lips with the back of his hand. He glanced up at Dominic with bloodshot eyes that dared his best friend and manager to make him go home.

"I'll be fine," was all he managed to say before his head was back over the toilet, letting loose and wreaking havoc on his frail system. His whole body shook as he heaved up copious amounts of bile, the only thing left after lunch had disappeared ten minutes ago.

"Did you have a glass of chamomile tea today? You know that helps calm your stomach?" Dominic asked, angry that Caleb wasn't being responsible enough to take care of himself.

"You watched me drink it in the car, Dom. Stop asking questions you know the answers to," Caleb mumbled into the shallow depths of the toilet.

Dominic knelt down and rubbed Caleb's back, soothing him as best he could. "You need to start listening if you want to get better, Caleb," Dominic advised.

"I know what I'm doing, Dom!" Caleb snapped. He flushed the toilet and, wobbly, got to his feet, shrugging Dominic's helping hands away. Again Caleb faced his image in the mirror: skin translucent, eyes bloodshot, and the circles under them more pronounced than ever.

"I'm not leaving. If I don't play, I'm—I'm doing it for her," Caleb said mostly to his reflection.

"One day of rest won't kill you. Living is better than dying, Caleb," Dominic replied.

"Until it's not." Caleb ran his hand through his hair. Strands clung to his fingers. Caleb looked down in astonishment and shook his head.

"You need to take a sleeping pill. I said the sleep deprivation you're experiencing can –"

"Alright, Dr. Montgomery, get off my case. You think I don't want to sleep?" he asked, eyeing Dominic in the mirror. "I can't help it, she's always there behind my eyelids," he whispered, seemingly faraway, his mind taking him back to a place he was better off forgetting.

Dominic placed his hand on Caleb's shoulder to rouse him from his past. "You know you can talk to me, right?"

Caleb nodded, fingering the strands in his hand, watching as they floated down into the sink.

~

The piano was an extension of Caleb, his way of channeling emotions and energy into one tangible object. It allowed expression in ways he could never convey through words. He felt he was more relatable when he sat behind the piano to perform. He was blessed in so many ways, but he was always plagued by what he sacrificed for those opportunities of expression. He loved the music, but sometimes he couldn't necessarily say the same about the instrument.

A lone tear ran down his cheek. Occasionally, tears would slip by at the most inopportune moments, and he wasn't sure why one was running awry today. He had moved on in a way, but sometimes things had a way of bringing back the memories. Being back in Chicago calmed Caleb but made him anxious at the same time. Everything had changed twenty-eight years ago. He had changed, and since then, he felt as though he'd been on a countdown, waiting for the clock to strike twelve. A Cinderella without the luxury of a fairy Godmother, he waited longer than he imagined, the news not coming as a shock, the disease his sentence for what he had done all those years ago. He took the news and ran with it, silently relieved that he need not wait any longer, always looking over his shoulder for it to catch up. Now that it finally had, he felt better. Like a weight had been lifted off his shoulders, allowing him to move freely through life, accepting of his fate. He had gotten away with twenty-eight years, years he dedicated to his mother.

He knew predictions were pointless. When would it all end? How? All he needed to know was that it was most certainly going to, and it wasn't going to be painless. These days all he could say for sure was that he was living an exceptional life under unfortunate circumstances. He wondered if things would have turned out the same if it had been just like any other day in the Montgomery household. Would he be the same shell of a person who waited for death to strike every day of his existence?

Caleb's morbid thoughts were taking him out of his professional mind set. Banishing them, he stood in the entryway. Closing his eyes, he sought to gather his emotions, to get in a place where there was only music, and to pool all the energy he had left in his body, which didn't feel like much, and focus it all to his fingers. Caleb could sense Dominic hovering behind him. Dominic's persistent nearness was unsettling, but Caleb knew Dominic took his role of big brother seriously.

"You okay?" Dominic asked when he saw Caleb turn from the stage and place his hand against the wall.

Caleb felt as if his head were going to explode. The buzzing returned, and a slur of muddled voices imploded in his head, but only for a brief moment before Caleb started to cough uncontrollably. Caleb's form slowly buckled as Dominic wrapped his arms around his brother, helping to hold Caleb up against the wall, making sure to keep up appearances.

"Caleb, I don't want to have to carry you out of here," Dominic whispered into his ear.

His words stung, but Caleb knew Dominic was right. Caleb shouldn't be there. It just wasn't that simple. Caleb refused to let his destiny take away the one thing that was allowing him to make up for being alive.

"If you even try to carry me out of here don't come back." Caleb pushed away from Dominic's chest and hid the blood on his palm by clenching his fist. He thundered past Dominic toward the stage, walking through the entryway. As discreetly as possible, he bent down to tie his shoes with an air of forced nonchalance. He wiped the blood from his palm onto the bottom of his pant leg, concealing the blood that stained his hand--the blood that always seemed to be on his hands.

The coughing was a new addition to his complications. He was a little under the weather lately. Headache-induced dizziness, elevated temperature, and labored breathing were followed by extreme bouts of coughing. However, seeing the blood in his palm scared Caleb a little. Perhaps the disease was progressing faster than they thought; yet from all the facts Dominic rattled off to him about the disease, coughing up blood was not on the list of symptoms.

Caleb looked amongst the players. The semi-circle ended with his eyes drawing near to her face, and when he found her he couldn't manage to look away. The way she swayed to the music, even when she wasn't playing, entranced him. She looked up for a brief moment, and their eyes met, her eyes a sea of blue that silently beckoned Caleb. Her brown hair was pulled back into a ponytail and the lavender V-neck blouse made her porcelain-white skin look radiant against her spruce-wood cello.

He stood quite still, not fidgeting, slightly apart from backstage where he could disappear at any second lest he feel the need. The orchestra warmed up only a few feet in front of him, and although he was trying to blend in with his surroundings, she could see he was quite intense. She felt shocked to find his gaze upon her, as if he were dissecting her with his eyes, roping her in. But, a moment later, as she overcame her initial shock, he looked away.

Caleb shook his head to clear his mind of the dangerous thoughts he could barely control. Clearly the therapy was affecting some sort of brain function. There was no time for games, just work. Time, the word pulled his attention, making his thoughts return to the darkened cave in his mind. Fleeting was a perfect word for it. Her eyes were burned into his memory, and when he closed his own to prepare, he saw only them. Not allowing himself a moment to dwell on her, Caleb broke the connection by looking at what he was eternally connected to—the piano.

Pulling his shoulders back and stiffening his back, he lifted his head high, confidence radiating from every pore of his body. He knew why he was there and that he deserved to be. He had done the work, and this was his payoff. He had charisma and showmanship; two things that helped make him stand out as a performer. He played with a keyed-up intensity, always wanting the audience to feel the music through him. He wanted to perform to the best of his ability whenever he stepped out on stage, whether in rehearsal or a concert. In the end, there was nothing left. Everything was left out on the floor—like an athlete—always wanting the crowd to believe in every stroke he took. Caleb meandered past the orchestra to the piano and took his position on the bench.

The orchestra was commanded to stop by its conductor, Riccardo Muti. He was dressed casually in a pair of jeans and a button-down, tailored shirt with the first two buttons undone. His black hair, with a few strategically placed strands of gray, licked the back of his white collar. His intense eyes smiled at Caleb as his star sat down at the piano.

Instruments were lowered, bows were dropped, and all eyes were on Caleb as everyone put their hands together in a round of applause. Caleb felt awkward when he first took the stage. People applauded the talent he worked so hard to achieve, and he silently wondered if they could see him the way he saw himself. If they truly knew the person behind the piano, would they still applaud him?

Caleb answered the question—no. He flipped his hat back around so the bill covered his eyes, and once he was comfortably in position, Caleb ran his fingers over the keys. Looking up at Riccardo who arched his eyebrows in question and gave him a lazy smirk, Caleb nodded for the director to begin. Riccardo tapped his baton against his podium for attention. Pages were flipped, instruments positioned, and fingers aligned. Brahms Piano Concerto No. 1 was first on the playlist, and they were off with the movement of a baton.

He was at liberty to choose the pieces that would be performed throughout his two months with the symphony, unless Riccardo was against any particular piece. Caleb was going to show the orchestra what he could do, why his fingers were insured, and why he held records as the fastest piano player in the world. He was performing a concert series of the most intricate and demanding concertos by Brahms, Grieg, Stravinsky, Tchaikovsky, Mozart, Chopin, and Beethoven. He would end with the most complicated, Rachmaninoff's Piano Concert No. 3—his finale.

Caleb was exhausted just thinking about the two months that lay ahead of him, but he craved the challenge and excitement of the pieces and the difficulty they presented to most performers. The last two weeks of his concert series were going to be hard on his body, but he was going out big, ending with Rachmaninoff, the World Series to most pianists.

Focusing on Brahms, Caleb began the piece, and a moment later the orchestra chimed in. When behind the piano, Caleb radiated life. Thoughts of the world outside those auditorium walls did not exist. His disease was a distant memory, and with the music pulsing through him, the visible marks of fatigue and nausea disappeared. He was normal. He was safe. He was healthy. He was alive.

Music helped Caleb focus on what was important and purge his thoughts of disease, of what his life would be if he weren't able to play the piano, of penitence for his sins. To Caleb, playing music was a movement toward freedom, his mind escaping the ailments of his body and darkened thoughts, allowing him to push his own limits of reality. The music he created and performed gave him a sense of accomplishment, but he knew that burying himself in music had more to do with his past than just his selfish desires to escape.

Three hours later, Caleb was drained. He took off his red hat, now darkened crimson from perspiration, and ran his fingers through his slicked-back hair, examining his hands for any strands, finding none. His fingers ached, and his eyes were even tired, drooping as he sat in the bathroom, the toilet seat down and his body hunched over, making his back cry out in pain.

Normally, he would have talked to some of the orchestra players and enjoyed conversation with Riccardo, but he was letting Dominic take care of everything while he hid in the bathroom calming his body after the draining rehearsal. He was pushing hard, but when he played he didn't feel tired. He didn't feel as though his body were shutting down. Instead, he felt nothing, and that was one of the reasons he played.

~

"My condition," Caleb said through clenched teeth. He didn't want to believe his brother could betray his confidence without even mentioning it to him. He paced back and forth in a remote corner, backstage. His mind was going a mile a minute as he tried to figure out a way to assess the need for damage control before him. It was a secret, a heavy burden. One twitch could possibly give him away, and expose his frailty. That was not something Caleb wanted in the open.

"I had to tell him, Caleb," Dominic replied, shifting his weight.

"Dominic, you —" Caleb looked around to make sure they were alone. He could hear the faint whisper of a cello, but no one was within earshot. He lowered his voice to a bitter whisper. "Why don't you just shout it from the rooftop?" Caleb stormed off, fuming at the thought of someone knowing what he was going through. He trusted Riccardo, but to think he was one step closer to his secret being leaked, Caleb couldn't comprehend the ramifications.

Dominic followed closely behind trying to find the words to make everything right. "Look, I'm sorry, but he needed to know in case there was an emergency," Dominic cried, grabbing Caleb by the shoulder and spinning his brother around to face him.

Caleb swatted at Dominic's hand. "And you didn't think that I should be let in on that decision?" Caleb snapped.

"I know. I was an idiot for not consulting with you." Dominic bowed his head, the picture of contrition.

"Understatement, Dom." Caleb tried to calm down by taking slow, shallow breaths. "Look, I just ask that you consult me first, instead of undermining me. This isn't something I want to get out. I don't want another person's pity on my conscience."

Dominic's head snapped to attention. "I didn't tell him so he could pity you, Caleb. It was solely based on possible risks. He needed to know in case anything happened while I wasn't around." Dominic reached out, putting his hand on Caleb's shoulder.

This time, Caleb didn't shrug away. He tapped his fingers on a snare drum, trying to rationalize what was going on around him. He knew Dominic was right, but he didn't want to give the satisfaction of saying it aloud. "I don't see that happening," he sighed. "You're always around. Even when I'd rather you weren't."

"But what you're really saying is…I'm right."

"I didn't say that."

"Out loud you didn't."

"You read into things, and most of the time, like now, you're wrong." Caleb smiled knowing it made no difference what he said. "Are you coming over to watch the football games?" he asked.

"Yeah, but is it alright if I stay tonight?" Caleb frowned hoping Dominic wasn't asking so he could watch over him. Dominic threw his hands up defensively before Caleb could argue. "Whoa, not checking up on you, just plan on having a few drinks. Don't want to drive. Plus, I have something being delivered."

"Seriously? What is it?"

"Can't tell ya."

He smiled his devilish grin, challenging Caleb to try and get the truth out of him.

"You know I don't like surprises."

"We'll see about that tomorrow."

"I hate you," Caleb mumbled.

"I know. Love you too." Dominic patted him on the shoulder. "I'm going to pull the car around and take you home." Caleb opened his mouth to object, but Dominic put his hand up to stop him. "Don't even think of trying to fight me on this. I'm taking you home and that's that. You can drive yourself on a day you haven't been throwing up."

Caleb watched Dominic snake his way around the corridor, pondering what useless gift Dominic was going to give him now. He hadn't hinted at anything he would like. It didn't matter what it was. If Caleb even looked at something for more than a second, Dominic went out and got it for him. There was a room in Caleb's house devoted solely to Dominic's useless gifts, from the Hawaiian Chair he saw on Ellen, to a Snuggie for Arnie. The thought brought a smile to his face, knowing his brother was so insistent upon making Caleb happy, even if it meant buying him something so outrageous that they got a good laugh out of it for an hour then never looked at it again. The room was full of useless junk, but it was full of memories and laughter. He could do nothing but thank Dominic for that.

Caleb was just about to go to the lobby to wait for his ride when he remembered the cello music. It had stopped for a moment but started up again. He listened to a few chords. Bach's Cello Suite was coming from a lone performer on stage. Caleb walked out from the constricting white corridors that wound backstage as the music glided through the air, compelling him to follow.

The playing was beautiful, precise, and passionate. When he came upon her, he saw it was the same woman that first caught his attention before rehearsal. Her hair was no longer restricted in a ponytail but now spread across her shoulders, elongating her face and making her eyes stand out more clearly. Her gaze was intent on her instrument, nestled between her legs, the bow gliding gently over the strings, and her head swaying to the melody Bach had first introduced hundreds of years ago.

Caleb was behind the piano before he realized he had moved, still watching the unsuspecting cello player's solo. The song was nearing its conclusion, but before he would allow it to end, Caleb followed along with the piano, adding to the superb tone of the cello. A song, rich in its loneliness, was now brought together with Bach's instrument of choice.

The piano lifted the piece to new and extraordinary heights. The woman remained unfazed. She made no movement to stop, and as Caleb's hands struck the last chord of the composition, he continued on, his fingers mapping out a new course. Now, instead of being the follower, he was the leader.

He looked up from the keys to find her now watching him. She continued playing, matching his passion and pace. The duet they were composing together acted as a conductor for their attraction. Intent on each other's gaze, they played as if one—connected in their extraordinary quest.

Caleb felt the need to go on, but his urge to stop and speak to her was more overwhelming. His fingers slowly came to rest, his hands dropping to his sides, as her bow came to a slow conclusion, putting a fitting end to the piece that could have continued for hours.

They were silent, feeling no need to speak, the air already heavy with their emotion. Her stare unnerved him, now that they were no longer playing. She looked at him as if through a telescope, seeing every cell in him racing along, stirring up an uncomfortable commotion, tormenting the disease that was spiraling in chaos throughout his body. It almost felt as if she already knew his deepest, darkest secrets, and the fear that spread through made him break into a cold sweat.

She stood and came to him, seeming to glide on the static air between them. A smile spread across her face, making her eyes light up like the

Northern Star. Caleb wanted to unglue himself from his bench and run, but she had spelled him and moving was not an option.

"Hi," she said waiting for Caleb's greeting in return. When he didn't answer, she continued, undaunted. "You play beautifully. It's a pleasure to perform beside you." She held out her hand. "I'm Rylen Price."

Her voice was elegant and soft. He wanted to speak to her, but Caleb's throat constricted. He opened his mouth, but nothing came out. Her teeth were gleaming in the stage light, and he couldn't take his eyes off of them.

"You have really white teeth," he blurted out.

"Excuse me?" she said, a hint of a giggle in her voice, wondering if she had heard him correctly.

Caleb snapped his mouth shut, and instead of greeting her in the proper manner, his fight or flight response kicked in. He was finally able to make his legs cooperate and lift him off the bench. They shook underneath him, so close to giving way, undermining his intent to run. He moved around the bench, avoiding her entirely and dropping his eyes to the ground as he took one step at a time. He avoided the impulse to look back, afraid she'd draw him in.

While Caleb slept, it all played in his head: the sun shining brightly as the music filtered throughout the car, the windows down and the breeze ruffling their hair like smooth fingertips gliding along his scalp.

"Did you have fun today?" she asked the boy next to her, running her hand over her tiny belly.

Laughing. Smiling. Happy. Their faces were always a blur, but he knew they were happy in that moment, a moment in time he'd never get back, a happy family, singing along to the music of the oldies station. Then, the blow. Blood, sparkling red blood, poured from open wounds and gashes. Glass shards covered the seats. He didn't hear the screams. They were inaudible. The taste of the fear was palpable, but everything was too hazy to grasp the situation at hand. Cold. Pain. Unconsciousness.

Sirens blared in the distance, but they were drowned out by the deafening sound of the music; the music that was playing only moments ago putting smiles on their faces, smiles gone now, hidden by the mask of blood. He tried to conjure up their faces before they were struck, to keep the smiles, but they were always replaced with the blood. The blood he spilled, blood that was running through his veins, mocking him because he had escaped death. This time, he was within its grasp, and the fingers were slowly tightening around his body, squeezing out every last ounce of blood—the blood that was smeared on his hands.

His body was cold as he whimpered, calling out in the night, their eyes mocking him, the only part of their faces that was in focus—eyes that were seared into memory. Caleb loved them, and he was frightened by them, but he carried their pain with him, seeing their eyes as they lay in front of him. And even though he cried out, his cries went unanswered.

Caleb tossed and turned, trying to wake himself from the dream, but he was stuck in limbo. Stuck where the memories could hurt him, and they always did. They pulled him from the warmth and shrouded him in the inevitable coldness and despair. He gasped for breath, the icy fingers of death on his throat. He clawed at them, kicking and jabbing, trying to pull away, but it was too late. The eyes were staring at him, waiting for him, whispering to him that his time was near. The fingers loosened, marking him for later, but his heart still raced with the discovery of what was lurking behind the curtain of his mind. Caleb wasn't sure if he was able to bear the shame of it all, knowing what he had done.

Chapter Four

Studying the directions, Dominic could have sworn his eyes were failing him. Everything they said was foreign. Even the picture made him cringe. It looked nothing like his finished product. Putting a crib together shouldn't be rocket science, and yet, it was. This was a new low, but the excitement that it created in him was astounding. He was putting together his child's crib, a baby–his baby. Was it a miracle? His second chance to do right? In Dominic's case it was more a miracle that he even found out about the baby. He had Arnie to thank for that.

He had stayed at Ashley's that day until two in the morning, just talking. She was scared, and she didn't want him to feel obligated. She knew his feelings toward his job and his allegiance to Caleb—especially now. What she didn't understand was that Dominic saw this as a way of mending things, putting the pieces back together—mom, dad, and baby–a family.

Frustrated, Dominic looked at the lopsided crib and threw the directions across the room. It was the most expensive one on the market and the most complicated. Lying back amongst the screws and leftover pieces, he felt a crick in his back as he stretched out. Why were there left over pieces? He was going to have to take it apart—again. Or pay someone else to do it. No, it was his baby. He was going to put it together. He needed to get used to putting things together. The next few years would require plenty of all-night projects—toys, bikes, and furniture. This was only the beginning of his new life as a "dad".

"Son of a bitch," he murmured, looking over at the crib that mocked him. Sighing and wiping the sweat from his brow, Dominic set to taking the crib apart for the second time.

Ashley walked into the room. Leaning against the door frame, she watched Dominic disassemble the crib. This go-around was worse than the first. She shook her head. He was going to be there all day, and when she woke up tomorrow the crib would be lying in a heap. He insisted on doing it, so enthusiastic to take part in the preparations she had yet to complete. He had painted the room a light shade of green since Ashley was intent on the sex of the baby being a surprise. There were not enough surprises in life anymore, but then again, she hadn't intended on Dominic finding out about the pregnancy. For that matter, she hadn't intended to become pregnant. Surprise!

The Winnie the Pooh boarder she bought two months ago now sectioned the room in half and the ceiling fan rotated above him, trying to keep him cool. Still, his shirt was plastered to his back, sweat seeping through in patches between his shoulder blades.

She hadn't wanted to let him in, but he had stood outside her door with bags full of baby necessities. There was now no point in having a baby shower. Dominic had covered everything: bottles, diapers, a changing table, high chair, stroller, toys, stuffed animals and Baby Einstein tapes that she wouldn't need for a while. He was trying, she gave him that, but she preferred that he not put forth so much effort. She wanted to be mad at him, to keep the anger she felt toward him inside. She didn't want him tending to her needs, caring for her.

Against her better judgment, she had reluctantly let him in, unsure of what she should do. Since he'd found out about the baby, she had been able to sleep better. Her secret no longer weighed on her mind, but she was afraid Dominic would take things too far and think they were reconciling. Opening the door meant opening the door to that possibility. He had put her through enough. She was straddling the line. She couldn't decide which frightened her more: going forward alone or falling back into their easy routine.

Dominic worked intently on the crib, pulling the screws out and letting them fall on the carpet until they were needed again. To make things interesting, Ashley grabbed Dominic's new camera off the changing table. Pictures of the room before he attacked it with his enthusiasm were documented and now she wanted to turn the lens on him. Besides, she wanted to get this experiment on film. He would deny his struggles with the crib, but she would have the undeniable proof.

She was having fun taking pictures of him without his knowledge, the frustration evident in his shoulders, his fingers easily pulling the pieces apart instead of putting them together, and his face contorted in a humorless humiliation. She inadvertently laughed, causing Dominic to turn around. His surprised expression was perfect, just as she pressed the button. That was going to be a great picture.

"Hey!" he said, surprised to find her watching him, let alone taking pictures. "I believe that's my job." He leaned back on his hands, his chest heaving from the strain. Crib 3, Dominic 0.

"Thought you'd like to look back and see how bad you were at putting a crib together," she laughed, the camera quiet in her hands.

"What are you talking about?" he played dumb. "I'm putting it together for the first time."

Ashley put her hands on her hips and cocked her eyebrow. "You never were a good liar, Dominic."

"No, I suppose not." He stared at her for a long moment. "You eat all your lunch?" he asked, wanting to make sure she was well nourished and taken care of.

"Yeah." She stood up from the door frame.

He lazily grinned at her, hoping she would see how happy he was. "Good." He stood up and went to her, almost reaching out to pull her towards him, but he restrained himself. "You look beautiful by the way. It's true what they say about a woman's glow when pregnant."

"I look like a whale," she demurred rubbing her belly.

"A gorgeous whale though," he laughed. "You know, I should be taking pictures of you. That way, you can look back at this time and show our son what his mommy looked like when he was chilling in her belly."

"Son?"

"Just dreaming out loud," he grabbed the camera from her and broke out into his pretend fashion photographer persona. "That's perfect, beautiful. Fling your hair over your shoulder," he started clicking for his nonexistent assistant. "I need a fan pronto and a bagel!" He went back to taking pictures. Ashley tried to shy away, but his enthusiasm was intoxicating and she played along, modeling against the door frame and running her hands through her hair. "That's great. Growl for me," he laughed.

"I draw the line at growling," she stopped their impromptu photo shoot.

When he broke down into his puppy dog face, the face that used to make her putty in his strong hands, she swatted at him. He grinned and started to take more pictures of her.

"Could you put your hands on your stomach for me and lean against the door frame?" he asked directing her. Ashley did as he asked, secretly wanting these pictures as well. These would be an improvement from the pictures she had been taking on her camera phone as her pregnancy had progressed.

Dominic hastily snapped pictures, trying to get as many as he could. Then suddenly it all became very real, and he stopped, letting the camera slowly fall to his side. The way she caressed her stomach made Dominic picture her holding their child, and Dominic couldn't help but feel left out, even though he was doing all he could to fit in. He wanted to put his hand there, feel the life under his fingertips, the life that he helped to create when she used to love him. But he didn't think she'd like that. He read that pregnant women didn't appreciate people rubbing their bellies. A person could lose their finger poking and prodding at a pregnant woman.

She must have caught him staring and registered what he was thinking because she grabbed his hand and placed it on her stomach. He was so shocked by the gesture that he started to pull away, but she kept a firm grip and kept his hand in place.

"It's okay, Dom," she reassured him.

His eyes lit with the anticipation of feeling his baby move beneath his fingers, but nothing happened. He frowned, a little let down, but Ashley's hand remained on top of his.

"I almost forgot how small your hands were."

She removed her hand. "Doesn't look like she's in the mood to entertain today." She stepped back, Dominic's hand slipping off her stomach.

"She?" He lifted an eyebrow, doubting she actually knew for sure.

"Just dreaming out loud," she said glancing around the room, taking in the full scope of the mess he made. "Maybe you should call it a day. I'm kind of tired." Ashley turned to leave, afraid to let him get close again, but she wasn't fast enough.

"Wait." He put his arms around her, pulling her back against his chest, his hands on her stomach and his head resting on her shoulder, nuzzling her neck. The strong scent of sweat and burgers radiated off him, but that could be because she wanted to eat a burger. His scent was all man. Something she always loved about him.

Closing his eyes, he enjoyed the feel of her again, a feeling he had tried to recreate with other women, but it was never the same—they weren't Ashley. They didn't fit like she did.

"Dominic, you should go," she whispered.

He could feel her pulse quicken where he kissed her on the neck. He grabbed her hand in his.

"I don't want to," he replied, pulling her tighter against him. His mouth was against her ear, the smell of his after shave pulling her back to the days when she would watch him getting ready in the morning from the comfort of their bed. She caressed his arms, reveling in their strength as she leaned into him. This is what she needed, someone strong. She didn't want to go through this alone.

Dominic turned her to face him, pulling her close until their lips met for the first time in longer than he cared to remember. They missed each other, that much was evident. She wanted him to stay, but the thought, "he didn't pick you," weaseled into her mind forcing her to end the connection.

She pushed him away, their lips swollen and their breathing heavy. She saw the question in his eyes. "You didn't pick me," she said aloud before she disappeared down the hall.

"Let me make up for it," he yelled after her just as she slammed the bathroom door.

Dominic pulled himself together. She was right. He hadn't picked her. He had been living with that decision every day of his life since she left. Wondering how different everything would be, especially now that there was a baby on the way. No matter how long it took, he was going to make it up to her.

Closing the nursery door behind him, Dominic decided to leave his things there. He'd be back. The crib still needed to be reassembled, he had a room to finish, and a home to build—one strong enough for a family.

For a brief moment, everything felt the same; yet one piece of the puzzle had forever changed—Ashley. In the past few months, she had built a new life. She was teaching second grade again, had her own place, and even started using her maiden name. She had ripped him from her life, replaced him. Except now there was a baby involved. That was a constant reminder. He had no right to be mad at her. He had pushed her away first, and it was evident to him now that he hadn't moved on as well as he had imagined. She didn't need him like he needed her.

Dominic was numb inside by the time he reached the front door. The lump in his throat was trying to dissolve into tears, but he wouldn't cry there. He opened the door and walked into the hallway. Stillness surrounded him. Normally, he was glad for it, but lately his world was full of stillness, and he hated it.

There were two options before him, he could leave or he could sit down and talk to her. He needed someone to talk to. He was tired of not being able to let out everything that weighed on him. The world was on his shoulders, and there was no one there to listen. She used to be his rock, lying in bed with him for hours, simply talking. Talk about nothing. Talk about the world. Talk about life. They might discuss the latest episode of some reality series he was embarrassed to admit he watched. It didn't matter what it was. They talked, and Dominic missed that. When he was away he'd call her, and if he wasn't able to talk to her before going to sleep, he was guaranteed a night of endless tossing and turning.

Running his fingers through his hair he expected to find strands clinging to his fingers from stress, but his hand returned only wet from perspiration. He loved two people, and it hurt to breathe without them. He shivered as he realized how much he had hurt both of the people he held dearest to his heart, the chills a reminder of how much he had come to disappoint and fail them. It was easier when there was no one to hurt, easier to love someone from afar than it is when they were right in front of you. You were less likely to see the disillusionment in their eyes when they realized you weren't who you purported to be.

The hardwood floor creaked under her weight and pulled Dominic's attention from the door he had left open behind him as he contemplated which way to turn. She almost looked relieved to see he hadn't left, making the easy decision to walk away, like he had before. This time he wasn't going to be so easily persuaded by his inner voice.

Chapter Five

"Why don't you go for a swim?" Caleb asked Arnie. "We're at the beach. Everyone's just about gone," he said as he sat on the cement stairs looking out over Ohio Street Beach to Lake Michigan. Arnie's head didn't move, but he looked at Caleb with disinterest. "Just a thought." Caleb shrugged and immersed himself in his book.

Droplets started to bounce heavily on the pavement next to him. It was a relatively cool day, and the remaining people on the beach were either reading or playing in the sand. A few times Caleb felt his attention waver toward the playing children and quickly turned back to his book. No need to dwell on the impossible.

Arnie whined beside him, bored by what the beach had to offer. Caleb leaned back against the step and glanced at his watch, wondering if he should stick around since Arnie wasn't enjoying their lazy day together in the city.

Arnie sat up and stretched his back legs. He stood at attention and looked around them, listening to the traffic on Lake Shore Drive as it whizzed by. The sky darkened, and Caleb knew they didn't have much longer until the downpour began. It was probably time to go, but as soon as the thought crossed his mind, Arnie barked in excitement and took off toward the beach. Caleb lunged for the leash just beyond his reach.

Now that it was starting to rain steadily, the beach was practically void of life, with the exception of a lone woman sitting in the sand by the water. She was molding sand together, and it appeared she was taking a stab at building a sand castle, a sand castle that didn't stand a chance against Arnie. He tended to be a destructive little shit. Caleb hoped the woman wasn't attached to what she was building.

The sand was cold and gave way easily beneath his feet as Caleb trotted down to Arnie who jumped side to side on the pile of sand that had moments ago resembled a castle. The woman was laughing which boded well for them. An apology was always easier to make when the other party wasn't angry.

As he got closer, he saw she was decked out in running gear. Either she was an avid runner or she just bought the clothes with the intention of blending in with the running crowd. She stood up and splashed along the water as Arnie chased her, and as Caleb watched, he knew what was going to happen before it did. All Caleb could do was watch, knowing there was no way he could stop the disaster unfolding before him.

The leash drug over the surface of the water, and when Arnie turned to circle around the woman, the leash loop wrapped around her foot. Arnie jerked to get away from her grasp, taking her legs out from under her. Caleb cringed, watching as the woman face-planted in the water.

If Arnie had jumped on her sending them sprawling into the water, that would have been playful compared to the pain this appeared to cause. She pushed up out of the water on her hands and knees. A few clumps of sand fell from her head while she coughed up the lake that had entered her lungs. Arnie assaulted her with his tongue. Try as she might to push him away, she had made a new friend—for better or for worse.

This was not how Caleb imagined his relaxing day would play out. He shook his head at Arnie and padded into the water to help the distressed woman. Reaching down to assist her, Caleb failed to announce his whereabouts. Startled by his presence, the woman's head flew back, straight at his face. Black spots exploded in his vision as the sickeningly loud crack of his nose mingled with the splash of lake water in his ears.

"Oh, my God," she yelled.

Caleb's hands instantly went to his face as blood started to pour from his nose and down his chin, staining his favorite Floggin' Molly t-shirt and ruining his jeans. He lay back, his head on the safety of the shore, and the rest of his body soaked as the water lapped over him. He was dazed, but he could still make out Arnie hovering above him. Crawling over to his side was the woman. He squinted at her, not sure if what he was seeing was his imagination playing tricks on him. When she spoke, he couldn't believe it. Of all the women in Chicago to break his nose, it was Rylen Price.

He tried to sit up, but she forcefully pushed him back down.

"Stay down," she said her voice laced with worry.

Caleb's body tensed at her voice. He wasn't sure if he could speak. Not only was his mouth filled with blood, but he had come face to face with the woman he ran from just the day before. Karma was, in fact, a bitch.

Rylen couldn't believe she was staring down at Caleb Montgomery. She stared in shocked horror at what she had done. She prayed she hadn't broken his nose, but with so much blood, she had doubts.

"I think you broke my nose," he said sounding congested.

Rylen's face contorted and she broke into tears. Holy hell. He didn't know what to do with a crying woman. Where was Dominic when Caleb needed him? Damn this day, damn tears, damn Ohio Street Beach, and damn Arnie. He turned toward Arnie who was sitting next to him, his tongue hanging out of his mouth as he panted, his fur ruffled from the water.

While Rylen was distracted by crying, Caleb sat up, gently squeezing his nose to stop the bleeding.

"It's okay, don't worry about it," he tried to reassure her, his voice nasally.

She tried to speak, but everything came out as gibberish—a far cry from the cool, collected person standing before him yesterday. Caleb was mad but not mad enough to make a person cry. The sheen of her tears glistened up at him.

For a moment, the voice in his head told him to run, but he had already done that and felt it would be unbearable to experience the humiliation of doing so again. Somehow, she was thrown back into his line of vision, hazy as it was.

He stood up and held out his hand. When she ignored it, he cleared his throat to get her attention. She looked up at him and stared at his hand, unsure of what to do.

"Let me help you up," he said.

"You speak." Rylen smiled, realizing how she must look, wiping the tears from her eyes and pushing her wet hair back from her face. She composed herself. "I'm sorry. I don't know why I broke down like that." She took a deep breath. "Is this your dog?" she asked, pushing Arnie away from her face as he tried to attack her again.

"Yes, Arnold." Hearing his formal name, Arnie looked up. "I'm sorry about what he did."

"Oh, no, you're sorry! I just –"

She felt the tears coming again but took a deep breath.

"It's okay." He anxiously shook his hand at her. "Would you like help up?" he asked.

"I can't. I think I twisted my ankle." She sat back, extending her legs out in front of her. Caleb crouched down beside her, trying not to look too concerned as some blood spots dripped in the sand next to her legs.

"You must have sprained your ankle when you got tangled in Arnie's leash." He carefully examined her foot. Gently, he took his hand away from his nose, but blood dripped down into the sand. Before he could reach back up, Rylen lightly pinched it to stop the bleeding. They looked odd: both drenched, her ankle swelling rapidly, his bloody nose held closed by her hand. He surveyed his ruined clothes as he tried to breathe and speak through the blood pooled in his mouth.

"Good thing it doesn't take an ankle to play the cello." She smiled, seeing a hint of a grin on Caleb's face. He examined her ankle like a professional as she asked, "Do you know what you're doing?"

"If I said yes, would you believe me?" he asked, a glimmer of mischief in his eyes.

"No. A pianist and a doctor? That's like finding a unicorn."

Caleb laughed at the analogy but cringed in pain. "I am a man of many talents." He watched her, forgetting himself for a moment, but averted his gaze before she noticed. Just help her up and go home, that's all he needed to do. She was a part of the orchestra, and Caleb never fraternized, preferring to keep things strictly professional. "Here, let me help you up." Rylen's grip on his nose was replaced by his own fingers and with his other hand, he gently slid his fingers across her palm.

She winced in pain, trying not to put any weight on her right ankle and wrapping her arm over Caleb's shoulder as he guided her a few feet away to the cement steps where his book still sat. He carefully helped her sit, all the while holding her hand.

Arnie rested his head on Rylen's lap, his eyes radiating concern. She laughed and scratched his head with her free hand while unconsciously maintaining her grip on Caleb with her other hand. Caleb wasn't at all surprised at how gentle Arnie was with Rylen. If anyone knew what it was like to get hurt, it was Arnie.

A tingle rippled throughout his hand. He went to stretch it but found it intertwined with Rylen's. He panicked, lifting his fingers up one-by-one until his hand was no longer clutching hers and letting it drop to her side. He flexed his hand, a heat creeping up to his face, embarrassed at showing such intimacy toward someone he barely knew.

"Are you okay? I can't believe what just happened. I don't know what to do. I'm so sorry," she apologized, rambling on.

"I'm okay, it happens. Rarely, but it happens."

She hid her face in her hands. "I'm going to get in so much trouble. If I'm the reason you can't play." She shook her head in disgust. "Let me make it up to you." She put her hands down. "I have a doctor friend that could look you over," she offered.

"No," he said hurriedly. In the past year there had been nothing but doctor visits; he wasn't going to go to another. Rylen frowned, his answer surprising her. "I'll be fine, really, don't go through the trouble."

"Then can I buy you a coffee?"

"Don't drink coffee."

"Wash your clothes?" Odd suggestion, but it was something.

"They're old…probably going to throw them away anything." He had just bought the jeans three weeks ago to replace the ones that no longer fit. And if there was one thing he disliked, it was jean shopping.

"Then maybe I should have you come up with a way for me to make it up to you."

"Really, Rylen, it's fine." He shrugged it off. His nose was on fire, but he didn't want to worry her by admitting it hurt.

"You remembered my name," she said, pleasantly surprised. "I would have thought, with the way you ran off, you wouldn't have caught it." A smirk played across her lips.

"I didn't run. I casually walked with intent. There's a difference."

"Yeah, I guess." She paused. "Thank you for helping me up. I didn't realize how bad it was."

"It was my duty to make sure you were okay. Dog leash attack etiquette." She laughed at his wayward attempt at humor. "Does anything else hurt?" he asked.

Rylen looked herself over. "Besides my pride and self-esteem? No."

"Yeah, you did and do look ridiculous." He smiled, winking at her.

"If that's you trying to cheer me up, it's not working," she said, casually flirting and laughing lightly under her breath. He liked the way she laughed. "And you," she shook some sand from his hair, "don't look much better."

They sat in a comfortable silence, listening to the water lap on shore as the sun started to peak back out. It was comforting sitting there with her, but something nagged at the corner of Caleb's conscience.

"Umm...look, about yesterday," he began.

"Yes, about yesterday." She studied him, waiting for an explanation. Her eyes turned regretful when she looked at the bruising setting in under his eyes.

Caleb thought for a moment, trying to come up with a reasonable excuse, but telling her that she made him nervous and that her eyes were hypnotizing didn't seem proper.

"I had 24-hour bronchitis. Horrible, hurts like hell." He implored her with his blood shot eyes to believe his ridiculous excuse. She wanted more, but Caleb's creativity eluded him and he was struck dumb. "I'm sorry," he rattled off, thinking an apology was best.

"Thank you, that's all I wanted. I forgive you." She returned her full focus to Arnie who was basking in the glow of a woman's caress. Caleb felt jealous of the dog. The way she was looking at him, touching him. "But do you forgive me?" she asked.

He stretched out his right arm and lay back against the step, feeling lightheaded.

"Yes, it was just a reaction. You couldn't help it."

"You need a doctor, Caleb."

"Just bruising. I heal quickly," he lied. The bruise from last week's run-in with a doorknob was still pronounced on his right hip.

"Are you sure?" she asked concerned.

"Yes."

Resting against the step, Rylen was surprised to find Caleb's arm lying behind her. The nape of her neck touched his forearm, sending an excited chill down her spine. She rolled her shoulders and touched what felt like a slight bump above her eye. She looked like a real prize, not exactly the look one would sport when they wanted to seduce someone. Hold up. Did she want to seduce him? She barely knew the man, and yesterday he had no intention of getting to know her. She was always compelled to go after what she couldn't have, and Caleb struck her as someone she couldn't have.

A laugh bubbled up, and Caleb felt a calm wash over him like he had never felt before. This was going to be a problem, but after today, he was going to ignore her. Today he'd be polite, and when he saw her at rehearsal next, it would be back to business. There was work to do. Avoiding social fraternization was a practice he not only engaged in but emphasized to Dominic, who liked to do more than simply fraternize.

"What happened to his leg?" she asked, breaking the silence with her curiosity about Arnie's injury.

"When he was a puppy, he saw a kite, wandered into the street, and was hit by a car. Leg needed to be amputated. He has an aversion to kites now."

"That's understandable," she said, planting a kiss on Arnie's head. "You're so cute," cooed Rylen in a baby voice.

"Ever since, he's been on an expedition to rid the world of the kite variety," Caleb laughed. "Very much a love-hate relationship." He ruffled Arnie's hair. "Don't ya, buddy? You love to hate those nasty kites," he laughed. Arnie barked and glanced around, knowing full well what they were talking about.

"Maybe he's the better for it."

"How so?" Caleb frowned, not sure how such an injury could be for the best.

"He learned his lesson. Sometimes, it takes something bad to happen to us to get us moving. Like a kick in the butt. The Universe's way of saying; Time to get going. You've been standing still long enough."

"And what would a dog need to learn from the universe?"

"To look both ways and to sniff more butts, of course," she laughed. "Live life to the fullest."

"I don't think a dog knows the difference," Caleb said, not sure he was on board with her logic.

"Sure he does. You need to give him more credit." Arnie tilted his head to the side and watched Caleb. Caleb studied his companion and wondered if the dog was keeping track of the conversation better than he was; the Universe's expectations beyond him.

"I don't know if I necessarily believe your line of reasoning."

Rylen turned to look at him. "Oh?" she asked. "Well, look at it this way. Are you living life or just living?"

"It's the same."

She shook her head. "No. Some people just exist."

Caleb thought about her comment. Was that what he was doing? "Existing is living."

"I can see I'm not going to get anywhere with this argument."

"So you're conceding?" He grinned taking his hand away from his nose, relieved the bleeding had subsided.

"No, I know when I'm fighting a losing battle, but I'll get you to see the light." She patted his leg, wanting to leave her hand there. Rylen hesitated for a moment, wondering what he might do if she did, pushing the limits, but he shifted, and she removed her hand.

Rylen saw the tattered book next to her. Curious, she picked it up and was pleased when she read the title. "Out of Africa." She handed it back to Caleb. "Seems you've read it many times. It's one of my favorites. True story."

"Yes, that makes it all the more heartbreaking." Caleb clenched the book, its spine twisted so that it fit perfectly in his back pocket.

"Heartbreaking? No, it's a lovely story. A tale of finding one's own way, of finding love and loss."

"Loss is not lovely." Caleb looked out over the water. Now that the rain cloud was gone and nothing else threatened the afternoon sky, people started to take their sailboats out, and families gathered back on the beach. He wished to look at anything but her at this moment, fearing she'd see the truth in his eyes--what he had done, the monster lurking inside of him.

"It's the experience of finding. Wouldn't you rather have love in your life, even if it is for just a short time, than not have that experience at all?" She watched him, wanting him to look at her.

"No," he said, his eyes void of any emotion. The book twisted in his hand, the front page worn, slightly tearing from the spine in his vice grip. All his concentration was focused to his hands as a tingling sensation took over. His fingers started to drum on the book in forced motions so his movements didn't become jerky. "I have no time to experience things that won't last," he finally said, breaking their awkward silence.

"You mean you don't make time," she retorted, trying to read him.

He looked at her again. "No. I have no time," he emphasized. His voice was tight and barely controlled his fury. He stood with authority but did not run away like he had before. "Do you need me to call anyone for you?"

She looked up at him, his face aglow from the sun shining behind him, casting a shadow over her body, making the warmth depart and cold sink in. One minute he was making jokes and winking at her, the next he was harsh, cold, distant, and ready to leave. She shook her head. "No. I can take care of it," she said, disappointed by the turn of events.

"Very well." The book was crammed into his back pocket, and he walked away. Arnie remained seated, his head still on Rylen's lap, his eyes watching her while she watched Caleb retreat. "Arnie," Caleb called. Arnie whined, breaking Rylen's concentration.

She gave him one last pat on the head and rub behind the ears before she dropped her hands. "Better get going," she told him. Arnie backed away and sped off to catch Caleb.

Rylen watched a moment longer before she attempted to stand. Her knees throbbed. She wanted to go back to her apartment and lie in the hot shower for the rest of the day until whatever she was feeling passed through her system. She wanted to get away from Caleb and regroup.

Her knees had stiffened; sand scrapes ran across them and her shins. She tried to keep the weight off her ankle, but there was no way she was going to get far with just one leg.

Limping seemed like an indulgent weakness she would rather not let Caleb witness. She forged on, her head held high, but the pain was too great. Her lower lip quivered and all she could think was ouch. Putting light pressure on her ankle, she winced in pain. She didn't want to look hurt, but it was evident on her face that she was in pain. A forlorn and lost look crept in to make her look extra pathetic.

Was the man really worth this trouble? It didn't matter. The pain was too unbearable to focus on anything else. To keep her strength, she repeated in her mind the one word that seemed to sum him up—ass.

When Caleb was far enough away that he knew she couldn't see him, he turned to see if he could find her. He noticed the steps were empty, but not far from it, he saw her limping away in the opposite direction. Arnie barked and sat back, his arrow-straight tail thumping against the cement, demonstrating his displeasure over Caleb's actions.

"I'm an ass, I know," admitted Caleb. Arnie barked in agreement. "Thanks."

He wanted to go and help her, but he knew she wouldn't take his assistance. Not now. So he did what he did best. He turned and walked away.

Chapter Six

Caleb stared straight ahead as he drove, his only intent to get home and practice in solitude. Not only was he burdened with how callous he had been, but he was upset by the feelings she brought to life. He could feel the tension in his shoulders and rolled them to relieve it. Twice now, he had been unkind to her: the conversation, short; the change in demeanor, menacing; and the clear imagine of his back, prominent. He was sure that, when Rylen thought of him, she could only conjure up images of him walking away.

Why did he care? She was different. She probed, and he really hated that. He didn't ask questions of others for a sole reason: if he did, the other party would do the same, and Caleb would be forced to choose between lying and divulging too much.

Caleb rubbed his eyes. Looking in the rearview mirror, he was met by Arnie's ice cold glare.

"You have something you want to say?" Arnie continued to stare, unmoving. "I didn't think so." Caleb put the back window down so Arnie could stick his head out, flapping his tongue with the wind, as he liked to do, but he didn't take the bait. Caleb frowned. The damn dog always felt he had a say in Caleb's business. "If you're trying to make me feel bad, don't. I already do. And I don't need you judging me," he yelled into the mirror. "It's none of her business anyway. I say who can be in my life, not you." Arnie made no acknowledgement. "When we get home you can ignore me all you want." Arnie yawned, ready for the conversation to end. "I'm taking a nap."

Caleb would have to apologize somehow, and not in the normal "I'm sorry" way. He had to do something different. His plan to ignore her was evaporating as many different thoughts began stirring in his mind. The unwavering need to apologize bothered him. His own promise was already broken. He knew what he would do. It was going to expose him in a way, but he wanted to make things right. He needed to make things right. Then he could ignore her. His plan was formulated.

Dominic's Mercedes sat in Caleb's driveway. Now he was annoyed. All he had asked was to have a day alone. Arnie bounded forward from the back seat. His tail swished back and forth in excitement at seeing his Godfather, slapping Caleb in the head. Caleb was certain this was done purposefully. He sat with the engine idling, ignoring Arnie's cries to be freed. What was his brother doing here? Dominic knew today was his day to be alone.

The front door opened, and Dominic emerged with a smile on his face. The smile soon faded as Dominic got closer. He could see Caleb clutching the wheel in aggravation as well as the red stain that ran down Caleb's chin staining his t-shirt. In an attempt at closer inspection, Dominic swung open the door, freeing Arnie. Jumping out, Arnie hopped on his back legs begging Dominic to notice him, but Dominic could only focus on the blood-stained Caleb.

"What happened?" he asked, worried. "Are you okay? Did you go to the doctors?" Dominic absently patted Arnie, keeping his focus on Caleb. "You shouldn't be driving!"

He stood inside the passenger door waiting for Caleb to respond. Neither said anything. Arnie stopped trying to get Dominic's attention and returned to the car. Putting his paw on the seat, he looked at Caleb; then almost defiantly, he sneezed and trotted into the house.

The car door slammed as Caleb tried to escape the inquisition he knew was to come.

"You can't just show up with blood all over and not expect me to ask what happened! Your eyes are bruised. What the hell, Caleb?"

Caleb stopped in the doorway. "This is my house. I can show up whenever I want. And what are you doing here?"

"What do you mean what am I doing here? I told you last night I was staying. I had a new chess set delivered today. We have our weekly chess match."

Caleb looked at Dominic like he was a crazy person. "You never said anything to me. Now you're just lying so you can hover and watch over me. I told you I don't want you babysitting me," he said, trying to maneuver past Dominic.

"Caleb –" Dominic started in awe. "I was with you all night," he swung his arms around wildly. "When you had your nightmare about –"

Caleb pushed past Dominic with his head down. "I don't have those dreams anymore, Dominic, you know that."

"Are you serious? You don't remember anything from last night?"

Caleb stopped. "Fine, maybe I just forgot. I got hit in the head and I think my nose is broken."

"Think or know? Did you see a doctor?" Dominic tipped Caleb's chin up to inspect the damage. "Caleb, did you see a doctor?"

"No, alright! Just realign it. You did it before when we were kids."

"Caleb you need to see a doctor, there's a ton of blood all over you." He scanned him up and down shaking his head. "I don't feel right just letting this go, especially since you don't remember anything from last night."

Caleb tried to push past Dominic. "Fine, I'll just have a crooked nose." Dominic threw his arm across the entryway and glared at Caleb. Positioning his feet shoulder width apart, Caleb put a wad of his t-shirt in his mouth and took a few deep breaths.

"You're like a child," Dominic said as he put his hands on either side of Caleb's nose.

Caleb blinked giving Dominic the go ahead. A blinding white light flashed and he heard the crack of his nose as it returned to position. Caleb stifled a scream into his shirt and leaned his head on Dominic's chest.

"That hurt," he said dropping the shirt from his mouth.

"Yeah." Dominic patted him on the back, grabbing him by the shoulders. "Now, go get cleaned up."

"Dom," Caleb fretted, now able to breathe through his nose without wheezing. "I don't want to play."

"Since when?"

"You act like I know how to play chess," he said exasperated.

Dominic stood silent for a moment. Caleb took this as his opportunity to weasel past him into the house. Walking in, he found Arnie was already lying on the couch with Mr. Puff at his side.

"What do you mean you don't know how to play chess?" Dominic asked, stalking down the hall after him. Caleb threw his outfit away. No need to try and clean the blood off anything except his face. "What do you mean you don't know how to play chess?" Dominic repeated sternly.

"Just what I said. When have I ever played chess?" Caleb splashed cold water over his face and washed the blood away. "I don't even know what the pieces do."

"This is a joke right? A bazaar joke to get me out of the house."

"Dominic, if I wanted you out of the house, you wouldn't be here."

"Then what do you call that chess board on your coffee table in the living room?"

"A chess board."

"Don't get smart with me."

Caleb wiped his face clean, the blood a distant memory. "What's your problem?" he asked, throwing on a new shirt. "Why don't we just go upstairs and play some Wii sports?"

"Because we don't do that. We play chess!" he exclaimed.

Caleb brushed past his brother and reemerged in the living room where Arnie continued to play with Mr. Puff. Not far from him, the chess board, pieces lined up in their assigned squares, sat on the coffee table. He stopped for a moment and looked at it.

"See, we play," Dominic said taking a seat on the couch, the white pieces in front of him.

"You really want to play?"

"Yes," he said softly.

"Then you have to teach me."

Dominic paused. "I've already taught you," he said defeated. "Though, I don't mind doing it again. Are you up for it?"

"I suppose. I don't have anywhere to go," Caleb said, just as his head exploded with the irritating buzzing noise. He looked around to find the source, but it seemed he was the only one hearing it.

"What?" he slightly yelled, the buzzing still affecting his senses. A blinding white light fogged his eyes, and Caleb could barely hear anything Dominic was saying over the voices screaming in his head.

"We should wait!"

"There's no time. We have to do this now."

"And after?"

"We'll cross that bridge when we come to it."

"No, I want to know what their plans are."

"You know perfectly well what's going to happen. I don't want to prolong a life that isn't there anymore."

"How do you know that?"

"This isn't your decision. You can't blame us for following through."

"You know what this means."

"It means we can finally grieve and move on."

"It's selfish."

"Selfish is what you're doing. We're the only ones in this room. I don't understand what you're holding on to when nothing is there."

"I'm holding on to a family that you're trying to separate."

"The decisions been made. Everything is in order. This is not our call. Paper trumps all of us. You'll realize that soon enough, you can't hold out much longer."

The shouting stopped, and Caleb could hear someone sit down next to him. The air puffed out of a chair cushion followed by a deep sigh and a strangled cry that Dominic held back. "They're gone, you ready?"

Caleb's eyes shot open and he found himself sitting on the couch next to the black pieces, his eyes hazy with tears. The buzzing had quieted, keeping steady in the back of his mind, always there, but muted some. Instinctively he moved a pawn forward.

I've missed this.

"Sometimes it's nice to be able to relax."

Nice to spend time with friends too.

"Sometimes," he laughed. He reached forward and pulled back quickly, taking notice that his watch was broken. "My watch is broken."

Time bandit.

"It seems," he sighed starting to undo the band.

Keep it on.

"There's no point, it's useless."

Time is what you make of it. Just to warn you, I plan on beating you in 3 more moves.

"You sound sure of yourself."

I'm confident in my abilities. I can teach you.

"I decided I'd rather learn on my own."

Another game?

"Yes," Caleb said, putting the pieces back in starting order.

You have to know what your opponent is going to do before they know it themselves. As well as their strengths and weaknesses. Do you have any weaknesses?

"I think if I were to divulge that information then that would be a weakness. Therefore, my strength is I don't reveal my weaknesses," Caleb laughed.

Well played. You know, I've never asked before, but what made you decide to be a pianist?

"I learned long ago that I couldn't possibly be anything other than a pianist. I wasn't offered the choice."

Now that's silly, we all get a choice. I believe the choices we make are what shape us, yet you say you haven't chosen to be who you are. That goes against my philosophy.

"Sorry to burst your philosophical bubble, but some are molded, forced, then left, and the only thing they know is what has been taught to them."

You were forced to be a pianist that plays beautifully, and yet you continue to do so with vigor. Why?

"Because it's all I know, as I said before. Circumstances have forced me to hide behind the piano."

Hide?

"I meant sit, sit behind the piano."

As opposed to what?

"Standing," he sighed seeing the board was not in his favor. "Even though your philosophy on life is flawed, your chess skills are far superior to mine. Two losses is my limit for the day."

My philosophy isn't flawed. We're all given a choice.

"Then I must have been the exception to the rule."

The buzzing stopped and his body calmed. His head hurt like hell. Vision returned to normal. Moments ago, he was standing in the hallway reminding Dominic that he didn't know how to play chess, while Arnie licked Mr. Puff. Finding himself in the same place, Caleb looked to see Arnie still on the couch, the chessboard untouched and Dominic gone.

Chapter Seven

Caleb waited at the main entrance to the Six Flags Park, tickets in hand and anxiety making him rock back and forth. The rush of kids and families breezed past him in their quest for a day of entertainment, sugary treats, and rides. Looking behind him, he watched as the Giant Drop plummeted 200 feet toward the ground. The sight gave Caleb heart palpitations. That was one ride he wasn't going on.

Rylen had no reason to show, but Caleb wanted to see her. With only three hours of sleep the night before he kept replaying the scene on the beach over and over until he hated himself enough for his actions that he got out of bed. He had debated endlessly if he was doing the right thing, standing in the yard for over an hour picking out the perfect bouquet. He tried to talk himself out of sending it, but in the end he shoved it at the messenger and told him to run before he changed his mind. Now he was terrified she wouldn't show up.

It was already half past two. He had been studying his new watch every second for the past half hour. A black town car pulled up to the entrance and Caleb stood up straighter. She had finally arrived. But it was not her, just some man and his daughter. He had ordered a town car right? It didn't matter. He'd stand there all day if he had to. Then again, maybe not. He didn't want to look like some amusement park creep.

More cars came and went, and eventually Caleb released a deep breath. She wasn't coming. Deep down he knew she wouldn't come. His body unclenched, his shoulders slacked, and his anxiety seeped away. He could go home now knowing he tried to make amends. He glanced at his watch one more time—it was only 2:32.

Rylen watched him from a few feet away. She had the driver let her out a little way off when she saw him waiting for her. She still wasn't sure if she wanted to stay, but as she watched him continuously check the time, she couldn't bring herself to leave.

He stood waiting in jeans that clung nicely in all the right places and a polo shirt. In the day that had passed since their last meeting his hair had been cut. She liked it much better than his shaggy, unkempt look. She could see he was getting antsy, and his shoulders slumped forward slightly, his fingers drumming against his leg. He had given up hope. Finally ready, she took the first step to relieve him of his anxiety.

Caleb's new plan was to give the tickets to the father and daughter. He started forward, hoping he could catch them before they bought their own tickets. Turning, he ran straight into her. He was shocked to see her looking up at him, her eyes twinkling with excitement, as he took a step back.

"Leaving so soon?" she asked, a smile broadening her face. He was clean-shaven, and, even with the slight bruising around his eyes and the red rim around his nose, he looked more handsome than before.

Rylen could tell by his intense gaze that her fun, seductress look was working. Since she wasn't sure where they were going, she had opted for a pair of slim-fit jeans, a white t-shirt, and a black leather jacket. Her hair was in loose curls on her shoulders, and she sported the medical ankle brace that had come with Caleb's bouquet of flowers. She preferred stylish heels but, in the light of her injured ankle, had opted for the more comfortable option of sandals. Now, looking at the park, she longed for the support of her sturdy tennis shoes. Luckily, she had taken Tylenol to keep the pain at bay for a little while, and she had pain medication stashed in her pocket for an emergency.

"I didn't think you were coming," Caleb said, still not believing she was in front of him.

"Believe me, I thought about not coming and while I was thinking about it I found myself here. Next time you have me kidnapped, tell me where we're going. I was clenching my pepper spray the whole ride," she laughed. "Why did you bring me here?"

"Because I felt you deserved an apology in person," he said, hoping he wouldn't find any apprehension in her demeanor.

"Thank you. But, you couldn't do that at rehearsal? It still doesn't answer why Six Flags?"

"Because …," he tried to remember why he had wanted to meet here. "Because flowers aren't enough and neither are words, so I thought we should start over. Meet here and enjoy each other's company. Try something outside of Chicago." He shoved his hands into his pockets, slightly embarrassed by his childish idea.

"Rylen Price. Nice to meet you," she said, holding out her hand. "Say, what happened to your face?"

He smirked, putting his hand in hers and shaking it firmly like his father had taught him. "Caleb Montgomery, it's a pleasure to meet you so randomly, Rylen." He tentatively touched his nose. "Some crazy woman at the beach yesterday tried to beat me up over a stupid sand castle." She swatted at him playfully making him laugh as he continued, "Here's an idea. Since we're both here and now acquainted, would you like to accompany me on a few rides, play some games, eat copious amounts of sugar, and enjoy the rest of the day?"

"Good thing that's exactly how I want to spend the rest of my day."

"Great," he beamed. Everything was turning out better than he had expected. His nerves calmed enough that a panic attack was no longer in his future.

They started to walk toward the entrance when he noticed her stride was slightly off. She was limping, and he felt foolish thinking she'd be fine walking through an amusement park. Suddenly, he was hit with the prospect of his own legs not cooperating. He had been experiencing such a rush of anxiety since he made the decision that he hadn't thought about how everything could crumble at his feet.

"I'm so sorry. I didn't think your ankle would be bad today. Do you want to go back home?"

"No, it's okay. I took enough pain relievers that I barely notice the throbbing. When we're in line I'll just lean on the bars."

"Hopefully we won't have to wait in line that long; I got the flash passes for us."

"That will make things easier."

He held his arm out to her so she could put some of her weight on him. She wove her arm through his, her hand resting on his forearm as they made their way into the park.

"Thank you for the flowers," she said as they joined the line of people trying to get through the entrance. "I love lilies."

"They're my favorite. Lilies of the valley in particular."

"Why?" she asked. Most men don't admit that flowers mean anything more to them than apologies or gifts for holidays.

"Lilies of the valley mean a return to happiness, good fortune. The legend of the lily of the valley is that it sprang from Eve's tears when she was kicked out of the Garden of Eden."

"That's beautiful. The ankle brace was a nice touch."

"I thought it would be funny," he cringed. "Do you have it on?"

She pulled up her pant leg revealing the white ankle brace. It bore his hand-written note inviting her on the outing and advising that a car would be waiting for her. "Original."

"It just so happens I'm an outside-the-box thinker."

"By the way," she turned to him, "I accept your apology."

"What? You mean I didn't have to do all this?"

"Don't push it pal, be happy with small miracles."

"Lucky me." He smiled down at her, his bruised complexion endearing.

His heart was racing. The nausea was getting to him, and he thought he was bound to throw up his hot dog and chili fries on the poor, giggling child in front of them. Caleb hadn't been on a roller coaster in years. He estimated the last time was probably when is father took them to Disneyworld when they were eight. The Dumbo flight had been the highlight. What was he thinking with the amusement park idea?

The Viper roller coaster was wooden and had an 80-foot drop in addition to ten other drops during the two-minute ride. As they creaked slowly toward the first drop, Caleb made the mistake of looking over the side. He could feel his stomach start to rise into his throat. Just as they were about to descend, Caleb pinched his eyes closed. He could feel the air rushing past his scalp and his butt rising out of the seat. Clutching the security bar, Rylen put her hand over his to remind him she was at his side.

The creaking of the wood underneath the box cars made Caleb anxious. It sounded as if it was going to splinter at any moment, plunging them to their deaths. Oh, yes, this was a great idea.

"Open your eyes. The camera is coming up," she squealed.

"I can't!" Caleb cried.

"Yes, you can. You don't want to miss anything!"

Her chiding comment prompted Caleb to open his eyes to the hellish ride before him. He wasn't sure what resonated about the comment, but he wished he had kept his eyes closed. She pointed at the camera just as their train dropped forward, the speed making his stomach do flips.

"Smile!"

Caleb gave his best frightened but attempting fun smile. It felt awkward. After the initial drop he somehow managed to keep his stomach intact, but with ten drops still to come, Caleb wasn't holding out much hope that its contents would remain there.

Alive, intact and his last nerve fraying, Caleb was worried he had left his gut somewhere at the bottom of the Iron Wolf's 90-foot drop or the 360 vertical loop. He was going to pay for all of this tomorrow he thought standing next to a trashcan in case what was left decided to make a quick getaway.

Rylen raced toward him with their picture in hand giggling the whole way over she shoved the picture in his face. "You look absolutely terrified," she laughed pulling the picture back before he decided to grab it and toss it into the trashcan.

"I smiled."

"I don't think that's what I would call a smile." She tilted her head trying to figure out the range of emotions plastered on his face. "Looks like you were going to hurl on that kid in front of us."

"I was scared for a moment."

"Ha." She clutched his arm. Her ankle was not hurting as much as she thought it would when she first saw her destination, but she wasn't going to tell Caleb that for fear he'd take his arm away. "So what's next?"

"Really? You want to go on another ride?"

She pursed her lips as she pondered making him suffer through another ride, but she decided against it. "How about a game? You any good at winning prizes?"

"You got me confused with Dominic," he snorted, thinking about how good Dominic was at everything.

"Who?"

"My brother. You'll eventually meet him at rehearsal. He's my manager."

They passed by a ring-toss game. Caleb stopped, his sudden halt pulling Rylen backwards and pressing her against his chest. She blushed, brushing a strand of hair behind her ear. She glanced at the game in front of which Caleb had stopped.

A jolt of electricity ran through Caleb's body as Rylen fell against him. He helped steady her, putting his hand on the small of her back but quickly pulling away fearing he'd let it linger.

"Up for it?"

"I hope you like watching me make a fool of myself," he sighed.

"Oh, I can hardly wait." She rubbed her hands together menacingly.

The day flew by, and in a flash, they were walking past crowded snack shops and gaming areas on their way to the exit.

It was difficult with Rylen's limp, but they were able to make it past the crowds easily enough without straining her foot any further. Fathers were carrying their sleeping children, and mothers were pushing strollers filled with candy and prizes as everyone started to head for home. The sun gone and the stars out, they watched as fireworks erupted over head.

Caleb carried a big, purple gorilla on his back. With Rylen's arm still looped in his, they stopped to watch the fireworks. He liked walking with her, her face alight by the explosions overhead. She didn't try to fill the air with needless conversation today, relishing the quiet nature of their thoughts. He found himself mysteriously drawn to her.

"Thank you for today," she said.

"So my apology worked?"

"I think you won me over when you spent twenty bucks trying to win that damn doll. Should have just bribed the man with your money and bought one without all the hassle."

"That's cheating. Besides, you wouldn't have been able to witness my supreme ring tossing skills. After all, it did win you this fine four-foot tall purple gorilla."

"Supreme isn't exactly the word I'd use." She squeezed his arm forcing the blood to his head.

"I think you're insulting me. If you don't want the gorilla, I can set him free." He set his sights on a little girl and veered off toward her.

"Don't you dare!"

She limped after him.

"I don't think you're in the right physical condition to stop me, Rylen. If he's not wanted, I think it's best to just give him to someone who can provide him a better home." He twirled the gorilla over his head and started talking to it. "I'm sorry buddy, but she doesn't think you're worth the effort like I do." He shook the gorilla's head, playfully listening to what the gorilla had to say. "I understand one hundred percent." Rylen tried to grab for the stuffed animal, but Caleb held him up.

"Give him back. He's mine."

Caleb stopped her by putting a finger up. "Technically, he's mine. My twenty dollars and ring tossing exhibition won him."

"But you gave him to me."

"I've been carrying him," he replied, nodding at her ankle.

"That's your dog's fault," she chided.

"Sure. Blame poor, defenseless Arnie, the three-legged dog." He looked back at the gorilla. "Sorry, Jetson, but it's time for you to go."

"You named my gorilla Jetson?" She put her hands on her hips, offended he would take the liberty to name her gorilla; and of all things, Jetson.

"You weren't pulling your weight. The guy's been in the family for thirty minutes, and you haven't named him. So, I took it upon myself to bestow the first name that popped in my head. I wish I could have given him a name that befits his heritage, but it's too late."

"His heritage?" she asked.

"He's Asian."

"Uh huh, and how would you know that?"

"Says so on his ass. Made in China." They laughed. "Do you really want him?" She gave him her best sad face and nodded her head. "Will you take good care of him? Care for him like he deserves?"

"Girl Scout promise." She held up her fingers and saluted him.

Rylen grabbed the gorilla and hugged him, her face barely visible over the humongous purple fluff. She glanced up over Jetson and batted her eye lashes, swaying back and forth.

"Think you can carry him?"

Caleb laughed. "Absentee mother. I bet you weren't even in Girl Scouts."

Rylen tossed Jetson to Caleb and grabbed for his arm, but instead of locking arms, she wove her fingers through his, brazenly pushing him into

55

uncharted waters. Caleb's heart raced. He wasn't sure if this was how he wanted things to go, but he was too afraid to drop her hand. She smiled at him and squeezed his hand in reassurance. They continued toward the parking lot to call it a day.

Waiting for the town car to arrive and take Rylen home, Caleb stood on the curb at a loss. Standing with the smell of funnel cake clinging to them and the stars shining brightly above, he was uncertain of his next move. Their time together had been great, and now that it was over, he wasn't sure if he should kiss her goodnight or just help her to the car. They waited in silence, her hand still in his and Jetson still on his back. His stomach protruded from the funnel cake he had decided he needed before they left, hoping it would make the emptiness go away. She was looking at their roller coaster picture and laughing.

"You're not going to leak that to the press are you?" he asked.

She hid the picture behind her back. "Depends on what you're willing to trade for it."

"Wow. You're looking for a bribe. I didn't think you were that type of girl." He took a step toward her.

"I don't think you know what type of girl I am at all." She stood her ground defiantly. "I'm willing to negotiate."

Caleb loomed over her. "I have ways of making you bend to my will," he joked, pointing at Jetson for her to get the message.

She took a step back. "Perhaps, but maybe that was a ploy."

"No. Eyes don't lie." He took another step forward, forcing her to take one back. She was halted by the steel beam holding up a sign for the ticket booths with nowhere else to go. He leaned in, his face only inches from hers. Her breath smelled of strawberry cotton candy and it hitched in her throat as he drew his finger down her bare arm. "I have ways of making you talk." His mouth was by her ear, his finger finding its way down to her hand where the picture was grasped loosely. "Or...I can just take it," he whispered, grabbing the picture from her hand and stepping away.

Her eyes were wide in disbelief as he blew on his fingertips like they were on fire and wiped them against his shirt. "Sometimes I impress myself."

"You're horrible," she said making a grab for the picture.

"Now, do you really want to play that again? I do have Jetson and the picture. Maybe it's time for you to negotiate the release of your possessions."

She crossed her arms over her chest. "What do you want?" She tried to tap her foot on the ground, but from walking all day, it was finally starting to give out on her.

"I want –"

The car pulled up, and Caleb's thoughts swayed back to his predicament. Should he kiss her? "I want to give them back because I know you'll take good care of them." He extended the gorilla and the picture out to her.

There was an instant where she wasn't sure if he was playing with her, reluctant to take the bait, but he placed both articles in her hands and folded his behind his back. "Thank you, again, for showing up. I wasn't sure about the whole idea, but I'm happy you were able to enjoy the day with me." He walked her to the car, the driver staying behind the wheel while Caleb opened the door.

"I had a great time," she said.

It was now or never. Caleb had made his decision. He was going to kiss her even though he knew it was a bad idea. The worst idea he had ever had.

She silently waited for him, hoping he'd kiss her goodnight, but she wasn't sure if this had been strictly a friend thing, just an apology or some sort of undercover date.

Caleb leaned in, uncertain if he was supposed to lean in ninety percent and she came ten or was it 80/20? He tried to remember the rules, but his mind was a conflicting mess of warning signals and applause for what he was about to do. Rylen was leaning in, mirroring the extension so they would meet, but a minivan behind them honked its horn in aggravation. Caleb stopped and glanced over at the man in the minivan who was waving his hand for them to get going.

Caleb pulled back. "Goodnight," he said, putting an end to the evening.

"Night," she whispered to hide her disappointment.

Rylen sat down in the car, and Caleb closed the door. The car took off, and traffic flow resumed its crawling pace.

Maybe he had dodged a bullet. What would have happened if he had kissed her? What would she expect from him? His plan was to ignore her existence. Things had been set right by apologizing, and now there was no animosity. The original plan was now set in motion. There was no Rylen Price. The only thing that existed on that stage was the piano and the orchestra, no individual players. Things were as they should be. Although, he couldn't help but think, in the few wondrous hours they spent together, not once did he have a tremor or a speech impediment. Nor did he feel the restlessness start to consume him. He felt normal.

Chapter Eight

Nothing felt real. Everything was going according to plan; yet even though he knew this was real, he was praying to wake up. He was helpless, and no one would listen to him. Perhaps they were right, but miracles happened every day. Why couldn't they hold out? Surprisingly, after all their arguments, they had allowed him in the room. It was only fair in his mind.

For thirty minutes they stood around while the procedure was completed, and for that half hour Dominic stood in a daze. He wanted to weep, but the tears only pooled in his eyes and did not flow. Once everything was done, she'd be gone. This wasn't how it was supposed to go, the order of things, not how someone he loved so much was allowed to disappear from his life without even a goodbye.

"He's here," he heard the doctor say.

The room was solemn except for the cries of the baby boy. Dominic stood by her and didn't look at the child. He brushed her hair back and kissed her cheek. "You did so good," he whispered into her ear.

The nurses cared for the child, taking measurements and swaddling him in a blanket, protected from the cold. A blue cap was placed on his matted head.

"Would you like to hold him?" the nurse asked him. He didn't acknowledge her, only caressed the mother's moist cheek, his tears coming steadily now. "Sir?"

"No," he said gruffly, "she should hold him first."

"Dominic," the doctor said putting his hand on his shoulder. Dominic shrugged the hand away.

"She should have a chance to hold her child before you take him away," he cried.

"But she can't," the nurse said.

"No one holds that baby before his mother does," he swung around, his eyes blood shot and stern, glaring at any who dared make eye contact. "Does anyone object?" The room went still, and the baby cried for his mother. The monitors beeped while the ventilator compressed air into her lungs. "Good," he said beckoning the nurse to bring the child. "Just place him on her chest." The nurse did as she was told and took a few steps back. All eyes were on them, but he didn't care. She deserved to feel her baby's skin against her own. "Here's your son," he said to her taking her arms and cradling them around the baby.

Strangled sobs echoed throughout the room, and he wasn't quite sure if they belonged solely to him. Dominic's heart was breaking watching the baby snuggle up to his mother, the last time the child would feel her warm skin against his own. In a few short moments she'd be gone, and the baby in her arms would never have any memory of her. Dominic supposed that's where he came in, sharing memories of her so her son would have a chance at knowing the woman that carried him for as long as she could, the woman that protected her baby from harm giving him a chance at a life. Dominic wouldn't allow him to forget. She'd be there every day watching, and he'd be there every day protecting and sharing all he could.

"It's time," the doctor said.

"Just let it be for a few more minutes. Hasn't she earned the right?" he asked with his back to the room. No one answered. "I believe she has."

"We all knew this day was going to come," her father Joseph said.

"What's going to happen next?" Dominic cried.

"You're next," the new grandmother answered, Debbie's words penetrating.

"What?" Dominic questioned still trying to process the situation.

"You're his Guardian. It's in her documents," Joseph huddled up next to him.

"I was never told," Dominic mumbled his legs shaking almost giving out on him, the new responsibility frightening.

"I'm sure they never thought it would come to this," Debbie whispered looking fondly at her daughter.

"We're not going to fight it. I want to respect her wishes. She wouldn't have done it if she weren't sure that you could handle it. I just ask that we get to see him," Joseph pled praying that Dominic wouldn't keep their grandchild away.

"Whenever you want; I swear on my life," Dominic assured him.

Chapter Nine

"You shouldn't be here," Caleb said as he walked toward the stage. It had only been a week since their Six Flags excursion, but he had kept to his promise and ignored her. They hadn't spoken since then. He avoided her at rehearsals, disappearing afterward until the hall was empty, but his walls could only go so high. She was always in his sight, but he only ever ventured a glance when he knew she was unaware.

His hands were clenched together in a tight fist. The blood rushing to his head was making him feel dizzy, and he felt every charged atom in his body zipping around in agitated fury. He had sat in the audience waiting for Rylen to leave so he could practice alone, but after a half hour he had finally given up. Here she was, interjecting herself into his world again, waiting for him after rehearsal, knowing full well he waited until everyone left so he could practice alone.

Anger and jealousy rippled through him as he watched Rylen take a seat at the piano, her fingers lightly touching the keys-his keys. A primal urge to take back what was rightfully his surged through his body and the anger only intensified it. Whispering the notes out loud she tapped the floor with her foot carrying the composition in her mind. He knew the anger had to do with her insatiable patience to wait him out, but he didn't know if the jealousy was because she touched his instrument or that he wanted to touch her.

The sheet music in Rylen's hand flew into the air. His voice startled her making her go hot and cold, something only he could do. Caleb walked into the light and looked up at her with a hard expression, his mouth set in a tight line and his eyes cloudy. Behind his cold expression, he looked pale and tired. Caleb, it seemed, was going to continue on as if their day together never happened, but Rylen wasn't about to let him forget. The tension between them would remain until Caleb changed his attitude. She had so much to say; yet she could never manage to say it. She had waited for this very moment. Today was the day she was going to make her decision. Either he'd recognize what they could have together or he'd turn his back. Whichever, she was leaving the auditorium with an answer. Either Rylen would be keeping her current position or taking the offered position in the London Symphony Orchestra.

He was next to her in a second helping to gather up the sheet music she had thrown. He didn't look at her, set in his task, but stopped when he saw the piano sheet music she was searching for.

"Why do you have these piano pieces?" He picked them up and looked over the Rachmaninoff piece he was to perform for his finale.

"Ahh..I dabble a bit here and there. Practicing." She tried to grab it from him, but he held it out of reach, standing to full length above her.

"So you think you can do what I do?" He turned his back and went to the piano, setting the music down.

She could tell from his tone he was upset about something. Maybe today wasn't the best day to catch him, but she wasn't going to stand down now, not when he was actually in front of her and speaking.

"No, I —"

He spun around on his heel to face her. "Wow me," he said with flourish and a sarcastic undertone. He walked back offstage and took a seat in the audience where Rylen couldn't see him.

"I'm not any good!" she exclaimed, trying not to cause further embarrassment in front of him. He said nothing as he sat down to watch her, the only sound that of his creaking seat.

As Rylen hesitantly walked over to the piano, Caleb noticed her limp was gone. Her ankle was healed, and he felt bad that he hadn't noticed before. Still, if he was going to ignore her he had to do it completely. At this moment, he was doing anything but ignoring her.

Rylen looked down at the intimidating baby grand piano holding the sheet music to Rachmaninoff's third movement, one of the most difficult pieces ever performed or attempted, especially for a novice. She sat down, already unsure—her first strike. She scooted the bench in, making sure her hands were a comfortable distance away as she placed them on the keys.

Caleb leaned forward in his seat, clasping his hands in front of him, waiting for her to perform. Her chest heaved one last time as she took a deep breath. Her fingers started to stroke the keys. She concentrated heavily, too heavily, making the movements look mechanical. Her fingers fumbled and the mistakes rang out through the auditorium. As the piece continued, Rylen was able to pick up steam and move along with the notes relatively better, which surprised Caleb. He didn't expect her to get far, but the mistakes dwindled, and she was able to gain momentum.

He leaned back in the seat and closed his eyes as the music ran through him, soothing his nerves and quieting the slight tremor that was making his leg bounce up and down.

He had been angry when he first saw her at his piano, but his anger conflicted with stronger feelings she stirred in him. Caleb had an unbreakable bond with the piano, one she was intensifying by placing her fingers atop the keys. Now that she had possession over his instrument Caleb felt they were bonded and in his eyes it was clear she had taken possession of his attention. There was no mistake that Caleb would feel her presence beneath his hands now when he played. It was bad enough she was within his sight when he played and some days he caught himself focusing on her more than the music.

An astounding energy bathed over him when he saw her. She was beautiful and alive and though he wanted to deny it, she inspired him in a way that only music had before. She made it difficult to stay away, to forget everything about her, silently drawn in by her strange pull. Caleb knew it'd be impossible, at least for the duration of his stay there to ignore her, but he desperately wanted to reign in his overzealous emotions, remembering every sensation he felt when she was around him. He didn't feel like himself when he was around her, his emotions too openly displayed, gradually evolving, but Caleb was too complex and knew she'd always be there floating, attached to his every thought, a painful throb that he'd never be able to sedate. What didn't kill him would likely try again and Rylen was very persistent.

The music stopped, awakening and releasing Caleb from its thrall. "I told you I'm not good." Rylen grabbed for the sheet music in an attempt to put an end to the madness, but Caleb had appeared at her side. Standing next to her, he placed his hand over hers, securing the music where it sat upon the stand.

"Humor me. You weren't butchering it as much as I thought you would," he said, not a hint of a joke in his voice or in his expression.

"Thanks," she mumbled, mortified. She had a sudden urge to punch him. She looked back at the music and started from the beginning. She hoped to work out the kinks, but practice did not make perfect in her case. Again, she fumbled through the piece, missing even the easier runs she had performed correctly before. His presence annoyed and discouraged her. She had been looking forward to talking to him, but now she desperately wanted him to leave.

"Focus," he said into her ear, making her trip over a few keys. "Stop thinking." He sat down on the bench next to her. "Feel it. You feel the music when you play the cello. This is no different. Let it come out through your fingertips. Move with it."

Caleb placed his fingers on the keys and began playing with her, four hands on the keys. The concerto came to life beneath his masterful fingers. Slowly, Rylen let her hands slip away, leaving Caleb to play the piece on his own, no missteps, the notes memorized and synchronized in his mind. Caleb was now captain, helming the piece as Rylen watched, enthralled. He had the amazing ability to move a person with the passion that moved through his body and commanded every key stroke.

"You listen for the orchestra. You're not the only one on stage." Caleb imagined the orchestra. "It's rapture." His key strokes started to pick up steam, his fingers playing tirelessly, his body settling into a familiar rhythm. "It's soothing melody." His fingers became a blur. "This is life. Playing is like breathing. Our fingers are the heart. As long as they keep going, the music never stops breathing. It's a feeling of freedom." Beads of sweat started to drip down his face, blurring his vision, but he didn't need his eyes to perform the piece. He closed them and concluded the portion Rylen had fumbled through. "Passion. The music lives in you because it's what feeds you."

Caleb was a mess. Sweat was pouring down his face, and his cheeks were blotched red from his heavy breathing. Caleb ended the phrase gracefully but did not continue the concerto. He didn't want to go on with her watching. In no way was he in any condition to play the entire piece yet. He needed to practice, to set his breathing pattern like an athlete preparing for the big game.

Caleb opened his eyes trying to slow down his breathing until it returned to a steady rhythm. Rylen stared at his profile, waiting for him to look at her, but he remained transfixed on the keys. Hands shaking, he folded them at his sides so they couldn't be seen.

"That was beautiful." She placed her hand on his shoulder prompting him to straighten his posture and pull back slightly. Rylen shied away and stood from the bench, grabbing her sheet music.

"I'm sorry," Caleb murmured, hunching over as he waited for his hands to stop shaking.

"That was amazing. I could never do that."

Caleb swung around on the bench and stood up facing Rylen, pushing his hands into his pockets, looking at her serenely. "You already do but with your cello." His eyes lit up, and a smile spread over his face. He imagined her playing. "You think what I do is remarkable, but you do the same, only your fingers and bow are on strings. Mine are on keys."

"That's different."

"It's music."

Rylen felt like she was back at Six Flags coexisting peacefully. She was about to ask him if he wanted to get dinner, but she was stunned into silence when he ran the back of his hand down her cheek. He laughed, his hand no longer shaking, even though her skin under his fingers made him want to quake.

"You're breathtakingly beautiful," he whispered.

Caleb's heart pounded when she smiled, but once he realized he had spoken out loud, he wasn't able to smile back. There was no doubt about it now. He was clinically insane. With each step he fell further, getting in too deep. The prospect of continuing what they had started was a great force, pushing him into unchartered waters he felt were better left unexplored. He knew what was best, what was right, but deep down in his bones he wanted to throw caution to the wind, even though his mind told him to be reasonable. He had no room for error, no room for more people in his life. The closer she got, the closer she would get to knowing he wasn't who she thought he was. Inside he was dark. His soul was spoken for, and his body was dying right before her eyes. She didn't know it, and that's how he wanted to keep it. This way she was safe.

"I have something I need to tell you," she said, waiting for him to respond, but he just waited for her to go on. "I've been offered a position in London."

His heart stopped. The air around him froze, and he felt his dream slipping away before it had truly formed. Perhaps this was for the best. She'd leave and forget about him and go on to bigger and better things. But could he forget her? The answer was clear, but he didn't want to face it.

"There's something about your eyes." She watched as his mind reeled behind them, every emotion passing, but too difficult to distinguish. "Truth. Sadness."

Caleb's demeanor changed in an instant, a flash of irritation passed across his face quickly fading into indecision.

"I think you should leave." His voice was as unforgiving as his glare. A wall of ice had been resurrected right before her eyes. Rylen knew when she wasn't wanted. It was possible her feeling was a girl's infatuation with a celebrity. When she was offered the position, she had been indecisive about what to do with her future. Now he made it easy. If he didn't want her, she didn't want him.

She grabbed her sheet music and shoved it into her purse. Caleb had already gone back to the piano, and without looking back, Rylen walked off stage and down the center aisle as fast she could. She was trying to get away, but there was no place she could go to escape her thoughts of him. How could she have been so stupid to think he wanted her? There were moments of sweetness, but the moment she got close, he closed up and turned his back on her. Today showed her just how stubborn and self-destructive he was.

The lobby doors opened. Light from the lobby shined through, silhouetting the man's body before her. His face was darkened by the blinding light.

"I'm sorry," Dominic said, moving out of the way. "Is something wrong?" he asked, genuinely concerned.

"Your brother is a manipulative asshole," Rylen yelled loud enough for Caleb to hear clearly before she stormed through the lobby doors.

Dominic jumped on the stage to find Caleb lying on top of the piano staring up at the ceiling. "What was that about?" he asked, confused. "Hey, you okay?"

"Do you think there'll be stars out tonight?" Caleb asked, trying to take his mind off of Rylen.

"Why? Do you plan on making a wish?"

"I do want a milkshake. Think I can persuade you to go get me one?"

"Maybe." Dominic paused. "Are you going to tell me what happened?"

"No," Caleb said, not in the mood to rehash the devastating news Rylen had just told him and replaying his breathtakingly beautiful words over in his mind. He could feel the heat rising up his neck, and his hand twitched at the conflicting thoughts.

"Do you want me to pick you up at your place tomorrow for therapy?"

"I'm not going."

"Are you not feeling well?"

"No, I'm fine. I just don't want to go."

"Why?" Dominic's stance stiffened.

"I don't have to go if I don't want to."

"You made a deal with me, Caleb, you can't renege on it."

"Just forget it, Dominic."

"I'm picking you up at 8 tomorrow," he said with finality.

"I won't be there."

"Where are you going?"

"You don't need to know my every move, Dominic. I'm my own person. If I say I don't want to go, I don't have to. I'm a grown-ass man."

Dominic let out a quick puff of air. "You sure as hell haven't been acting like this grown-ass man you claim to be." Caleb's face was complacent with no emotion, but Dominic wasn't going to let up until he knew Caleb got the message. "If you don't go tomorrow, don't expect me to help you anymore. You've worn me out, Caleb. I can't keep doing all this if you're not willing to help."

"Fine."

"That's it? Fine?"

"Go away," he whispered.

"Caleb, are you okay?" Dominic took a step toward him. "Does this have something to do with that woman that just left?" Caleb remained vigilant in his silence. "You like her," it dawned on him. "That's why you're so angry."

Caleb shot up into a seated position. "Dammit, Dominic, leave!" his voice echoed throughout the auditorium.

"I'm picking you up at 8 tomorrow. Your ass better be ready." He sternly pointed his finger at Caleb's chest.

Caleb's eyes glinted with fight. "I told you, I won't be there," he said through clenched teeth.

Dominic leaned in and pressed his finger against Caleb's chest. "Yes. You. Will."

Caleb could feel his body vibrating with the force of an impending fight. He tried to move forward off the piano, but Dominic pushed him back.

"Why do you keep picking fights with me, Caleb?" he asked, confused by Caleb's actions as of late. Dominic waited for a response, but Caleb didn't seem to want to, or didn't know how to answer. "If you're not there tomorrow, Caleb, I'm done," Dominic whispered.

"You're replaceable," Caleb said, his voice colder than the Arctic wind.

Dominic took a step back and smirked. "You're unbelievable." He shook his head in disbelief. "Alright." He thought carefully about what to say next, meeting Caleb's glare, his voice steady. "Then I'm done."

Dominic jumped off stage and started toward the doors. His gait was slow and methodical, waiting for Caleb to react, to take it back, but he didn't.

When the auditorium doors slammed, Caleb slid from the piano and onto the bench where he started to pound on the keys playing Franz Liszt's Un Sospiro.

Caleb's hands shook. A tremor cascaded down his body. He wasn't sure if it was the anger that was boiling over inside of him or the disease taking a stronger hold. He tried to get control over them, taking a breath and focusing his energy to his fingers, trying to control the tremors. And his hands went limp, something they've never done before, lying lifeless on the keys that were his life.

"I wonder, can you feel my pain, suffering, and utter resentment when I sit behind you and place my fingers on your soul?" he talked to the piano. "Bending me at your will and forcing my hands to do your bidding." He waited for an answer, but knew an inanimate object was never going to answer to his craziness. "I don't know why you should care if you did." He collected himself, slouching behind the piano, placing his head down on the keys. His hands may not have been working, but his arms were. Coercing his arms to move, he ran his fingers over the keys one last time for the day. "I'll see you soon," he bitterly whispered to the piano, placing a soft kiss to the ivory keys.

Chapter Ten

*C*aleb crouched down on the balcony overlooking the living room. He watched the crowd through the rails of the balcony, feeling as though he were in prison—exactly how he envisioned it—a prisoner in his own home. The party started without him, just as he had hoped, not wanting anyone to linger longer than need be. The house was full, but Caleb felt all alone. Dominic had yet to show, if he was even going to. He hadn't spoken to Dominic in well over a week. His brother had come to rehearsal, but they didn't even glance at each other. This was probably the longest they had ever gone without butting into each other's lives. He felt bad for what he had done. His brother had only wanted to help, but Caleb had now moved on to annoyed—annoyed with how thoroughly Dominic was avoiding him.

Sticking to his guns, Caleb didn't go to his appointments, aerobic swim and physical therapy. A driver even came to pick him up, Dominic's roundabout way of getting him to go, reminding him he had priorities, but Caleb couldn't be bothered. He was too tired. He had sat at the piano the night after their argument, staring down at the keys. He wanted to play Franz Liszt Piano Concerto No. 1 in E-Flat Major, but his brain couldn't process it. His fingers lay helpless on the keys with nowhere to begin because he didn't know how it began, where it progressed, or how it ended. The whole musical composition was lost to him, and he sat, the entire night, staring at keys that he could not press. If he didn't know how to play concertos he had grown up playing his whole life, what was the point in going to therapy?

Things had been falling apart for quite some time now, but he was failing to take notice of the goings on around him. Dominic's life was spiraling out of control and Caleb was to blame for it all. He saw what happened after everything fell apart in Europe, the depression that led to him pretending nothing happened. Caleb chastised himself for not helping his brother when Dominic was in need. After all, Dominic had always helped him.

He tried to hide in the shadows, sitting on the ground with Arnie lying across his lap whining, his face pressed up against the rails, searching the crowd for any glimpse of her. He was angry for even thinking about her, but he couldn't stop. It bothered him that she somehow managed to find her way into his thoughts and daydreams. She was invading his space, emotionally and mentally, and he wanted to resent her; resent her for the way she unnerved him and how she unknowingly made him want her.

Arnie whined again, his eyes staring up into his master's, trying to regain Caleb's attention.

"I know, me too, buddy." He kissed the top of Arnie's head, bringing his focus back to his three-legged partner in crime. Arnie wasn't accustomed to so many people in one place and felt out of his element with all of them invading his home. Caleb could understand. He too felt ill at ease, an unpopular kid spying on the cool kids at recess. Petting Arnie, he tried to soothe the big baby of a dog. He found himself reasoning with his loyal friend, assuring him it was okay to be scared and coaxing him to meet their guests. In reality, Caleb was actually trying to soothe his own fears. Big baby.

Her brown hair was full, lush, and long, complementing the contours of her body. The dress she wore was the color of her eyes, a pale blue, and elegant in its simplicity. It flowed against her graceful body in a way that mesmerized Caleb. He spied her through the railings of the balcony and contemplated sitting there for the remainder of the evening just to watch her. It would be so easy to stay there and forget the rest of the world around him. Looking at her wasn't a betrayal of his plan to ignore her. He was allowed to look—just this once.

He took a deep breath. "Here goes," he murmured walking down the stairs, making his way to his guests. At first, he was able to make it into the living room without anyone the wiser, but as soon as one person spotted him, the room erupted in applause. He could feel his face turn red. Embarrassment blotching his neck, he waved his hand for all to stop.

"Thank you," the room quieted down. "First, I want to thank everyone for making it out here tonight. I know it's a long hike from the city, but it's a pleasure to have you in my home. Second, I want to thank the donors for so graciously contributing to the wonderful Symphony. Without you, well, we'd just hit someone else up for the cash." Laughter sounded throughout. "Last but not least I'd like to thank Riccardo and the orchestra musicians for taking me on these next two months. It's a pleasure to be back in Chicago. So, let's get drunk and fat tonight." He clapped his hands together while others laughed and hoisted up their champagne flutes. Caleb wasn't much of a speaker, but he knew if he threw in some jokes it would ease the tension he felt and it helped the flush on his cheeks diminish to a lighter shade of red.

As soon as he was done with his speech, he was thrown into conversation. He grabbed a glass of champagne to fit in with the crowd and to keep his hands busy instead of in his pockets. Every chance he got his eyes flitted through the crowd just to find her. He hadn't seen her since he came downstairs, but he could feel her lingering presence.

The crowd parted for a moment and she materialized. She was talking to one of the tuba players. Smiling, sipping a glass of champagne ever so slowly, she threw her head back in laughter as the man put his hand on her back and whispered something in her ear. Strange. Caleb had the sudden longing to be the one making her laugh, to place his hand on her back, and to whisper in her ear. A surge of jealousy coursed through him at the mere thought of her with anyone else. Crazy thoughts ran rampant, making him shutter. It's true the harder you push something away the more you want it, but Caleb had enough in his life without needing to pursue more.

Was he being guided by his heart or his head? She was well worth the effort, but so much more was at stake and the effort needed to win another person's heart required time, so much time that Caleb wasn't sure he had it. Close the door and throw away the key. She was just another part of this world that was not on his side of the equation. In Caleb's case, one plus one did not equal two.

The whole of the evening was spent barely eating, pretending to drink, and performing the social niceties—making the rounds, greeting the guests and striking up little conversations that left Caleb spent. The entire affair felt like a waste of time. From the moment she arrived, Rylen had continued to stay in the furthermost corner of the room, and if Caleb came even remotely close, she retreated into conversation. Caleb continued to stay away, fearing he'd be pulled into conversation and scare her off. It wasn't as if he wished to talk to her. She had a terrible, unnerving effect on him, but he was like a moth to a flame. He wanted to know her decision. Was she going to London or would she continue to stay in Chicago and plague him with her presence?

"Caleb, play something for us," a voice in the crowd shouted.

He forced a smile, taking his place, knowing this moment would come. "And what shall I play?"

"Play something you've written," someone suggested. "A real Caleb Montgomery masterpiece."

Caleb nodded and ran through the compositions in his head. He wanted to play the song he had been composing the past month, but it was yet to be finished, and he wasn't sure he wanted anyone to hear it. He was territorial, and the song felt as if it was meant for someone, but he wasn't sure who. He wracked his brain, but nothing felt right for the occasion.

"It seems I have drawn a blank," he laughed, hoping he would not have a repeat of the other night.

In the crowd, Rylen carefully made her way closer to the piano. She wanted to watch him, his strokes, his eyes, his face, and the movements of his body. Caleb caught sight of her just as she came to the edge of the crowd. Their eyes met. Then, instead of playing something he had done hundreds of times, Caleb composed something entirely new in that moment. He only prayed his body cooperated as he improvised.

The feelings that ran through his body were the motivating factor behind the composition. It started out soft and gentle, a heavily romantic melody: glimpses, stolen moments, touches like quivers on the piano strings that reached a loud swell where everything came to a head. Then, he played through the realization that he could never possess what he was imagining. He could never actually act on his desires. He drove the piece louder and louder, his fingers pounding the left side of the keyboard with few soft touches played here and there. He returned to the softer version of the beginning, the song starting to die down as he imagined how his life would be if she hadn't been on that stage, but his mind turned to how empty it would be if she were not there to take root in his thoughts. He delicately sent his hands back down the keyboard where he intended to end it, the melody transitioning to a tonic major as his thoughts drifted to her, leaving forever. He pounded his fingers on the deeper chords, letting the song emote his anguish.

It was as if all else faded away until only the two of them remained, their senses heightened and attuned only to each other. He was intensely aware of her, but as aware of her as he was, he was more alert to his own body's reactions to her nearness—as though he might become fluid and pour into her. He could barely believe the incredible sensations she evoked within him. How did she manage, with nothing more than a look, to completely undo his world? Caleb could feel his breath hitch in his throat as he felt her stare upon him, allowing him to end the piece gently. The ending that flashed through his mind was not his destiny, so, instead, he ended it properly, letting her go.

Everyone was staring at him wide-eyed. Sweat started to bead down his forehead, his fingers aching. He looked in Rylen's direction across the piano, the hood obscuring part of her face. For a moment they stared at each other. She looked away, embarrassed for being caught. Applause broke out and he was able to let out a deep sigh of relief, one he wasn't aware he was holding.

"That was amazing!"

"Encore!"

"Stupendous!"

Caleb gave the customary bow, suddenly surrounded by a swarm of people, glancing over the heads of the crowd to find Rylen, but she was gone. Though, wasn't that what his song was about, finding someone you couldn't have and then letting them go?

Chapter Eleven

*T*he dark line of the water lapped against the sand, pooling at Caleb's feet. It was cold, but it didn't bother him. What bothered him was how much stock he put in his need to see her. The sinking feel of the sand under his feet as the water retreated back to its home made him feel as if he were sinking, the sand slowly taking him down, inch-by-inch, as everything around him disappeared. He wanted to keep walking, but the music and conversation of the party made its way down to his sanctuary.

"Time to get back to reality," he sighed. "They'll be gone soon." Arnie whined and followed Caleb's retreating steps.

She was there before him as he came around the bend of the path. His breath caught for an instant, an instant that had Arnie gazing at him thoughtfully. She stood on the gazebo, looking out beyond the brush. She closed her eyes against the evening breeze, letting the wind soothe her as it brushed the hair from her face. A snapping twig broke her meditation as Arnie trotted up the path. Caleb shook his head at his three-legged friend—traitor.

"Hey boy," Rylen called, welcoming him with pats and scratches. Arnie turned back to Caleb and barked, giving away his position. Rylen halted when she saw him standing a few yards away from her like a stalker in the brush.

Caleb approached but stopped before the gazebo not wanting to appear too eager to be in her company. She stood straight and still, her arms at her side. Her eyebrows were arched gracefully in surprise and her blue eyes travelled, unafraid, to his. Their connection made him feel as if he had always known her, as if she had always been a part of him. The softness of her gaze held him, as if seeking from his soul the answer to some hidden question between them.

He couldn't stand there all night. The door awaited him just behind her. She was the only thing between him and the safety of the party. Beyond that door, the pressure of her presence would be offset by the many people in the room with them. Caleb summoned his courage and strode up the stairs until he was next to her. Neither of them spoke. The silence was maddening to Caleb's senses.

He meant to walk away, but he couldn't. She was smiling down at Arnie but took a moment to glance at him, her smile still in place. Before he could allow a smile to play across his own lips, Caleb frowned in disapproval. Arnie was none too pleased with Caleb's attitude, whining as he curled up at Rylen's feet. Caleb glared at Arnie and motioned to the door with a slight nod of his head, but Arnie would have none of it. Tomorrow, Caleb would put those dog training books he'd purchased to good use.

It would be best if he just left and returned to the party, but he knew if he went inside he would just be running away. "Just talk to her," a little voice in his head said. What was the harm? He did want to know what her final decision was, to apologize and fix the rift allowing her to stay or go. Caleb turned back to Rylen who had now taken a seat on the stairs and was petting the traitorous Arnie. Settled in contentedly, Arnie spared Caleb a reproachful, disappointed look.

"Can I join you?" Caleb asked. She shrugged her shoulders indicating she could care less. Her brush-off was well deserved. "Too good for my party?" he said lightly as he sat, leaving a comfortable distance between them.

"Just want to enjoy the quiet. Don't get much of it in the city," she answered, absently stroking Arnie's back.

"Yes, it's relatively soothing until the quiet drives you insane. Probably why I got this mongrel." Arnie whined, putting a fleeting smile on Caleb's face.

"And here I thought he was just here to help you pick up chicks."

Caleb laughed. "If that is his sole purpose, he's not very good at it." He watched as Rylen rubbed Arnie's belly. "Careful, he becomes attached easily once you pet his stomach."

"I can handle it."

"Have you made a decision yet?"

"I don't know," she sighed looking out into the darkness. "What do you think I should do?" she asked glancing over at him.

"Do you have a reason to stay?"

Rylen remained silent, thinking over his question and watching him closely. She wanted to answer yes, but he gave her so many reasons to say no. "I'm not sure yet." She paused, searching for more to say but succeeding only in creating a deeper silence.

A moment of uncomfortable silence passed between them and suddenly he felt his company was no good for her. Caleb came partway to his feet. Waves of heat rolled from his body as anger pulsated through him.

"I'm going to go back in," he cut the words off with a finality meant to push her away, but before he could retreat, she grabbed his wrist. She studied him, a hint of aggravation playing across her face.

"Boy, you're exactly what I imagined a brooding pianist to be." She pulled Caleb back down to his seated position.

"Which is?"

"An egotistical asshole." She grinned, and Arnie gave what sounded like a snicker.

Pulses of energy hung in the air forcing Caleb to talk when he wanted nothing more than to run away. Her body language told him she didn't like him, but when he looked in her eyes they told a different story, a story he wasn't sure he wanted to hear. He didn't want to venture down a road he'd never see the end of.

"I wasn't always like this. I'm not like this. It's just...a complicated situation has presented itself."

"Would you like to talk about it?"

He knew she meant it. She genuinely wanted to hear what he had to say. "No," he said and turned away so that he wouldn't see her disappointment.

"How do you do that? You can be charming one minute, and then you walk off the next without any explanation."

"Years of practice. You don't know me, Rylen. Don't pretend to." Arnie growled, prompting Caleb to flick the dog's ear to silence him.

"I've never pretended to think I know you, even though I've been trying. You just don't like to let people in." She saw the truth.

"Sometimes we're better off alone."

"Then explain Six Flags to me," she countered. "I thought we had a good time, that we could be friends. What happened in the last two weeks? You know what, never mind," she said with defeat in her voice.

He wanted to tell her he'd had a wonderful time, so great in fact that he never wanted it to end. But it had ended, and the fog had lifted. It was time to leave. He needed to walk away and let her think the worst of him. She needed to stay away. Caleb stood once more and looked out toward the beach. He closed his eyes taking in the smell of the lake, but her perfume intermingled with the air and intoxicated his thoughts. "Are you coming?"

"This isn't one of your better off alone times?" she asked, sarcasm dripping from her words, her face surprised at his invitation.

"It could be, but why waste such a beautiful evening by spending it alone?" He was a walking conundrum.

It was actually calming walking along the beach with her. The water lapping up to their ankles, the breeze whisking her hair, while Arnie followed close behind as chaperon. Rylen rubbed her arms indicating she was cold. Caleb wrapped up in how magical she looked walking along the shore, took off his jacket and put it around her.

"It's cold. Would you like to go back?"

"No. It's fine."

"Careful, it's a Tom Ford suit jacket, not exactly cheap."

"Snob," she laughed.

They continued on in quiet, the noise of the house a distant memory as they continued down the beach.

"Would you like to see my favorite spot?" he choked out before he lost his nerve. Logical thought screamed in protest, but he couldn't take it back even if he wanted to.

"Is this you letting me in?"

"Do you have to question everything?"

"I'm rational."

"And slightly annoying," he joked.

"Wow, big charmer." She pushed him away playfully, their banter helped to reassure Caleb that he wasn't making a mistake.

Caleb stood before her, stopping their progress down the beach. She looked up at him questioningly, but she knew better than to persist. There was conviction and tenderness in the way he took her hand. He slid his fingers awkwardly into her palm as if he'd never held hands with a woman before. And yet, there was more to his hesitance. She frightened him.

He gave himself a mental shake. He was letting his feelings have free rein. Something inside warned him he was venturing down a treacherous path, but he stayed and led her out into the lake. He was being foolish, like a sailor caught by a sea nymph. It was best to walk away, but she gripped his hand, and he wasn't going to let go just yet.

He slipped the jacket from her shoulders and held it out to Arnie who gently took it in his mouth. The faithful dog waited as Caleb showed Rylen his spot. "Close your eyes." She looked at him in questioningly. "Close them. Trust me."

It took her a moment, but she closed them. He led her to just within the water, standing in calf deep, her dress and his pants soaking in the water. The water was cold, but her hand warmed him.

"You're not going to drown me are you? I have Arnold as a witness."

He laughed. "One more question and I might entertain the thought." She smiled keeping her eyes closed. "Do you feel that?"

"It's cold." The waves lapped up to their legs making them sway with the movement of the water. Caleb positioned himself behind her, letting go of her hand. The warmth disappeared, but the heat radiating from her body kept him from going far. He leaned in from behind, putting his lips to her ear.

"Do you hear that?" She quivered at his proximity. "The lap of the water? The crashing of the waves? Nature is playing for you. The spray as it rushes along the rocks. This is music in its purest form." Rylen's hair blew in the wind and lightly caressed Caleb's face. He summoned the courage to touch the tips of her hair, fearing they may burn him, holding his hand up as the wind played with her hair against his palm. The smell of her skin matched that of the crisp lake, and Caleb felt the urge to lose himself in her. "The wind as it glides along the surface. Can you hear it?" He dipped his hand in the water, letting it drip down her arm, making her body shiver and amplifying his forbidden need to touch her. "Do you feel that?" He opened his eyes and found that he was now standing in front of her, their faces almost touching. He could feel her breath against his skin. "It wants to play for you. Nature is always playing for us." Caleb leaned in, his mouth only inches from hers. Fear crept nearer with his vulnerability, but he pushed it down. In a sense, it was too late.

Rylen could feel his intensity as he spoke, the electricity pulsing from his skin as his hands rubbed the water up and down her arms. She almost leaned into his body, asking him to engulf her with his. Was he playing cat and mouse? She frowned, inwardly, thinking she was that easy to trick, but for some reason, she knew he wasn't playing games with her. Whenever they were remotely close she could feel his stare upon her. When she played, when she was in his house, when she spoke to others, she could always feel him watching her. Was it wrong of her to enjoy tempting him with her smiles, the playful jabs, the music, the banter? And now, she admitted, allowing him to touch her, to be so close, was exciting.

They stood there in silence for the longest time. He was watching her now. Had they remained just as they were until the sun came up, he would still have been watching her just as he was. She relished the thought. Rylen was slowly melting inside. Would he just make a move already? Her breath hitched when Caleb's hands stopped caressing her arms. His cheek was now against hers, and she could feel her arms start to rise and embrace him.

Caleb had no idea what he was doing. His cheek was against hers, and he could feel her arms on his waist. He needed to do something, anything, but all he could do was breathe in the scent of her. His hand snaked around her body and traced a line down her spine. Her body froze when he touched her, and he could feel her shaky breath against his ear. Did he want this? Her? Most importantly, did she want this? Questions raced through his mind as he tried to regain control of his body, his thoughts. He truly had no idea why he was doing this, why he was touching her. What frightened him the most was how much he craved this. Their bodies were so close, like they fit together perfectly, almost as if he already knew her intimately.

Rylen couldn't take it any longer. She wanted to moan. His hand glided up her back, along her neck to her throat and collarbone. She stifled a giggle. And yearned for his mouth to replace the fingers lingering on her body. Her hands tightened on his waist, and she rubbed her hands up his torso. He moaned lightly in her ear making her smile. She steadied her breathing and silently screamed with longing. She wanted his lips on hers, to know what he tasted like. His lips connected with her skin, sending a tremor throughout her body. His kisses followed the path his finger had traced from shoulder to throat. His hand caressed her cheek and tilted her head back.

This time, she moaned aloud, snapping Caleb from his dreamlike haze. His body went ridged. His hand stopped moving, and his lips retreated from her beautifully pale skin. He released his grip and took a step back.

Rylen automatically felt the chill of his absence and wanted nothing more than to have him back. Her mind reeled as she held onto the lingering feel of his touch.

"I'm sorry. I shouldn't have taken such liberties," his voice was gruff. He cleared his throat. "You can open your eyes now." When she opened them he was still in front of her, but he was looking down at the water, avoiding any eye contact. "Now, after listening to nature's music, what is the first thing you want to do?"

It took her a minute to grasp what he was talking about. To get out of the haze he put her in. "Play," she choked out.

"It works every time. Whenever I don't feel like playing or can't bring myself to look at the piano I just come out here and listen, and then my world is right again." Caleb continued to look down at the water lapping at his legs. He was nervous to look at her. Would he see disappointment or hate? After what he had done, he hated himself. He should never have brought her out here with him. This was his place. He never shared it with anyone. Now he would pay for it. His heart pounded as he tried to work up the courage to look at her. When he did, he found her eyes burning into his. The tears in her eyes made her anger evident. He wanted to reach out and comfort her, to apologize for his ignorance. He never meant to hurt her. "I can't begin –"

He didn't know what to say. He just wanted to break the unbearable silence. The wind came upon them, blowing Rylen's hair into her face. Before he knew what he was doing, he took a step toward her, compelled by his body's need to feel her against him once more. Mere inches of lake air separated them. She moved in as well, her eyes slowly closing, but Caleb, again, pulled back. The movement made her start. Caleb could not allow this luxury.

"We should probably –"

Galloping from the beach, Arnie came toward them like a tidal wave. He flew through the air pouncing on Caleb, knocking his master off balance into the water. Rylen's attempt to help Caleb did nothing but send her into the lake with him.

Satisfied, Arnie trotted back to the beach and watched as they floundered about in the knee-deep water, soaked and cold.

"Are you okay?" Caleb asked, wiping the water from his eyes and helping her sit up. She was crying, God what an evening. First, he makes inappropriate advances toward her, and then his dog makes her cry. Arnie was so grounded. Caleb wanted to drown, but as he struggled to sit up amid the commotion, he realized she was laughing; laughing so hard tears were flowing down her face. "See, now you're hysterical. We should get you back inside before you get sick."

"For the record, Arnold is the one that ruined your jacket," she cried as Caleb's Tom Ford jacket slowly floated by. Some fish would be well dressed tomorrow, and he couldn't help but laugh right along with her. Feeling good, he playfully splashed her. She sputtered, water spilling from her mouth. Intent on revenge, she splashed him back, a splash war commencing. "Hear that splash?" she asked mockingly.

"Are you making fun of me?" he asked, laughing hysterically. He felt better than he'd felt in far too long.

When the splashing stopped, the laughter died with it. Rylen's pale skin stood out in stark contrast with the shadowed lake. The moonlight shined upon them, lighting their position. Rylen's blue eyes studied his as he gazed at her. The water had carried wisps of her hair across her face, forcing Caleb to once again put them behind her ear. Rylen quickly put her hand over his, gently tugging his hand to her mouth where she gingerly lay a kiss upon his palm. Her smile was unexpected, and it warmed him, softening the edge of his fear. He hesitantly caressed her cheek.

Rylen moved toward him, her lips parted in need, but stopped short. She wasn't sure if he would run again. She feared she would try to give too much and get none of him in return. Her mind had little time to wander before Caleb closed the distance between them, hesitating but a moment. She parted her lips, inviting him in, and closed her eyes. Caleb took heed not to rush into anything, but he wanted her. That was the reality. His thumb lightly traced the outline of her lips, and shutting off his mind, he kissed her.

It was a first kiss that would surely haunt him until the day he was laid to rest, but even if that day came tomorrow, he couldn't imagine ever taking it back. His hand explored her face, outlining every curvature as he sweetly kissed her. Rylen kissed him back, her arms wrapping around his neck, pulling him closer, pressing her lips against his as the kiss went from sweet to urgent and hungry. Caleb was afraid it'd be the last time he'd kiss her.

Caleb pulled her to him, lifting her up out of the water, moving closer to shore where he could lay her down. Rylen's hands ran rampant, running along the lean flesh of his torso. He pulled her up, reaching around her back to unzip the dress. The thought of her body against his made him hunger for more. He ripped his shirt off, buttons losing themselves in the lake, tearing away any inhibitions. He laid a trail of kisses down her neck and along her collarbone as he removed her dress strap. Rylen arched into him, her body taking wresting control from reason.

Rylen was fumbling with the belt of his pants. She knew what this was leading up to, and even though she shouldn't have wanted it, she felt as if her soul knew him, that it was somehow guiding her toward him, placing her squarely in his path.

Rylen was so caught up in what this all could mean that she hadn't realized Caleb had suddenly stopped. She opened her eyes to see him breathing heavily, his eyes aggressively seeking her attention.

"Is this the reason you're looking for?"

"What do you mean?"

"Me," he said feeling her hesitation beneath him.

"Ye – Yes," she stammered, her hand caressing his cheek, corralling him back to her.

The smile that crossed Caleb's face was heartbreaking, and he could see that if she stayed in Chicago she'd be missing out on bigger and better opportunities. "I wish you the best of luck," he said, draping the straps of her dress back over her shoulder before kissing her on the forehead.

Caleb stood, the water and Rylen releasing their grasp upon him. The dipping of the stars in the night sky prompted his attention. He tore his gaze from Rylen's beautiful form for just a moment, but the stars in her eyes could light up the sky. Looking away for but a moment was all he could afford. He wanted to remember her face just as it was--full of lust and wanting. He wanted to see it when he closed his eyes that very night and all the nights after. She was his starry night, but he wasn't hers. He wished the memories of her face would remind him that some things were just beyond his grasp. That no one was supposed to have everything they wished for. He had already received word he wasn't meant for this world anymore and that he should focus on what he did have in his life right now.

The water soaked Caleb to the bone, his clothes weighing his body down as he made his way back up to the beach. Rylen stirred behind him, standing up, her dress no longer swaying in the wind, now heavy with water.

"Caleb?" she called.

"Arnie, take Rylen home." Arnie licked Caleb's hand acknowledging his chore before he trotted down to the water's edge to guide Rylen away.

Caleb chose not to look back, feeling her eyes burning into his back as he walked further down the beach, his back a sign of his leaving forever. She needed that image so she'd stay away, not so that she'd follow.

Caleb was shaken and he no longer felt whole. He walked down the beach kicking the sand and stones, imagining what it would have been like to follow through. If it was anything like the kiss, he was missing out, and a piece of him felt as if he had given some part of his soul away. It was true. When you kiss someone you give them a little bit of yourself.

~

The morning breeze was cool as the waves lapped soundlessly to the shore, a welcome respite after the heat and noise from last night. Caleb took a deep breath of fresh air. Today he was free of the previous evening's motives, free of expectations. He let his thoughts pour over him one last time before he banished them from memory into a file that he would never reopen.

Had he lost his mind? Caleb thought he had a firm grasp on his sanity, but doubt crept in. He was foolish, there was no doubt. The night before he had taken a terrible risk, and it backfired. She was not his to handle the way he did, but she had kissed him back and responded to his touch. Or had he just imagine it?

Caleb had awakened to the soft sand under his hands, Arnie at his side, and a blanket draped over his body. Arnie snored beside him. Caleb petted his companion, rousing the faithful dog from his deep sleep. Underneath Arnie's head was his pillow, Mr. Puff. Even with Arnie at his side and the blanket Caleb could not control the cold that seeped into his bones causing him to shiver. It didn't feel that cold out, but sleeping outside in wet clothes hadn't been the most intelligent of ideas.

Caleb slowly stood, stretching the weariness from his body. He felt the cold deep in his bones making it difficult to make his muscles cooperate. He looked to his house, silent and safe.

"Ready for your morning walk?" he asked Arnie. Caleb picked up the blanket. Arnie dragged Mr. Puff in his mouth, and they set off for their home looming in the distance.

The house was undisturbed as if nothing had transpired the previous evening. The caterers had taken their supplies. The leftovers were tucked securely in the refrigerator, and the house was relatively clean with his furniture back in place. Arnie padded over to his corner of the room and put Mr. Puff back in his rightful place among the rest of the toys.

"I'm going to take a shower," he told Arnie.

The shower needed to be scalding hot. A shower didn't feel right if the water didn't burn right through him, burning away the touches from last night and, if he was lucky, the memories. Arnie sat in the doorway as Caleb looked in the mirror.

His shirt no longer had any buttons making it all the easier to take off. Tentatively, he touched the bruise on his hip. He had sustained it running into the doorknob weeks ago, and yet it looked like it had happened yesterday. The bruise was still dark and painful. Adding to the marks upon his body, Caleb found red splotches on his chest. With a frown, he lightly touched the spots. They weren't bumps, merely red marks, possibly from sleeping in the sand. Or were they marks mapping Rylen's fingertips?

"It never ends, does it buddy?" he said to Arnie. Caleb took a deep breath, his frail body lean, and the skin taunt against his muscle, the bones now starting to show.

He tested the shower spray, the water scalding to the touch. He unbuckled his pants when a sharp pain coursed through his body causing him to hunch over. He cried out in pain, his mind fuzzy. Arnie whined next to him. Looking over, Caleb saw the concern in his dog's eyes. To put Arnie at ease, Caleb grinned and patted his head.

"It's alright, nothing to worry about," he coughed.

Standing up straight and getting his breath back, Caleb set to getting in the shower, but the coughing started up again. It felt as if something was caught in his throat and someone was punching him in the gut at the same time. A frighteningly cold shiver ran through his body and he wanted nothing more than to still it with the heat of the shower spray, but the coughing forced him down to his knees. Gut-wrenching coughs had him leaning over the toilet, fearing he'd throw up. He pulled his hand away. Blood smeared the inside of his palm and he vomited in the toilet.

Once the vomit stopped, he pushed away from the toilet and opened up the medicine cabinet, looking for anything to help. The pounding in his head worsened, his eyesight blurred, and the coughing remained crippling. Arnie was pacing outside the bathroom.

In frustration, Caleb slammed the medicine cabinet shut and stumbled toward the shower. He reached for the shower curtain, his feet getting tangled up in the yellow smiley face mat. He fell, pulling the shower curtain with him and wrapping it around his body as he tried to catch himself. The scalding water splashed against his face, but the comfort didn't last long because a moment later he couldn't feel anything. His head bashed against the soap dish and he crumpled in a heap in the corner of the shower.

Arnie ran to Caleb's side, barking at Caleb to wake up, but the unconscious man didn't stir. Blood dripped from Caleb's lips. His palm was filled with blood from coughing, and the back of his head was gashed. Blood dripped down the shower wall. Arnie didn't know what to do. Disappearing out of the room he came back a moment later with the house phone in his mouth. He put it on the bathroom floor and nosed Caleb's leg to get him to move. Only, Caleb didn't, and for the first time, the buzzing was gone.

"Swelling."

"Nothing can be done."

"Blood is irritating the brain tissue from the pressure."

"So you have to go in again?"

"I'm not sure it will help any. With the trauma sustained –"

"I want answers, not your giving-up speech."

Chapter Twelve

The light drizzle did not affect Dominic. He stood under the canopy and watched the cars pass by. Visitors stood outside getting their nicotine fix, a fix he almost wished he hadn't given up ten years ago, feeling the need for something other than dread to course through his veins. He swayed back and forth, from the tips of his toes to the balls of his feet, and listened. Only, he didn't hear anything other than the beeping of the machines that were nowhere around him. He had come to hear those beeps wherever he went--in his sleep, driving in his car, going to Lamaze class with Ashley. He couldn't seem to shake them. He needed something to drown them out, but no matter what he did, they were always there, beeps in the background causing him to slowly go insane.

"Hey, Dominic," said a voice from the doorway. "I've been looking for you." Dr. Erdman walked out of the hospital entryway and outside to Dominic. For a moment neither of them said anything, Dominic's head full of beeps that did all they could to smother all thought from Dominic's head.

Dr. Erdman hesitated, taking in a deep breath before beginning. "I've talked to the lawyers." Dominic shook his head. "They asked me to talk to you."

Dominic was exasperated by their calls and annoyed by their arrogance at thinking he could come to such a decision in only three-and-a-half months. "I have no reason to talk to them."

"They're just doing their job, Dominic."

Dominic turned to him, agitated. "And I'm not? I have a duty to my best friend. I'm the one that has the authority to do as I please."

"And what about his wishes?"

"I'm doing what is right."

"For whom?" Dr. Erdman asked, knowing full well that Dominic was only doing this for himself. But it wasn't his place to judge.

Dominic lowered his head, looking down at the rain as the droplets bounced up from the sidewalk, splattering on the lower hem of his jeans. "I need more time." He reached for the flowers sitting on the bench, trying to keep his thoughts at bay, and his emotions in check. There were just some things he couldn't bring himself to talk about. "I don't know what to do," he finally admitted pausing for a long moment. "I should go see him."

When Dominic walked into the hospital he wound his way through the maze of corridors, a maze he could solve in his sleep. He was conscious of what Dr. Erdman and the lawyers were asking him to do. He knew the wishes that Caleb had conveyed to him, but he couldn't let go. There had to be some fight left in his brother. He had found it impossible to go a day without thinking about the promises he wasn't keeping, and the dear friendship he was neglecting. But wasn't he trying to keep it alive? Trying to give him a fighting chance? He ran his fingers through his hair, wondering where he should put the flowers. He believed deep down he was doing the right thing, keeping hope alive, but no one else looked at it like he did. They didn't know what he knew. They couldn't see that, even though Caleb expressed certain wishes, deep down, it wasn't what he truly wanted.

It was odd that those papers they had signed over a year ago would now come into account, signifying an end to everything he held dear to his heart. The power those papers of legal jargon wielded. They weren't his best friend, his brother. They hadn't spent their lives with Caleb. They didn't know his personality, bear witness to his talent. No, they were not going to govern Dominic's decision. He was going to take all the time he wanted until everything was put right and balance was restored.

Dominic felt a tinge of guilt. Caleb had the papers drawn up for a reason, as if he'd seen the future and was getting ready to combat it. He put Dominic in sole possession of his life and property. Only, Dominic didn't want the burden it placed on his shoulders. He wanted his friend. He wanted his brother. That was all he wanted, and it was the one thing he couldn't have.

Standing on the threshold of the hospital room, Dominic looked around feeling almost disembodied. It was like he hadn't left, but now there was an empty bed. Summoning his nerve, Dominic opened the shades. He was surprised to see the sun peeking out from behind the clouds. He hadn't remembered the last time he saw the sun, but he was grateful, if only for a moment. He felt a slight headache beginning, the throb of his temples and the base of his head making his eyes play tricks on him. Or maybe it was just the insomnia that had taken hold of him. He was going on only three hours of sleep a night. He spent most of the night staring at the ceiling, listening to Arnie as he snored, running scenarios through his mind. What would they do once this whole ordeal was over?

He walked into the bathroom, not recognizing himself in the mirror. He sported black circles under his eyes. His cheeks were hollowing out, and he'd lost at least twenty pounds, pounds he could afford to lose, but his body was eating away at his muscle mass. He hadn't been to the gym in over three months, and he took no care with his eating habits, if he ate at all. In fact, he tried to remember the last thing he'd eaten, but it only made his head throb harder.

He turned on the faucet, letting the cold water glide over his palms. This didn't feel right. None of this felt right. He had so much to tell him, so much to share. At a time in his life when things were falling into place, he should have been happy. Ashley was pregnant. He should be glowing with the prospect of parenthood, but he almost hated himself when he tried to smile. He felt as if he wasn't allowed this moment of happiness.

Gently patting his face with the cool water, he turned off the faucet and rubbed his eyes to keep them steady and awake. He pushed aside his doubts and smiled. It didn't reach his eyes, but it was all he could manage at the moment. He straightened his shoulders and cracked his neck, ready for battle.

"Hey buddy," he walked out of the bathroom, his strides longer and more confident than when he walked in.

He waited for Caleb to make the slightest movement, any sort of response, to let Dominic know his worries were naught, that normal was right around the corner, but nothing happened. The silence was cold, but he continued to watch, afraid he'd miss any sort of reaction. As he watched, he memorized Caleb's every feature. He needed the memories, even if this wasn't something he wanted to remember.

Dominic took a seat in the chair by the bed and reached for his friend's hand. Caleb's skin was pale, his veins more prominent on his hands. His body seemed smaller, as though he was reverting back to a child. Still, in spite of the changes that were taking place, Caleb still looked like the little brother Dominic had looked after. This was the boy Dominic had ensured never got into trouble, or even got a paper cut on his precious fingers. His longest relationship to date, possibly the longest one he would ever have. He cherished their time together, even their fights. Every relationship had its good and bad days, and they had stuck with each other, even in those moments when they hated each other.

Dominic looked out the window. He often found himself staring up at the sky, looking for answers in the clouds. He felt his resolve slipping away. There were never answers--no smoke signals. He was on his own, and that frightened him a little too much.

He squeezed Caleb's hand for comfort. They were finally alone. Not a day went by when there wasn't someone lurking about the room with him. Now, with the new arrival, they made sure to keep watch, taking shifts.

Dominic sighed deeply. He wanted to leave, let the questions he needed to answer stir about. Instead, he gathered himself, put the side of the bed down, and gently moved Caleb over, making sure not to disturb the tubes. Dominic slipped off his shoes and lay in bed beside Caleb, pulling him close and resting his head on his shoulder. He clasped Caleb's hand, attempting to find clarity that just wouldn't come.

Dominic had drifted off to sleep. The sun was no longer in the sky, and a nurse was in the room checking the machines. She smiled sympathetically at Dominic. They had come to know each other well.

She scribbled her notes down and closed the chart. "Sleep well?"

Dominic sat up, stretching, amazed he fell asleep. "It seems. I didn't even realize I drifted off."

"Drifted off about 3 hours ago," she smiled, hugging the chart to her chest. "You should go home, Dominic. You look like you need the sleep."

He carefully got off the bed and started to position Caleb back in the center with Mary's help. He wiped the sleep from his eyes, ignoring her suggestion. "How's the family?"

"They're better than you," she observed.

"I'm fine, Mary. Just need to eat some dinner and get some caffeine in me. Don't worry yourself."

"I can't help it. I'm a mother. It's my job to worry," she laughed. "When you're done, you better go home and get some sleep. Promise?"

"Slave driver, but yes, I promise," he lied.

"Alright, and don't play the music too loud," she turned and left the room, closing the door behind her to give them privacy.

Dominic went over to the little CD player he had brought with him from Caleb's home and pressed play. It was a compilation of all his favorite composers and including some of Caleb's own compositions. There was no reason to think Caleb could hear what was going on in the room or even feel Dominic squeeze his hand. Still, Dominic couldn't help imagining what he would do if Caleb ever squeezed his hand in return. Who knew what was going on in Caleb's mind? There was the possibility that Caleb was dreaming up compositions in his head, a multitude of melodies ready to take shape once he awoke.

"Arnie is doing okay," Dominic began. "He doesn't like not having you around, but I think he's adapting. I take him out to frolic on the beach," he laughed. "Frolic's your word isn't it? Such a dumb word." He cleared his throat, forcing it to sound normal. "I know I say this every day, but I want to apologize." He started to tear up, but quickly composed himself. "I hope you can hear me," he murmured, grabbing a tray that had their chess game on it and rolling it over to the bed between them.

I hear you. You sure you're not a girl with those soft hands of yours?

Dominic laughed, "You're an ass. Don't get on my bad side, I'll tickle you."

Then you'll have to clean up the mess my bladder leaves behind when you do.

"Is that a threat?"

No, I'm just telling you what will happen. My bladder muscles aren't what they use to be. Hey, you think you can turn the music up?

"Why, don't want to talk to me? Besides, I can't, it's late."

Fine. Fine. You look like shit.

"Wow, thanks for the vote of confidence."

Just an observation. You need sleep…in your bed, not mine. This bed isn't big enough for the both of us. You take up most of the room, and you spoon.

Dominic snorted. "I don't spoon." He thought about it. "Okay, I spoon, but –"

Its fine, Dom, spoon all you want. I know it makes you feel better.

"We always shared when we had bunk beds. Whenever either of us was scared, we'd jump into bed with each other." He laughed at the long-forgotten memory. "You remember that time we watched The Blob? Oh my God, I was so scared. I didn't put my feet on the ground for days. You carried me or I walked atop furniture. Mom wasn't really appreciative when I broke her ceramic bunny collection," he laughed remembering his mother's face.

Yeah, I remember. I think that's why my back is out of whack, fatass.

"Boy, you're in rare form today," Dominic wiped the sweat from his forehead, exhaustion finally starting to take its toll. His eyes fluttered for a moment.

Where is everyone?

"Taking a break," he mumbled glancing at the door before taking a seat. "Are you ready? It's your move."

When did I ever give you the impression that I like chess?

"When did I ever give you the impression that I care whether you like it or not?"

Just because you were on the chess team in high school doesn't mean you can use me as your practice dummy.

"I'm sorry. Did you say rook to a4? Sounds good." He moved the rook, pondering his own move now.

Now you're just going to ignore me? Classy. I'd rather you read today.

"Are you sure? We haven't finished our game."

What book do you have?

"I was thinking Out of Africa since you like it so much. It's the only book here. I forgot the rest at home."

That's fine. I love that book. So does she.

"Yes."

Where is she by the way? Her hand's gone.

Dominic tightened all over and clenched the book in his hand. "She took a break also."

Everyone but you, it seems.

"I'm not going to leave you."

I'm sorry.

"You haven't done anything wrong."

I think about a lot of things here. What with all the time I have, seems I may as well put it to good use. Are you upset with me?

Dominic stood at attention, clasping Caleb's hand in his, "There's no way I could ever be truly upset with you. You're my family, and I love you. You could never get rid of me no matter how hard you tried or pushed." He bent down, kissing Caleb on the forehead. "Unfortunately for you, you are never out of my thoughts."

Go home and get some sleep.

"I'm fine, Caleb. I want to be here."

I'm not going to wake up.

"Don't you dare say that!" His lip quivered wondering if this was just his mind playing tricks on him or if it was truly what he knew deep down inside. "Don't ever say that to me again. You just need time."

Caleb said nothing, and Dominic knew he was putting too much weight on his brother's shoulders. Expecting Caleb to wake up for him, to quell all of Dominic's unease.

The conversation was imaginary, but Caleb's voice seemed to rise from nowhere whenever Dominic was in the room with him. Sometimes, when he was at home and it was just him and Arnie sitting there, he'd talk to Caleb as if he were in the room. He was going crazy. It was in his eyes when he looked in the mirror. It was in Arnie's eyes when he watched the one-sided conversations, but there was no way Dominic could stop. He needed the conversations to keep him sane, which made him sound all the more crazy.

"I need you to wake up. I miss you." This time, he let the tears run down his cheeks freely. Putting his cheek against Caleb's he whispered, "I love you."

I love you, too.

Dominic drew in a long shaky breath, his face still against Caleb's as his other hand caressed his brother's cheek. The voice faded away, leaving Dominic alone again.

He sat back in the chair next to the bed, their hands still clasped. He resigned himself to staring out the window. The sun had gone. The clouds in the sky hid the stars that Caleb cherished, but tonight, the city hid their luster.

"I had a farm in Africa, at the foot of the Ngong Hills," he read.

Chapter Thirteen

*C*aleb awakened with a swift start. His head felt heavy and his body exhausted. What had happened? Where was he? He tried to focus on the walls of the room, but everything was hazy. Colors blurred in front of his eyes. The sweatiness of his palm had him pulling it up to his chest, but with it came another hand. Looking over, Caleb saw Dominic snoring peacefully next to him. They were in bed. In his bed, he now realized from the feel of the sheets and the permanent flatness of his pillow.

Arnie's head popped up from the ground, and he looked at Caleb with glee. He barked loudly, and Caleb's free hand flew to his head. Intense pounding at the base of his skull caused a sharp intake of breath. Caleb's hand came to rest on gauze that, upon further inspection, were wrapped around his head.

The bark didn't wake Dominic forcing Arnie to jump on the bed and paw the sleeping man. Dominic swatted at Arnie to go away and mumbled incoherently into the pillow.

"Dom," Caleb whispered, his voice barely audible. Dominic didn't move. Caleb squeezed his brother's hand, and Dominic's head popped up in frantic surprise.

"What?" he yelled to Arnie before noticing Caleb was staring at him. "Caleb?" he cried scooting over across the bed until he was practically on top of him. "Can you hear me? Nod if you can. Actually, can you speak?"

"If you'd let me," Caleb muttered pushing Dominic's face out of his personal space.

"Shit," he cried sitting back with his hands over his mouth.

"What's wrong?" Caleb asked.

Dominic remained silent, his hands covering half his face and his eyes welling up and spilling over with tears. "I just," he sputtered, "I just didn't think you'd wake up. I had this horrible dream," he continued, "you were…gone."

Caleb sat up on his elbows but stopped suddenly, closing his eyes as the movement caused his head to pound. "What happened?" he asked, not knowing why he was bandaged up and in bed.

"You don't know?" Dominic asked, perplexed.

"All I remember is being on the beach with Rylen."

"Rylen? The cello player?" Caleb nodded. "The cute cello player?" Dominic asked with a smirk. "I knew you liked her. What were you doing on the beach with her?" Caleb didn't answer and averted his gaze. "You naughty boy," Dominic laughed. "Tell me everything."

"After you tell me why I'm an invalid."

"You hit your head in the shower. I came over to apologize for not making it to the party, but I was angry with you. I thought about it, and I shouldn't be. I was being stubborn, but you were too," he pointed out. "I found you unconscious in the shower. I don't know how long you were like that, but the water was freezing. Long story short, I took you to the hospital, and luckily, it wasn't anything too bad. You had a concussion, and few stitches were necessary. I brought you back home since I know you don't like hospitals all that much."

"That's it?"

"That's it. Now," he leaned in with a devilish smirk on his face, "tell me about Rylen."

It was the thunder that awoke him from the heaviness of the day. The flash of lightning illuminated the darkened walls surrounding him, and the outline of his body reflected on the wall across from him. A shadowy figure watched. The branches from the tree outside reached for him like deadly fingers ready to choke the life from him. Was that death creeping toward him, intent on finishing what the disease consuming his body had started? Caleb shivered. Before, he had sought death, and it had not scared him. Now, he was frightened it would take him before he was able to see Rylen one last time. It was excruciating to know he might never get the chance, but Caleb had been hard-headed and he was only getting what he deserved.

Caleb heard the piano music slithering through his sleepy fog. He scanned the room, confused, and listened intently making sure he was truly awake. Rising out of bed, he slowly made his way into the living room toward the music.

He blamed the lack of sleep on the figure he saw in front of him. The sliding glass door was open, the curtain swaying in the wind, leaving the room chilly. As he moved across the room to shut the door, he found himself stopping next to the woman at the piano. She played beautifully, and he recognized the piece as Liszt, reminding him of his mother. The gentleness of her touch on the keys brought a sad calm over him. In that moment, he felt his fear of her wane.

The profile of her face seemed familiar, and when she turned to smile at him, Caleb felt as if he'd been struck by lightning.

"Caleb." The woman smiled sadly, showing in that smile how much she loved and missed him.

His mind raced trying to grasp what was happening, unable to fit what he was seeing with what he knew. This couldn't be. It was impossible.

"Mom?" he breathed in a whisper.

She gracefully stood from the piano bench, and arms he knew but barely remembered slipped around him. The comfort of her touch brought tears to his eyes.

"Oh, Caleb," she said soothingly, "how I've missed you." She ran her fingers through his hair, stilling him. "A day hasn't gone by when I haven't thought of you."

Reeling, he fought to control his emotions. He struggled to focus, to make sure what he was seeing was reality and not one of his nightmares. But she felt real. She smelled real. The emotions she evoked within him were real.

"How did you get here?" he asked.

"You wanted me here," she caressed the side of his face with the palm of her hand. Her hands soft and cold to the touch and he held her palm to his cheek so he could be sure she wasn't a figment of his imagination. She was standing there with him, nothing changed. Her eyes still twinkled like the stars and her forehead still wrinkled with worry lines that only came out when she listened to Liszt. She was his mother and he had never needed her more than he did now.

"I met someone," he said into her palm.

"I know. She's beautiful." She sat down making room for Caleb to join her.

"She plays the cello," he added while his mother turned her focus back to the piano, running her fingers over the keys. Caleb knew the movement, for it was one he practiced regularly.

"She has awakened something in you, Caleb." His mother started to play the song Caleb had improvised the night of the party. That night... those feelings...seemed so long ago. "Why now?" she asked, ignoring his gaze while he stared longingly at the mother he had lost. He longed to make up for those lost years.

"Why now?" He frowned. "Because I only just met her," he rationalized. He had so much to tell her, but the words he wanted to speak evaporated. Twenty-eight years of stories, memories, and things he wished she was around for could hardly be spoken in such a moment.

"Why haven't you told her?"

"I'm afraid."

"It wasn't your fault, Caleb."

"What?"

"The accidents, they weren't your fault. Stop blaming yourself."

"You mean accident. And I do blame myself. If it weren't for me, you'd still be –"

"And what about your accident?"

"I don't know what you're talking about."

"You do. Deep down it lurks, but you don't want to remember."

"Mom –"

Thunder made the walls shake, and the lightning shed light upon Kathryn's face. She was crying, tears streaming down her cheeks and falling on the piano keys. She wiped them away, one by one, as she continued playing the song composed for Rylen.

"I don't understand. Why would you say such a thing?" he was scared. He had waited years for a moment like this: to finally have his mother back; for life to go back to how it was supposed to be; to have his family whole; to be cleansed of the permanent scar on his soul. She was dead because of him, and she acted like he hadn't done anything wrong, weeping for him.

"I don't want you to end up like me," she lamented, shaking her head.

Caleb put his arm around Kathryn's shoulder and tried to get her to look at him, but she refused. This wasn't how he wanted to remember his mother. He wanted to remember the sweet, gentle woman that would play Beethoven on the record player and glide down the hallways waving her arms like a conductor. Something didn't feel right, didn't add up. Kathryn didn't know how to play the piano.

"Ma-" he began, as Kathryn suddenly went limp in his arms.

When he looked down at her, she was bleeding. Blood poured from an open wound at her side, and her face was scraped up, pieces of glass sticking out from the gashes. They fell backwards off the piano bench, and Caleb tried to revive his mother. Her eyes stared lifelessly up at him. He put his hand over what he thought was the wound, wishing for the flow to stop and for her eyes to blink back the life that was just in them.

Yet, how could he save a life that had already gone? He couldn't bring her back. Caleb was the reason she had died in the first place. Faltering, Kathryn no longer in his arms, Caleb curled into the fetal position. His limbs went numb and his eyes rolled back into his head as he tried to remember a time when everything felt right. Thunder crackled once more, and Caleb's body shook. Perspiration covered him, and he sucked in gulps of breath to keep from falling back into the nightmare. With the shaking came the buzzing once more. It had been some time since he last heard the noise, but he could feel it in the back of his mind. It was always there.

"The fever is too high."

"Then do something."

"We are."

"We're taking him home today."

"Both of them?"

The obnoxious buzzing was replaced by the sound of glass shattering. He could see the man's eyes in the rearview mirror staring back at him. The eyes seemed so familiar and for an instant he caught glimpses of the man driving the car and the woman in the seat next to him. She had a small protruding belly, barely noticeable, but it was there under her shirt. The man gripped the woman's hand, the glass falling in around them, their heads whipping back and forth. The airbags deployed just as the car started to flip. Water began filling the car, drowning the music. Their cries ceased. All was silent, but those eyes still stared back at him. For a moment Caleb thought they were his.

Chapter Fourteen

ʃying in the hammock, Caleb pushed the early morning events from his mind. He was tired and didn't need to drain the rest of his energy by dredging up nightmares. Dominic would be back soon for an afternoon cookout. His head still hurt, but he took the gauze off and lightly fingered the small bandage on the back of his skull. He'd just have to deal with it and move on. The accident wasn't going to change what was happening. If anything, it gave Caleb the knowledge that time was creeping toward its end.

Closing his eyes, Caleb breathed in the splendors surrounding him. He opened them just as quickly to avoid sleep. Today was the day for enjoying nature in the sanctuary he had built himself. Amongst a wild flower garden, Caleb watched the butterflies and bees as they fluttered about, pollinating the garden that was his pride and joy. He laid his book down and lifted his hand over his head. A butterfly circled and finally descended upon the tip of his index finger. Caleb studied the yellow and purple patterns on the wings, amazed at nature's creation. From a caterpillar to this astounding winged-creature that took flight and whisked through the breeze of the day. The wonder of it all overwhelmed Caleb.

Arnie barked at him, ascending the path from the beach. His fur was matted from playing in the lake. He loved to worry the ducks and be a general menace to the lake dwellers. The happy pup shook the water from his fur as Caleb covered his face. The butterfly sought solace among the flowers, no longer taking refuge on his finger.

"Arnie!" Caleb yelled, pushing the mangy mongrel away from him. He was now wet, sprayed with lake water, and reeking like wet dog. "You're so getting a bath today." Arnie whined. "You have no one else to blame but yourself. Don't play in the water and slosh it in my face." Arnie blinked, extending his tongue and slobbering down Caleb's face in apology. "Yeah, yeah, you're always sorry, but you continue to do it." He ruffled Arnie's fur and laughed at the precocious dog. "Damn you're cute. I can't be mad at you." Arnie's ears perked and his body went ridged. "Hear something?" Arnie barked and took off around the corner of the house toward the front yard.

Caleb sighed. Carefully, he extracted himself from the hammock, making sure he didn't flip and fracture anything. "Never a dull moment with that dog," he said.

Walking through the wild flower garden down the stone path, Caleb lightly ran his hand over the flower blooms. The house was flanked by wild flower gardens on both sides. He liked to meander through them, imaging a huge field he could run through, Arnie chasing after him, rolling around in the flowers, the smell perfuming his clothes.

From around the corner he could hear Arnie barking playfully as the dog ran around kicking up the gravel in the driveway.

"Arnie, be good," he called as he rounded the corner expecting Dominic back from his grocery run, but it was Rylen. She was outfitted in a beautiful pink sundress that made her skin glow in the bright midday sunshine. Her hair was draped over her shoulders, cascading in a dark brown pool between her shoulder blades. She was playfully bouncing from side to side as Arnie jumped at her trying to get her to sit still so she could pet him.

The sound of Caleb's voice had her turning toward him. Her smile faded, and the shine in her eyes disappeared when she laid eyes on him. She must not have expected to see him, which was surprising since she was at his house.

Arnie seemed baffled, looking from Caleb to Rylen, waiting for one of them to speak.

"Hello."

"Hi."

Caleb stopped, waiting for her to go on, but she didn't continue. "Sorry, go ahead."

"Oh, well," she scanned the property. "Is Dominic here?"

"No, he had to do some errands."

"Oh," she said with a hint of disappointment in her voice. Her reaction surprised him and made him wish she would leave. If she didn't want to see him, why was she here, especially now when he was trying to get over her after their night on the beach together? The intimacy of the night on the beach was a memory that he feared was no more than a dream, afraid she saw right through him. Seeing her there, in front of him, he yearned for her. The memory of her reaction to his touch made his body cry out for hers as it had that night.

"He called me up. Said there was a cookout here and to bring some burgers." She picked up the grocery bag sitting on her car.

"The plan was for Dominic and me to have a cookout together." Damn Dominic and his meddling. Caleb cursed his brother. As he walked past her, the wind kicked up the smell of her skin. Sometimes he hated nature.

"Well, I'll just get going then," she said, pulling her keys from her purse and returning to her car.

Retreating to the porch, Caleb set his rocking chair in motion with his toe as he stared down at the wooden planks of the porch floor.

The gravel shifted under Rylen's feet. The sound grated on Caleb's nerves. He felt bad she had come all this way. He had a pretty good idea what Dominic was trying to do with this planned rendezvous, and it made him smile. Perhaps, he'd finally go along with one of Dominic's ideas.

"Wait," he called out, spinning away from the rocking chair. She was halfway in her car, her head straining over the wind shield waiting for him to go on. "You came all this way," he walked down the driveway to her car. "How about you stay for a bit?" He kicked at the gravel, forcing himself not to make eye contact with her lest she say no.

"With you?" she asked surprised.

Caleb smirked. She was going to say no. What they had on the beach was gone. She didn't have feelings for him. It was time he ended this.

"If that's a problem, I could sit in a different room while you hang out with Arnie," he offered up a solution.

"No, that's okay."

Caleb nodded and turned around to retreat back into the house, the rejection stinging more than he imagined it would.

Her car door closed and he expected to hear the engine rev to life, but her footsteps followed up behind him. When he turned he was again confronted by her. She stood before him with her chin held high and her back straight. There was a determination on her face that baffled him.

"When I said no, I meant Arnie could join us."

"Oh." He furrowed his brow. "I just thought you -"

"I know what you thought, Caleb. I would like it if we could talk."

"Talk. Right." He searched for something to say. He was hoping they could just relax, sit in silence, maybe watch a movie, but things rarely played out the way he imagined. "I suppose a little conversation can't hurt."

She smiled. "No, I suppose it can't."

He led her into the house, opening the door for her. He stopped for a moment and looked out over the five acres of property that spanned out around him. For some reason today felt different to him, it felt...right.

When Caleb opened the door for her she was faced with a much different house from the night of his party. It felt welcoming in a way it hadn't the first time she'd come. Maybe her nervousness was gone, but now she felt a little more at ease. Things were still awkward between them, but Caleb had just invited her to spend time with him, to talk with him. This was a step in the right direction, but now that she was there she had no idea what to say.

She felt overdressed next to Caleb who sported a plain t-shirt and short. Caleb walked past, his hand brushing up against her. The hair on her arm stood at attention, and she flushed with embarrassment.

"Would you like anything to drink?" he asked hospitably. "I have water, tea, lemonade...maybe." He shrugged, not entirely sure of his refrigerator's contents.

"Lemonade would be nice, thank you."

Caleb walked into the kitchen, and unsure what to do, Rylen followed. "This is beautiful, Caleb," she said, putting her grocery bag on the counter.

Caleb pulled two glasses from the cupboard. "Thank you. Though, unfortunately, I'm not much of a cook, so everything is basically brand new and unused, almost a waste. I was thinking of turning it into a theater room and just keeping the refrigerator."

"What?" She pulled herself up to sit on the island, her legs swinging off the ledge. "The kitchen is the heart of the home."

Caleb opened the refrigerator and pulled out a jug of lemonade. "Not mine." He poured her a glass and handed it to her.

"Then where?" she asked, sipping the ice cold lemonade.

"I'd probably say the living room. It's where I compose most of the time." He poured himself a glass and gulped it down. His mind raced uneasily thinking of the ease with which he had regurgitated personal information.

"I can understand that."

Caleb absently pulled himself up beside her on the island, his glass of lemonade clutched in his hand. They sat side by side without touching, each watching their feet sway over the ledge, swirling the lemonade in its glass, feeling suddenly uncertain. She wasn't sure how to proceed. Rylen glanced sideways at him. "You don't like answering questions do you?"

He smiled at the question. "Is that you asking a question?" he laughed nervously.

"Let me rephrase. You do not like answering questions," she stated.

"Your hypothesis would be correct." He jumped off the island counter and held out his hand to help Rylen down. "I propose I take you around the grounds before the sun goes down. Then, after, grill up some burgers." He looked about his kitchen. "Long as you promise to help. Unless you're into murder-suicide, since I'm sure whatever I make will end up tasting like poison."

"I promise," she said.

His smile spread across his face, lighting up his eyes and making him look utterly handsome. Rylen took his hand and carefully hopped down from the counter. She felt like spreading her fingers in his, but he let go before she could give it a second thought. Oddly enough, they were comfortable around each other right now, and it felt good to know he was enjoying his time with her.

Caleb escorted Rylen through the grounds he had so meticulously landscaped: the wild flower gardens; the oak, maple and pine trees that lined the property; the porch that wrapped around the house, turning into a massive deck with the pool, hot tub; and a gazebo with a private boardwalk that led down to the beach. It was glorious in the waning light of day, not just to see everything, but to touch and smell the scents that welcomed them. What Rylen found the most fascinating was the rock garden.

"My memory garden." A memory garden that one day he may no longer remember. He had piles stacked everywhere, and each represented a different memory. "Would you like to build one?" he asked, slightly perturbed by the suggestion. It was his rock garden, his memories. Should he allow another to take refuge in it?

"I couldn't. It's your garden. I'd be intruding." She looked among the mounds, finding each was stacked differently and grouped closely together, except one that sat in the far corner, almost hidden from view. She pointed at it. "Why is that one all the way over there, away from the rest?"

Caleb knew which pile she was referring to. He needn't look to confirm. It was a pile of memories he wished to ignore, a pile he would rather not remember. He knew he had to take the good with the bad, and that pile was all bad.

The memory stones were a way to purge, make room for more without forgetting. He liked walking out here and remembering what each rock pile meant, whether it be his first day of school or the time he, with Dominic, were arrested for picking Mrs. Quinn's tomatoes and throwing them at her windows.

He shrugged. "There are so many piles I can't really remember what each one represents," he lied.

"Can you remember any?" She was asking questions again, but how was she going to get to know the real Caleb if he kept his walls up? She wanted to know more than what his music told her.

Caleb bent down and pointed at a grey and white swirled stone. "This one is the day I got into Julliard. I picked this stone because it had two distinct colors, and it represented the different emotions I had when I read the acceptance letter." Caleb had a faraway look on his face, almost as if he weren't in the rock garden with her anymore but back on that particular day. "I was so excited and so scared. I knew I was good, but I wasn't sure if it was what I wanted. Then, I remembered it was her dream for me and that put to rest all the quailing feelings." He lightly fingered the stone, careful not to apply too much pressure for fear the pile would tumble.

Rylen wanted to ask who he was referring too, but she didn't want to overstep every possible boundary in one day. Baby steps were needed.

"This sandy-yellow one with the knick in it represents Arnie because when it formed it was whole and then one day it just wasn't." Caleb looked up to see the faint rays of sunshine slicing through the sky. It was close to sunset and he wanted her to see its descent. He stood, turning his focus to the here and now. Arnie walked around the corner. He knew it was time for sunset, and their routine normally took them down to the beach to relax and watch, but today they had a stranger. "Blanket," he said to Arnie who turned and dashed into the house. "Almost sunset. Do you want to go watch it?" he asked.

"That would be nice. I don't think I've ever watched the sunset before."

"Then you're in for a treat."

Caleb and Rylen sat on the checkered blanket Arnie brought down to them. Once it was spread out, Arnie looked up at Caleb. Standing up, the faithful dog circled the blanket until he found the perfect spot. Once comfortable, he shoved his backside at Caleb, forcing his human to readjust. Moving over some, Caleb was now shoulder to shoulder with Rylen.

"Sorry. Arnie thinks he owns everything." He gave Arnie a sidelong glance.

"It's okay." She nodded, returning her attention to the sun barely peaking over the lake. She was surprised at how the sun disappeared in mere seconds, fully visible in the sky and suddenly, gone. "It's beautiful. Look at the colors reflecting off the water and the purplish hue in the sky," she marveled.

"It's different every time. Never the same sunset, and never the same circumstances while watching them."

"I'm amazed you ever leave this place. I could just sit on this beach and never care to move."

"It gets cold at night."

She picked at the blanket. "Blanket."

"Alright, I'll go in the house and stay warm while you sit out here with your blanket. I give you twenty minutes," he goaded her.

"Is that a bet, Mr. Montgomery?" She leaned into him, hitting him with her shoulder.

"No, but you're welcome to try." The sun had now gone for the day. "Ready?"

She shook her head. "I think I'll stick around. See how cold it gets."

"Alright, suit yourself." He stood up. Arnie stretched his legs lazily, yawning and shaking his body. "Come on, boy." Caleb started walking up the beach, leaving Rylen behind, but stopped. "Forgot one thing." He walked back over to Rylen, bent over and grabbed the edge of the blanket. He looked up at her and smirked, pulling the blanket out from under her, forcing her to fall over.

"Caleb!" she giggled, toppling over into the sand. She quickly got up and faced him, revenge in her eyes.

"Run, Arnie!" Caleb yelled, dropping the blanket and running toward his house.

"You better run." Rylen followed suit, running up the beach chasing after Caleb. Both were laughing as Arnie jumped around barking like mad. He tripped Caleb, watching as his favorite human face-planted in the sand. Caleb came up spitting sand, his face covered in it. Rylen stopped next to him, laughing. She grabbed Arnie by the scruff and hugged him, petting him in happy victory.

"Who's my good boy?" She straightened, looking down at Caleb, hands on her hips. "Looks like we know where his allegiance stands."

Caleb sat back on his shins, glaring at his traitorous dog and laughing. "He's a fool for a pretty face." He stood, wiping the sand from his clothes.

"You missed," she pointed at his face, making a circle. "All of it." She lightly wiped his cheeks, holding his face in her hands. "That was pretty funny." She scrapped the sand from his forehead, trying not to get any in his eyes. He just stood there, dumbfounded, his hands at his sides, enjoying the feel of her hands on his face. "There." She examined his face making sure it was clear of sand.

"Thank you," Caleb muttered. "It's ahh—it's getting dark out now."

"That's what happens when the sun goes down," her tone suggested sarcasm.

Caught up in the moment and unable to resist anymore, Caleb took a step nearer until his face was inches from her. Rylen's grin disappeared, and she now stood stonewalled. He wasn't sure if she wanted him to kiss her, but he wanted to. He leaned in, her eyes closing slightly, but before he could get to his target Rylen pulled back.

"We should go in. It is getting cold." She started walking up the path, Arnie helping guide her way.

"Yeah, cold," he said, stunned. The idea was so stupid and bold to even think about, let alone try.

Caleb walked back to the house, closing the screen door behind him to keep the cold from marring the cozy warmth left in the house by the afternoon sun. He was still mentally kicking himself when he found Rylen grabbing her purse and searching for her keys. He had truly been having a good time, and he went and ruined it by being an idiot. Had he messed up in reading the signs? Were there even signs to read? It didn't matter. He shouldn't have let her get to him again.

"What are you doing?" he asked.

"I think its best I go home."

She was right. It was probably best she leave. If she were gone, perhaps the urge to be near her would depart as well. "I would rather you didn't."

"I wish you hadn't done that."

"I'm sorry," he whispered. Deciding he didn't want her to go, that he wanted to follow through with the evening, he walked over and snatched her purse from her hands.

"Hey," she cried.

"We haven't eaten yet. You promised you'd help," he reminded her. "You're not the type of woman that goes back on her word are you?"

"I just think –"

"So you are," he nodded in disappointment. "Then if you want to leave, I can't force you to stay," he said, handing the purse back over to her. "I would just rather the evening didn't end like this. Give me a chance to make it up to you," he pleaded.

Rylen wanted to say no and run. He was roping her in again, and she refused to be hurt by him again when he turned his back. The evening had been perfect, like most of their time together normally was, until it wasn't, and he ran away. Now, the shoe was on the other foot, and she was attempting to run away. Perhaps, it was time for one final test. If he turned his back on her, she'd go through with her decision to go to London. She had given him the chance the night of the party, and the next morning she called and set everything up. She was almost afraid to tell him of her decision, but it was hers to make. She had the right to go if she wanted. As of right now, she wanted to, but with every minute she stayed with Caleb, it was getting harder to justify her decision to go.

"Alright," she said. "This is your last chance."

"You humble me," he said taking her hand and kissing the top of it. "I promise to be on my best behavior."

She yanked her hand away before it could burst into flame and went into the kitchen. "I think you should start by turning on the grill," she yelled over her shoulder. Rylen quieted for a moment and listened. When she didn't hear movement she popped her head out of the kitchen. "You don't know how to start it, do you?" she asked. Caleb shook his head. "Do you even know where it is?"

"On the deck," he answered.

"Great. That's a start." Caleb didn't move. "Want help?"

"That'd be very demeaning. I'm a man. Men are supposed to be masters of the grill."

"Most know how to turn them on."

"Good point. Help me, and I promise I won't put a gag order on you so you can't tell other men I can't grill."

"Threatening me is really how you want to play this?" she asked with her arms crossed.

"It's the only way I know how to play this."

"Then lead the way to the grill."

Caleb led the way to the deck and spied the grill on his right side just before the pool. The fact was, Caleb knew where the grill was, even knew how to start it, but did Rylen need to know that? No. It was more fun pretending he was helpless allowing her to participate, which meant more time together than having her in the house and him at the helm of the grill. This way she was close.

Rylen wound her way over to the grill and started it with little trouble. She could feel Caleb leaning over her shoulder, watching intently, but she knew he wasn't paying attention to her instruction. Rather, he was quite aware of the closeness of their bodies.

"Easy," she said, turning around to find Caleb barely a foot away from her.

"Seems to be," he said smiling down at her. "What do you propose now?"

"We need the burger patties."

Caleb glanced down at Arnie who was holding the bag in his mouth and bent down to retrieve it. "He's quite the chef assistant." They laughed at the perfect helper gazing at them adoringly.

Her stomach growled loudly, and Rylen tried to play it off as if she heard nothing. "Arnie, how rude," Caleb chastised the dog. "If you're hungry just say so."

Rylen laughed. "Let's put the burgers on before your neighbors hear my hunger pangs," she said placing the patties on the grill. "And what would you like to do while they cook?" she asked.

"Umm," Caleb thought not knowing what to do next, "I don't know," he said stumped. This was the equivalent of a date, and Caleb had no idea what to do on dates. That was Dominic's territory, and he was ill-equipped to proceed on his own. "Swim?"

"Don't have a suit," she said.

"Since when did that stop people?" he smirked.

"Next suggestion."

Caleb laughed. "We can stand here and stare at each other in silence while the burgers sizzle."

"Wow, you're a regular Casanova."

"It's how I roll."

Rylen busted out laughing and placed her hand on his forearm. "Don't ever say that again," she said, her hand innocently sliding down his arm until her pinky finger laced around his.

A jolt of electricity shot through his body at the simple placement of her finger. Caleb tried to contain himself, their earlier experience running through his mind. This time he didn't try to get more out of her.

"Movie? You said you liked 'Out of Africa.' Would you want to watch it with me?" he asked, watching her thoughts roll around. He offered up a movie less romantic. "Maybe some 'Goodfellas' would be better?"

"How about a comedy?"

"'Mighty Ducks?'" he suggested.

"You seriously want to watch 'Mighty Ducks'?" she laughed.

"I haven't watched it in a while. Good throw back to childhood movie. You down with that?"

"Yeah, I'm down with that," she squeezed his hand.

Caleb leaned forward and reached around her placing the grill hood down. His breath was on her shoulder. She leaned into him, her face an inch from his neck, breathing in his aftershave.

"Let's go inside. It's getting cold out here," he suggested.

"Right."

He could sense her demeanor had changed, and he hesitated for a moment with the thought of trying to kiss her again, but he resisted. She was cold and wearing a sundress. He wanted to get her inside so they could watch their movie and she could warm up.

An idea came to him. "I'll be right back," he said, closing the patio door, and taking off down the hallway. She could hear him open a door and rummage.

"You're joking, right?"

He shook his head. "Not when it comes to the flying V." He had thrown on a green Mighty Ducks jersey, the same from the movie, and had one in his hand for her to wear. He threw it at her, expecting her to put it on, but she only stared at it. "I thought you were down?"

"Yeah, down," she said, frowning at the huge green jersey in her hands. "It kind of clashes with my dress."

"Take it off." The words were out before he could mull them over in his head. "I didn't mean like –"

"Don't worry, I know." She pulled the jersey over her head, engulfing her like a parachute. "Not exactly my size."

Stretching his arms out, he showed her his was a few sizes too big as well. "Whose is? Are you ready to be a duck?"

"As ready as I'll ever be. Just as long as this duck gets to eat a nice, juicy burger."

Chapter Fifteen

Rylen and Caleb were leaning against the couch, their stomachs protruding from under their oversized jerseys and their eye lids barely open. Caleb's head nodded forward, and he quickly jerked it back, repositioning so it didn't look as if he were falling asleep. Sated from their burgers and snack pack of pudding, their side for the evening since he had nothing else in the house, Caleb noticed that the movie had finally ended. For the past two minutes, while he'd been trying to keep his eyes open, they had been watching the end credits. He leaned over to say something to Rylen but he'd lost her to sleep.

He lightly prodded her once and again when she didn't stir the first time. The second time her eyes flew open and she started chanting "Quack! Quack! Quack!"

For the hell of it Caleb joined in. "Quack! Quack! Quack!" He pounded his fists on his knees to make the chant feel more invigorating, helping to wake up.

Rylen started to realize her error when she saw that Caleb had turned off the movie and was only goading her. She stood up quickly, surprised she had fallen asleep. She had not realized she was so tired, but with the size of the burgers they consumed, she wasn't surprised.

"Who won?" she asked.

Caleb's smile disappeared, and his hands fell silent on his knees. "You mean, you haven't seen 'Mighty Ducks' before?" Rylen shyly nodded her head in embarrassment. "Then, I can't tell you." He folded his arms across his chest, shaking his head. "Nope. You'll have to watch it again. Do you know that it's a felony if you haven't seen 'Mighty Ducks' at least once in this state?" he joked. "It's unheard of, Rylen!"

"Wow." She was stunned. "I'm slightly perturbed at your passion for that movie." She held a hint of a smile, trying not to break character.

"And I'm perturbed by your lack thereof." He bounced up, fully awake now from their conversation. He was tired of talking about important things. Dominic always wanted to talk about treatments, therapy, and concerts. Talking with Rylen was like a breath of fresh air, and he didn't want to exhale. "You're welcome to take the movie home and watch it in its entirety."

"I think I'll risk getting arrested."

"Oh, I'm sorry. I led you to believe that you'd be arrested. No, you wouldn't be arrested, they'd simply just cut your hands off and possibly an ear for good measure." He tapped his index finger against his chin. "But... there may be one way to sway the court of 'Mighty Ducks' opinion," he chided.

"And what may that be, your Honor?"

He shook his head. "No, you wouldn't do it."

"You don't know that."

"Well, the tide could switch in your favor, if you simply wrote a heartfelt apology letter stating how sorry you are for having never seen such a fine movie and bathing the judge, me, with copious amounts of compliments."

Rylen stared at Caleb and decided the letter was out of the question. "I'll sacrifice my hands and both ears before I bathe you in undeserved compliments," she joked, putting her hands together in front of her to be cuffed.

"Geez, if I had a shred of dignity or feeling that would have stung." He grabbed his chest. "My heart is palpitating at your lack of respect for this court. However, you've made the decision quite easy." He grabbed her hands and started leading her toward the kitchen. "This is gonna hurt me more than you. Maybe not. I've never really cut off someone's hands before, so it may take me a few tries. It's safe to say this is actually going to hurt you more than me."

He put her hands on the island, opening a drawer below it and scanning the contents for a proper knife. "Any last words? Begging perhaps?"

"Begging is beneath me."

Arnie walked into the kitchen, and stood up, placing his one good leg on the island counter to watch the show.

"Arnie, you know the rules." Arnie slowly sat back on his hind legs and pulled his front paw from the counter. "Good boy."

Rylen looked down at Arnie. "Are you going to just let him hack off my limbs?" she asked. Arnie yawned and padded out of the room. "I thought you were on my side," she yelled after him.

"Now where do his loyalties lie?" Caleb continued wading through the contents of the drawer. "I give up. I can't find a suitable weapon. This probably isn't even the knife drawer." He let go of her hands. "You are free to go, but next time, I won't be so lenient."

"Awe...a judge with compassion."

"Hardly, I'm just tired."

He looked it, Rylen noticed. It was time to go. It was already well past midnight, and they both had a concert to prepare for.

"I think I'm going to go. It's late."

"You're more than welcome to stay if you're too tired to drive home. There are a few bedrooms upstairs that don't really get used." He stifled a yawn and wiped his eyes. "The jersey is yours for the evening unless you like sleeping in hot-pink dresses." He shrugged. "I prefer neon orange, but that's just a color that brings out my eyes." They laughed together.

"Thank you for the offer, but I have a lot to do tomorrow. Probably best if I just go home."

Caleb nodded in agreement. He preferred that she stayed. She was clearly tired, and it was a long drive home, but he wanted her to be comfortable. If she wanted to go home, he'd respect her wishes. "Keep the jersey, anyway. It's cold."

"Thank you."

Rylen retrieved her purse, a little disappointed she wasn't staying. The evening had been enjoyable, and Caleb was letting his guard down. She hadn't seen him this playful since the amusement park. She liked this side of him. Perhaps he wasn't emotionally closed off and dead inside after all.

Caleb opened the door, and following the lighted path, led her to the driveway. Lightning bugs littered the yard, sporadically lightning up all around them. She remembered chasing after the unusual bugs and catching them when she was a child.

They stopped in front of her car, the awkwardness now returning. "Thank you for letting me join you this evening. I had a great time." She smiled, gazing up at the outline of his face shaded by the night.

"Honestly, tonight was probably the most fun I've had in a long time. Really," Caleb opened up. The last few months had been hellish for him, and he was happy he had someone he could just sit back and forget the real world with. Rylen simply smiled, not needing to say anything.

"Goodnight, Rylen."

"Goodnight."

Caleb turned and left, afraid to make the same mistake he had made earlier. He had enjoyed her company extremely, and he didn't want to ruin it by being selfish. The path guided him back to the porch where he turned off the outside lights so she couldn't see him watching her pull out of the driveway.

Rylen unlocked her car, putting her hand on the handle she made a decision. She wanted to kiss Caleb today, but she was scared he'd pull away, so she beat him to it. She wanted to kiss him just now, but she held back because she felt vulnerable around him.

She dropped her hand from the door handle and walked back up the path. The house front was now dark, the porch barely visible. If not for the lighting on the path, she would have tripped over the stairs.

Facing the door, she tried to figure out what she was going to say; what she was going to do.

"Caleb…" she began, hoping to find the right words, but she didn't get very far.

"Yes?" he asked. The rocking chair creaked under his weight as he stood.

Rylen jumped back, startled by his presence. "I…" She was at a loss for words. He was standing before her now. She could hear him breathe, feel his proximity without really seeing him. Then she realized she hadn't necessarily come back to say anything.

Caleb still wanted to kiss her. She was so close, and she came back, but why? He didn't want her to think she had gotten to him, that just by a look she could make his insides squeeze into a tight, unforgiving fist. This was a test. She was tempting him, seeing if he'd break and ruin the friendship they were slowly building. He raised his hand, but afraid of her reaction, he dropped it back down to his side. He was not going to let her see his weakness anymore. Before he could step back, she leaned into him. Her lips parted, lightly pressing against his. It was simple. The type of kiss that left someone wanting more, but Caleb didn't act on his impulse. Instead, he let her pull away, walk back to her car and drive away. She was gone, but he could still feel her.

~

Tossing and turning, Caleb's mind refused to shut off. The evening replayed over and over in his mind, and the sensation that filled his body from the tip of his toes to the top of his head was so overwhelming that even his body was restless.

He punched at his pillow, making a crevice and shoving his head into it, trying to suffocate his thoughts of Rylen. He wanted sleep, needed sleep, but nothing he did would allow him the satisfaction. He flipped over on his back. A loud sigh escaped his lips prompting Arnie to roll over next to him, but the dog remained asleep. His light snore annoyed Caleb. Maybe if he watched the ceiling fan it would calm him, get him into a rhythm, like counting sheep. He started counting the circulations, but all that did was make him more aware of the noises around him.

The rhythm of the rotations combined with the symphony of nature. Crickets hummed and trees swayed in the breeze as a branch tapped against his window pane. He quickly lunged out of bed, a composition taking form. He raced to the piano, throwing himself at the bench. He almost slid off but gripped at the keys, his hands slamming hard down on them.

In his head, he rewound the beat and started to put notes to it. He grabbed a sheet of paper and started scribbling down the cacophony in his mind. He wrote ferociously, the pencil markings smudging as he wiped his hand across them, trying to keep up with the composition in his head. He had the song written before he even started running his fingers along the keys. This was the ending to what he had been preparing for the past few months.

Once he started to play, it was more beautiful than he had imagined. When he played, he saw her face, the face of the one for whom the song was written. The tune was now finished, and he realized that, even before he had met her, the song had been for her all along.

At the top of the sheet, Caleb wrote out the name of the song. It seemed natural that, at this moment, when sleep was eluding him and his mind racing with thoughts of Rylen, he would call it 'Sleep Sweet'.

Chapter Sixteen

His leg shook with such uncertainty until Dominic stilled it with his hand over his knee, but the nerves were so great his leg shook with the force of an impending avalanche. He'd tried to calm down by meditating, sitting out by the lake, but nothing helped. The mirror was playing tricks on him. Still wasn't right. Switching his outfit for the fourth time, Dominic stood at the closet and wondered why he was so nervous when it should have been a walk in the park. But she always made him nervous. For her alone did he strive to be better, and she deserved his effort. She was perfection in his eyes.

Again, he posed in the full-length mirror and debated between the green or black sweater. He recalled a conversation in which she had said she liked when he wore black. She thought the color made him look dark and mysterious with his black hair and deep hazel eyes. The decision was made. He ripped off the green sweater and pulled the black one over his head. This would be the last wardrobe change for the evening.

The turtle neck looked good. His hair lay just along the collar, skimming the back of his neck as she preferred. He felt silly, picking apart his appearance, but he wanted to impress her and help her to remember the good times. Maybe she would remember that he made her happy once upon a time.

The stairs disappeared beneath him as he took them two at a time, racing into the living room to make sure all was perfect. He put the remote to the stereo in his back pocket and scanned the spread before him. He had spent the afternoon racing around the city, getting her favorite treats from her favorite places.

The fire crackled at the end of the room casting shadows throughout the quiet house, a house that shouldn't be so quiet, he thought glumly. Time for some music. He grabbed the remote and pressed the corresponding buttons for the stereo. The music flowed freely through the house. He decided against classical. He couldn't let those thoughts in tonight. Tonight was too important for him to fall back into his old ways. He had already put others and trivial things before her needs. He wouldn't do that a second time.

Dominic went through his mental list of arrangements. Flowers adorned most of the flat surfaces. Candles and the fireplace were the only sources of light besides the waning rays of the sun. Milk was on ice instead of her favorite Riesling, and Neil Diamond crooned softly in the background. Everything met his specifications.

Clutching the necklace safely hidden away under his turtle neck, Dominic wished for the evening to go as planned, for that spark to be rekindled and a family to be put back together. The ring still symbolized his undying love. He had done things in the past few months to put that love in jeopardy, but nothing could take away the hurt of not having that ring still on his finger. Dominic knew there was only one person for him, and he had been lucky enough to be given a second chance to secure their happiness.

Patting his pocket, Dominic made sure the box was still safe. He checked continuously to make sure it was still there, the ring securely inside. He would give her the gift, not to win her back, but to honor the gift she was giving him by carrying his child.

The light knock on the door made him tense. Cracking his knuckles nervously he left the room content he could do nothing more. He grabbed a napkin from the kitchen and dabbed at his forehead. This was insane. She'd never go for this. She'd see right through it and never reconsider. He tried to hope for the best, but doubt gnawed at him. The door was within his reach. He pressed his forehead to it. She was on the other side, he knew, but he was afraid to turn the knob and face her. He was startled when she knocked again, his heart pounding with anticipation and fear.

"Here goes nothing," he whispered.

As he gathered his courage and opened the door, Dominic was struck by the sheer awe of her. It was as if he were seeing her for the first time. He gaped at her. Ashley's blonde hair trickled over her shoulders accenting her throat as her emerald green eyes dazzled. She was beautiful in an elegant black dress. Dominic hadn't realized pregnant women could wear such things. She was simply stunning. Every inch of skin glowed as he surveyed her like a hawk circling its prey. He couldn't manage words let alone move his legs so she could come in from the chill in the March air.

"Wow. Those shoes really show off your legs," he laughed, pointing at the footwear that completed the outfit.

Ashley kicked out her leg and wiggled her foot.

"Can't leave home without them," she smiled. "I don't think I ever hated walking so much before," she shifted her weight.

"I, for one, believe no one should leave home without a pair of winterized crocs," he extended his hand to guide her in.

This was the first time he had touched her since their kiss at her apartment. He was almost surprised she hadn't pulled her hand away. The cascading emotion of past happiness that ran through his body when she gripped his hand made Dominic hope Ashley felt it all coming back to her too. He didn't want to let go, but he didn't want to seem overzealous. She was there as his guest, not his wife. He exhaled when she released his hand, and now, the match was about to begin.

Like a gentleman, Dominic helped Ashley remove her jacket and held onto her hand as she kicked off the crocs. It was cute how she waddled around, but he would not dare point that out. Her belly looked bigger than her small frame, and the pregnancy added a little bit of extra padding in all the right places.

Ashley's nose perked up, and her pregnancy senses went into overdrive.

"Is that…it couldn't be," she sniffed. "Is that a Billy Goat double cheeseburger? And a Morton's steak? With Harry Cary's Vesuvio? Oh my God, Dominic, is that a Dolce de Leche cheesecake?" She eyed the cheesecake that was thawing for dessert.

"Yes to all of the above," he laughed, following after her into the living room where she found all her favorite foods.

The fork had just touched her bottom lip when she shyly looked up at Dominic. Her eyes were focused and playful, and she reminded him of that confident second-grade teacher he had met for the first time at Old Town Ale House. "You don't mind if we eat now, do you?" she giggled.

"Absolutely not." He took a seat across from her, choosing to eat the burger first so he could watch her eat the steak. "I hope you're not on some doctor-prescribed diet. I don't want you doing anything that he would frown upon or that could hurt the baby," he worried, just now realizing she could be regulated to a strict diet of salad and chicken.

"It's okay, Dominic. If I were, I think you'd know by now," she said, squashing his fears.

"Great, because I read in the book that you could get gestational diabetes if you don't keep a healthy diet or sustain a reasonable weight that's healthy for both you and the baby." He took a big chunk out of his burger and was about to go on when he noticed Ashley staring at him with a half gnawed on piece of steak in her gaping mouth.

"What?" he put his burger down and wiped his face, thinking he had food smeared all over it. "Did I get it?" he asked.

"You read the book," she said, astonished.

"Of course."

"Why?" she asked. Truthfully, she hadn't finished the entire book herself.

"Because I wanted to," he shrugged, afraid he may have crossed a line in telling her about managing her weight. He knew weight was a sore subject with pregnant women, especially, hormonal pregnant women. "I'm sorry if I said something wrong," he apologized.

"No, it's okay." They stared at each other for a few more seconds when, slowly, the half gnawed piece of steak disappeared. Ashley resumed eating.

"Oh, I wanted to tell you, I bought these new baby bottles. They're supposed to be better. They're called Milk Bank Baby Bottles, and supposedly they help the baby to eat without getting gas or colic. Something about a vented system and wider nipples." He never thought he'd be talking about bottle nipples. "And I got you a breast pump. Girl said it was the best one on the market. Don't understand the difference between them, but I wasn't sure if you'd want one or not. I got it just in case, I guess."

"You bought me a breast pump," Ashley gawked. Ashley put down her fork and knife. "This is too much," she wiped her mouth and leaned back in the chair.

"See, I should shut my mouth." He averted his face and debated changing the music to change the mood and, hopefully, the conversation. He was putting his foot in his mouth and probably talking too much about the needs of the baby. She was the mother. She knew better than anyone what was best for the baby.

Ashley remained silent, and Dominic tried to gather his wits about him to figure out what to do next. He could put more food in front of her to distract her that way, but that would only work for so long before she became full or he ran out of food. He was going to let her off the hook. He'd let her go home, and next time, he'd let her set her terms on her own territory so she'd be comfortable. He may not be with the mother of his child, but he was going to damn well be in his child's life. That would only happen if the mother was happy.

Before he knew it, he was pulling the box out of his pocket and tossing it across the table at her. Not exactly the way he planned to present it, but he was nervous that she'd leave, and the gift would only make him look desperate if given to her later.

"What is that?" she asked eyeing the box.

"Something that isn't for the baby. I know some people forget about the mother and only focus on the child, but I thought you needed a little something too," he smiled hoping she'd like it.

"Dominic, I really sho-"

"Please," he interrupted her, "it's only a gift. Nothing hinges on it. I only wanted to get you something."

Hesitantly, she grabbed the box and opened it. She stared at it for a long time, so long Dominic wasn't sure she was going to accept it, but when she choked up and took it out of the box, he knew she loved it.

"You like it?"

"It's beautiful." She looked up. "Thank you."

"You're welcome. Here." He jumped up, taking the ring from her and sliding it into place on her right hand. "Perfect." He sat down quickly so as not to linger too much, trying to keep to his boundaries. The diamond ring, the birthstone for their baby due in April, shone brightly. The chair scraped against the hardwood floor as Ashley pushed up from the table and walked back the way she had entered.

Dominic let out a deep breath trying to calm down. "One, two, three, four," he counted. Everything was going to be okay. Maybe it was all too much, too soon. He'd call her later to make sure she got home safe, and he'd find out if she wanted to see him again. There was still so much to do and so little time. He hadn't even finished the room upstairs yet, and they would be home in a few short days.

"Dominic," she called from the kitchen.

Dominic pushed his seat back, his strides long and determined, trying to keep his ragged breath under control so Ashley wouldn't notice.

"Yes?" he turned the corner, getting to her as fast as he could.

The light in the kitchen was off, and she stood in the soft glow of the moonlight that filtered in through the front window over the sink. She leaned over the counter, one hand supporting her and the other on her stomach, as she took in shallow breaths.

"Are you okay?" Dominic asked wondering what he could do to help her. If he had known that talking about bottles and breast pumps would make her feel this way, he would never have brought it up. First thing tomorrow he was going to take back everything and only get her what she asked for and absolutely needed. What was the point in fancy bottles and breast pumps? People before their time didn't have such luxuries.

"Ouch," she whimpered, her hands dropping to her underbelly.

"What's wrong?" Dominic asked, worry lines creasing his forehead as he grabbed her by the shoulders and watched her face contract in pain.

She took quick, shallow breaths and tried to harness her pain, but another contraction made her almost double over. Dominic gathered her up in his arms. The pain was too great to ignore, and she cried out.

"I'm taking you to the hospital." Dominic hauled her up and grabbed his car keys on the way to the door.

"No, I'm fine," she cried, knowing it was too soon for the baby to come. She was only a week shy of thirty-two weeks. There was no way she was going to let the baby come out before it was baked all the way.

"Too bad," he carried her out to the car and sped away.

Chapter Seventeen

The boat swayed with the wind, but he clung tightly to the dock, roped up for safety. The stars turned out in all their glory, shining like beacons in the distance, guiding Caleb in his endeavor.

He had been in the little row boat for the past hour since finishing his composition. Lying on his back with a blanket and pillow beneath him, his legs hanging over the side, he let his toes dip just below the water's surface where the fish could nip at his feet, if any were awake at such an hour.

Arnie lay patiently on the dock waiting for Caleb. His eyes opened and closed as he fought off sleep, the day taking its toll.

Caleb tried counting the stars, but whenever the boat rocked he lost focus and count. Lost in reflective thought the stars faded from sight. In life we come across people that walk in and out of our lives. If we're lucky, they leave us with something that we can carry. Something that helps us learn, actions that speak louder than anything they could ever relay to us. And when he saw her in his mind, even though they hadn't known each other long, she had taught him so much. She taught him the one thing he never thought he'd have in his life and it scared him to be faced with such a strong emotion. One he had scarcely felt before. He masked his initial feelings with disapproval, but in his heart he knew they were right for each other. Fit together better than puzzle pieces, better than macaroni and cheese, better than Fitzgerald and Gatsby.

However, when he opened his eyes everything seemed unsure. He wanted to be guided. To be pulled in one direction or the other. He didn't want to hurt her, but he knew the road ahead of him was as clear as the stars in the sky. He was scared. Death wasn't something most people welcomed, but he had accepted his fate. Though wholly unprepared for the change in circumstances, he was now questioning every decision he had made up until now. But those decisions guided him straight to her, and he was thankful for at least knowing her.

"What should I believe?" he asked the wind, but Caleb already knew the answer. Believe in everything, the unseen, yourself.

The wind picked up and the boat swayed back and forth, teetering so that his leg dipped into the water up to his knee. Then the winds changed and the boat twisted, rotating him in a circle. He sat up, his hands clutching the sides of the boat, Arnie's head popped up on the dock to watch. His heart raced, unclear of the sign he was being given, but he remembered his question, and the answer that came to him. Believe everything.

"Okay!" he screamed, the wind whipping the word from his lips and carrying it across the lake.

Caleb lay back down in the boat, wrapping his arms around his knees. The boat stopped moving and glided gracefully over the water knocking up against the wooden planks of the dock. Arnie peered over the side of the boat and looked down at Caleb, his eyes showing worry and confusion.

What Caleb was about to do was crazy. He was going to open up, to allow his frustration, anger, and fear to sail away with the wind, but he didn't know how to begin. The stars, they would guide him. He had faith they knew in which direction he was to go. He would let his heart and the stars take him to places he'd never ventured. He knew he was already in love with her. Now it was time to fall.

~

At the Chicago Botanical Gardens, wrought-iron framed, the sunlight filtered through the glass of the greenhouse, giving the plants a crystal-like glow. Caleb and Rylen walked among the plants, the ventilation system sending a light breeze through the greenhouse. They had spent the better part of their afternoon walking the gravel paths and pointing at the beautiful shrubs, flowers, and trees. They stood at the waterfall, watching the fish in the water lily and lotus area. Even though they planned on being there all day, they knew even in the hours they spent there, there was no way they'd see everything.

They continued on their way, walking through the Krasberg Rose garden where Caleb bought Rylen a rose. She brought it up to her nose, smelling its lush scent and cradling Caleb's arm, laying her head on his shoulder. They continued walking, basking in the beautiful spring day.

The magnificent purple hue of the blossoming magnolia trees swayed in the breeze sending flowers soaring through the air, falling at their feet. They stood among an urban Eden spanning a 385-acre tract of pristine forest. They were in another world, hidden off the beaten path of Chicago, a quiet oasis of lush green flourishing in the start of the season.

Every once in a while, when Rylen would venture off ahead of him or bend down to smell the fragrant flowers, he would snap a picture of her. He wanted to capture each memory in a picture, every happy look, every free-spirited smile. With pictures, he would always have proof of his memories, even as they faded. He might forget the woman. The garden may be a foreign memory. Yet, whenever he looked at the picture, he would be able to see the happiness of his past. Despite his precautions, Caleb was certain this day would never be forgotten. It couldn't.

She was smiling and angelic as she reached up to touch the blossoms of the crabapple trees. Scooping her up into his arms, Caleb whirled her around as she giggled, encapsulated in his embrace. Leaning forward, she kissed him, and Caleb snapped a picture of them in their embrace, the crabapple trees swaying behind them and the flowers springing through the air. Caleb knew that picture was going to be the memory he took away from this day.

Taking a rest, they sat on a bench surrounded by conifers. Rylen leaned back against Caleb's chest. He wrapped his arms around her and rested his head on her shoulder, watching families and tourists walking the paths through the lush forest.

"I'm going to tell you something I haven't told anyone yet. Not even Dominic," Caleb said.

"Go ahead."

The thoughts had been troubling, but now looking at her and seeing that she was there beside him made the answer seem clear.

"I'm going to retire after our last concert."

Rylen tensed, and her breathing seemed to stop as she digested what Caleb had just revealed to her. There was uncertainty in her eyes as if she were wondering if Caleb was just playing a joke on her.

"I'm serious," he said.

Trying to take solace in her skin, he ran his hand down her arm. Everything seemed so right to him. He had been contemplating retirement and had finally made a decision when she walked back to him and kissed him, setting his world atilt. He had never allowed himself to think seriously of retirement, or any other possible future, since receiving the news of his Huntington's Disease. Now, it was all he wanted, to slow down and watch the world instead of letting it pass him by.

"Why?" she asked.

"I'm tired. I feel I've done everything I've set out to do. There's nothing more for me to accomplish on the stage."

"You're sure this is what you want? No regrets?"

"I haven't been sure of a lot of things, but right now, I know this is the right decision," he let out a deep breath.

"Then if that's what will make you happy, I say go for it," she smirked.

Rylen pushed up and started walking. Caleb watched her and laughed, thinking of all the times he had left her with the very same image, but today it wasn't the same. She stopped walking, her back still to him, and the palm of her hand opening, waiting for his hand to fill the empty space. Caleb sprang to her side where he slid his hand into her palm. They continued on their walk in silence taking in the scenery.

Rylen felt safe. She had never had that feeling before with any other man, and knowing she could rely on Caleb, she thought about what his retirement would mean.

"Do you ever think of the future?" she asked, focusing on a woman pushing a stroller with a little girl.

"I tried not to," he frowned, "I wasn't sure if I was going to see one." He pushed his morose thoughts from his mind. Today was not a day to think of the looming questions he faced outside of the garden walls. He was happy. He felt good, and he had the woman he believed he was in love with in his arms. "Now," he kissed her cheek, his lips against her ear, "it's all I can think about," he told her truthfully. Things he never allowed himself to dream of were now foremost in his mind, and it thrilled and intoxicated him.

"There's hope for you yet," she laughed, rubbing her cheek against his, liking the feel of his scruff against her bare skin.

"You give me hope for a future I never allowed myself to imagine." He fell into the thoughts he had just tried to leave behind him, but they were always there lurking, waiting for their moment. He looked off into space, feeling the constriction of the sickness emanating through his body, waiting to strike at any minute.

Rylen watched him as he focused on something far away. His eyes darkened as though he was remembering something heartbreaking. She waved her hand in front of his face, worried, wanting to bring him back, to make him smile that beautiful smile he kept so well hidden.

"Hey, where'd you go?"

"Dare to dream." He smirked, leaning in and kissing her, hoping to calm her thoughts. "What about you? What do you see?"

"Hmm…," she threw herself down on the soft green grass. Stretching out on her back, she patted the ground next to her, inviting Caleb to sit. She placed her head in Caleb's lap, looking up at him, the sky a beautiful aqua blue and pure white clouds hovering above. "I see myself making beautiful music, getting married, and starting a family."

"How many kids do you want?"

"Two or three."

"That's it?" he frowned, shaking his head. "We'll have eight."

She shot up; alarmed at the number he threw out. She hoped he was only joking.

"Eight! And who said anything about 'we'?" She pinched her lips together in a fake pout.

"Too fast?" he cringed.

"No. I'll just be unrecognizable after having eight children."

"You'll always be beautiful."

"I better be." They laughed as she ran her hand through his hair and pulled him down to her lips. She couldn't get enough of him.

~

The stars were out in full force that evening as Caleb led Rylen out to the gazebo blindfolded. He had planned everything perfectly, had even considered telling her that he was in love with her, but he decided against it. Tonight was just about being together, having a nice time, and not throwing around words that may or may not be said back. That was what scared him the most. A chill ran down his spine, but it was anxious excitement that coursed through his body, not nervous dread.

A table sat in the middle of the gazebo lit by candles that surrounded the entire deck, guiding his way toward their destination. Dinner, special ordered from a caterer, was covered, and wine chilled beside it.

"Where you taking me?" she asked. "I hope you don't plan on chopping me into little pieces because that would just ruin the day we had," she laughed.

Caleb didn't laugh but answered seriously. "I'm taking you down to the beach. Then I'm going to cut you up into little pieces and feed you to the fish. You know too much." He suppressed a grin.

"Cute." Caleb remained silent. "You're joking, right?"

"Wow, no trust. I'm hurt."

She put her hands out wanting to touch his face. He was smiling. She could feel his grin with her fingertips. "Ass."

"I'm an ass? You're the one that asked if I was seriously considering offing you." He started to undo the blindfold. "When all I want to do is," he removed it, exposing his surprise, "have a special evening with you."

She gasped at the brilliant spectacle before her. The candles and the Christmas lights draped over the gazebo made it feel as if they were in their own little world, engulfed in white light.

She couldn't help but whirl around, her eyes sparkling in the light, and he felt a tug at his heart. It was perfect. She was perfect. He couldn't imagine being anywhere else with anyone else.

"This is beautiful. You did all this?" she asked surprised.

"Geez, don't act so surprised at my awesomeness."

"Now you're just making up words." Caleb folded his arms across his chest, tapping his foot annoyed. "Oh, don't pout," she cradled his face in her hands. "Your awesomeness astounds me," she laughed as she leaned in giving him a peck on the lips. "I love it."

He held out an arm for her. "Then allow me to show you to your seat." He escorted her to the table, pulling out her seat, acting like the gentlemen he could be on occasion.

Caleb leaned over her shoulder, smelling the scent of lilacs on her skin and kissing her neck.

"Hey buddy, don't get handsy. My man will be back any minute."

"Yes, madam, I apologize…but you liked it," he whispered over her shoulder. "Your man, huh?" he sat down across from her.

She hadn't meant to say it aloud, but she liked the sound of it. She wasn't sure how he looked at their relationship, but he didn't seem too angry at her assertion that she was in possession of him. And they had talked of children earlier in the day.

"Is that okay?"

He lightly tapped his fingers together, contemplating how he felt about the whole girlfriend/boyfriend title. "I think I like the ring of it." He grabbed her hand across the table, running his thumb across her palm. "I really like the ring of it."

She blushed, happy it was not only official in her head, but out loud.

"So, tell me. Should I be afraid?" She glanced down at the food that hid under the lids.

Caleb reached across, pulling the lid off of the plates. "Do you think I'd risk cooking? Grilling is one thing. I'm not insane."

"Then what are we about to eat?" She studied the food on her plate, trying to determine what was before her.

Caleb studied the same. "I don't rightly know. I told the chef to make his highest requested meal."

"It looks like liver." She scrunched her face together, not masking the look of disgust.

"Liver. That's not exactly what I had in mind for a romantic dinner. Better than cow tongue, I suppose." He gazed up at her, trying to make light of the epidemic, but she was still scrunching her face. "I take it you don't like liver?"

"What gave it away?"

"I think it was that ugly face you're making."

"You calling me ugly?" she gaped.

"Yes, now you have to eat the liver."

"No. Not gonna do it." She shook her head like a two-year-old refusing her vegetables.

"Come on, it's good." He picked up his knife and sliced a piece of the liver off, staring down at it on his fork, dreading the thought of putting it in his mouth, but he was going to prove a point. He closed his eyes and shoved it in his mouth, taking swift bites and sliding it back on his tongue, trying to force it down his throat, but it wouldn't budge. His gag reflex kicked in and the half-gnawed piece of liver came back up on his plate.

Rylen threw her hands over her mouth, suppressing laughter, but she broke down, screeching loudly. Caleb looked down on his plate. The saliva-encrusted piece of liver made him want to throw up. He turned his head and started coughing, grabbing his glass of wine and throwing back a swig.

"That has to be the most disgusting thing I've ever done," he choked out.

"You're ridiculous." She started making loud chomping noises. "Liver good." She rubbed her belly. "Me eat my liver. Nmmm. Nmmm."

Caleb straightened, his face returning to a lighter shade of red. He grabbed the lid and put it back over his plate, putting the sight of the liver out of his mind. Rylen was still laughing, and Caleb wasn't going to stand for this treachery. Cat-like, he jumped out of his seat and scooped her up into his arms, throwing her over his shoulder.

"Hey!" she yelled, slapping him on the back playfully as he headed back towards the house. "Put me down, mister."

"Sorry, I can't hear you. Too busy chewing. Nmmm. Nmmm. Don't you want to see your next surprise?"

"There's more?" she asked excitedly. "No liver, right?"

Caleb stopped, looking around, acting as if he were waiting for the next surprise. "It should be right here." He swung around. "Oh, I see it now."

Rylen looked up, trying to force her face out of the crevice of Caleb's back. "I don't see anything."

"It's just a step over to the left."

"Nooo!" she yelled, a moment before he plunged them both into the pool.

Chapter Eighteen

"Just a false alarm. It happens. The doctor said so." Dominic opened the door to Ashley's apartment.

"You'd think I'd know the difference," she mumbled, throwing down the hospital paperwork and going straight for the scissors in the junk drawer to cut off the hospital bracelet.

"How could you? Have you been pregnant before?" he asked, just to get her to smile. His effort was successful. "Now that's what I like to see," he nipped her chin with his thumb and forefinger. "I love your smile."

Their interactions were less awkward now that they were spending more time together. Slowly, they were getting back into the flow of being partners, even though the term was used loosely.

"Here," he pulled the ring he had given her hours earlier from his pocket. The ring held the birth stone of their child. He had taken it from her, fearing she'd lose it while in the chaos of Braxton Hicks contractions.

Ashley grabbed his hand and held it in hers. The diamond birth stone shone up at them. They were making progress, slowly finding their way back to each other. This was the relationship he cherished so much but had thrown away for another. If he would have known she was pregnant, he would have done what he could to be with her, but she had kept it secret. He still didn't understand why she would keep something so big from him. Maybe she was scared of being rejected again. Maybe she feared he would say no to her and the baby, but family was important to Dominic. He would never turn on them. For the same reason, he couldn't just walk away from Caleb.

"There's something I need to talk to you about, Dominic." She sounded serious.

"If this is about what happened at dinner, the breast pump and bottles, I can take them back."

"No," she shook her head. "It has nothing to do with breast pumps." She walked over to the coffee table where a pile of papers lay scattered over it. "It has to do with these." She pulled some papers out from under others, sitting them on top so Dominic could look at them.

"The divorce papers?" he questioned, both of them sitting on the couch. "But I signed them for you," he said despondently.

She clicked the top of a pen and sat it on the papers. When she finally looked up at Dominic, he could tell she was hurt and sad.

"You gave these back to me, but you didn't sign the last page." She pushed the pile of papers to Dominic. In a way, he was grateful for the divorce papers. They were the very thing that led to his realization of Ashley's condition, but they were dissolving a life they once had together. That was something he could not be happy about.

"I must have forgotten," he said, his voice tight with anguish.

Ashley reached into her purse and pulled out a small box. The box was inlaid with velvet, swaddling a ring. Ashley's wedding ring. She longingly looked at it and rubbed the empty spot on her left ring finger. Dominic wanted to reach out and pull her towards him to comfort her, but this wasn't the moment to do so. Not when their divorce papers were sitting between them, separating them like a vast body of water.

Ashley looked over at Dominic, but didn't make eye contact. She was looking straight at the small divot that his ring made under his sweater. She reached out and laid her hand over the ring.

Dominic tugged the neck of his sweater down and pulled the sterling silver necklace holding his ring over his head. He sat it down next to Ashley's wedding ring. Neither of them could muster the strength to speak. The rings were now circles broken by distrust, resentment, and promises not kept.

Ashley's hand flew to her stomach, and with her other hand she grabbed Dominic's, placing it on her left side where the baby was resting.

"You feel that?" she asked.

This time, Dominic was able to feel the kick of life under his fingertips, and he lit up. "It's amazing," he said in wonderment. "Are they always so forceful?" he asked. Astonished at how powerful the kicks were against his hand.

"All the time. Mostly when I go to sleep. He seems to think it's funny that I only get to sleep when he says I do," she laughed, her palm following the movement of the baby.

"He?" he arched his eyebrows.

"Just a hunch," she shrugged.

"Now you get on my bandwagon."

"We're in each other's lives forever now, Dominic," she said, the seriousness of the moment returning. "And I was trying to figure out how I felt about that." She took a deep breath. "When I was on my way over to the house last night," she gazed up at him, Dominic's hand still under hers. "I kept thinking about how you were when you were putting the crib together that day and the things you were saying during dinner… they all tell me something has changed. But then I remember how things were before, and it scares me to think that all that could happen again. I understand what you're going through right now with Caleb and now finding out you're going to be a father, but…"

Dominic stopped her, taking her hands in his and inching closer to her on the couch. "I swear that things have changed and will keep changing, but they'll continue to change for the better. I know I made those promises to you a long time ago, and I didn't keep my word." He shook his head and gripped her hands tighter. "I've been doing a lot of thinking, and I want to change. For you and the baby."

"I believe you, Dominic," she said, surprising him. "I'm going to let you make a decision." She picked up the pen and handed it to him. Silently, she slipped the sterling silver necklace from the hollow of Dominic's ring. She picked it up and ran her finger along the titanium band, a truly unbreakable band and bond. Reaching for his left hand, Ashley carefully slipped the ring back onto Dominic's ring finger. "You have a choice."

Dominic thought about what she was asking of him. He could sign the last line, dissolving their marriage, or he could have it all back. It would be like going back in time and righting all his wrongs. The answer was clear this time. He dropped the pen.

"I love you," she said with tears in her eyes. "I chose you before, and I choose you now."

She was telling the truth. Otherwise, she wouldn't make such a powerful gesture. The corner of Dominic's mouth quirked, and he took the ring he had chosen after scrutinizing every jeweler within a hundred-mile radius, he dropped down to his knee.

"Ashley, I love you," he grinned. "And to make this simple, I want you to be my wife every day that I open my eyes and every night that I close them. Again," he added with a lighthearted laugh.

"Yes," a tear trickled down her cheek.

Chapter Nineteen

Caleb sat backstage on a lone chair in the corner, facing the white walls, focusing on the black smudges and scrapes that it had sustained over the years. He had numerous odd habits, and this was probably the oddest of them all. He liked to focus, clear his mind, envision himself behind the piano, his fingers gliding over the keys, mentally preparing for the performance.

"Hey." Dominic slapped Caleb on the shoulder, startling him from behind. "Everything in working order up there?" he asked.

Caleb swiveled on the chair and stood up, walking with Dominic towards the stage entryway where orchestra players rushed through to their positions. "I'm good," he said, staring over at Rylen in her chair.

"I see that," Dominic said, following Caleb's gaze. His smile wavered when he saw his brother staring at Rylen. "Listen," he started, "I heard something from Riccardo and I thought you should know."

"Two minutes," a man said passing by.

"It's about Rylen."

Caleb turned to him, "What about her?"

"Riccardo said she took the position in London, but she wants to wait out your concert series before she goes."

Caleb faltered, not believing what Dominic was saying. She was going to leave him, and after he had given himself over to her. He gazed out onto the stage, and Rylen met his gaze. She smiled, but he didn't return the gesture.

"You're sure?" he asked, staring at her. Her expression now troubled.

"Yes. I'm sorry, but I thought you should know before –"

"Before I fall in love with her?"

"If it came to that."

"It hadn't. She's just a casual fling," he lied. "I know better than to do something as silly as fall in love with someone."

"How have you been feeling?" Dominic asked, changing the subject.

"Great actually." It was true. He hadn't had tremors or any problems since allowing Rylen into his life. She made him feel alive, but right now, he was feeling less than great. His mind whirled. How she could betray him, string him along like a puppy? To think he was so gullible and blind angered him.

"Lay off the high ones," Dominic said, giving Caleb a hug, their ritual before he went out on stage.

"I like the high ones," Caleb said, quoting one of Dominic's favorite movies, 'A League of Their Own.' It was something they did as kids for fun, and it stuck.

"Mule."

"Nag."

Dominic slapped Caleb on the ass for good measure. Caleb felt better already. His mind was free. The Rylen news was now a thing of the past. He'd do as he had promised himself before, ignore her. This time it was going to be easy. He had a tendency to be unforgiving.

Tonight was their first performance, and all Caleb wanted to feel was relief. Now he could go on as he once had, following the path laid out for him without any hindrance, but anger pulsated through him, so much anger. He couldn't help but glance at her as she strummed the cello. She had no idea he knew. The secrets they were both keeping were festering to the surface, but Caleb's secrets weren't public knowledge. They were private. Rylen was leaving town to join a new orchestra in a new country. Hadn't he a right to know? He had been sharing his life with her for weeks. He'd composed a song for her. His layers were being peeled back, exposing more and more each day, and she repaid him with lies masked by a kiss.

Caleb pounded the keys like he had never before, his anger throwing him into a pit of rage. Riccardo glanced over his shoulder, his eyes radiating concern, but Caleb couldn't control it. The anger had taken over. His focus was no longer on his fingers or the composition notes running through his mind. Everything he had learned to keep composed, to keep the disease from taking over, had been thrown out the window and now he could feel it moving through him. First his foot stopped and worry lines creased his forehead. He looked to Dominic in the entryway. Dominic lifted his arms in a shrug, but Caleb put his head down, persisting to go on. He would not lose the battle during the concert. Sweat beaded on his forehead, and droplets fell, splattering on the keys.

This was not happening. Everything he had worked for was in jeopardy. The disease didn't stop at his foot but traveled up his body to his fingers. He could feel them starting to shut down. The masquerade was coming to an end. His mask would be ripped off and all revealed. He needed to get out of there.

Just as his left hand was starting to go numb, he found Dominic and mouthed, "Help." Dominic knew all too well what this meant, and he rushed to draw the curtains as the piece ended and Caleb's tremors began. The orchestra was confused. Riccardo tried rushing to his side, but Caleb jumped up from the bench and limped to the entryway. He could hear the confusing shouts under the applause of the audience, but all Caleb cared about was safety. He could feel his stomach start to roll in an angry tidal wave.

"What's going on?" Dominic whispered as Caleb hobbled past.

Caleb's only answer was his rapid trajectory toward the backstage bathroom with Dominic in tow. Nudging the door open with his shoulder, he flung it closed and threw himself against it so Dominic couldn't get in.

"Caleb!" Dominic pounded on the door, trying to push it open. Caleb leveraged his feet against the wall pressing him against the door as Dominic persisted, "Tell me what's going on?"

The pleas for him to open the door went unanswered. This didn't feel the same as his normal tremors. It was the anger that infiltrated first, allowing access for the disease to spiral through unwittingly while he performed. The anger brought on because of Rylen's lies, and now a room full of people had to leave because the main attraction couldn't perform. So many promises were being broken, and it all started with the promise Caleb, himself, had ignored—the promise to avoid Rylen.

The room was spinning, and he had no way of stopping it. He gathered up his knees, hugging them to his chest. He tried to cry, to let everything out, but the tears wouldn't come. His body trembled and clenched in heated torment. There were some days where he hated the disease, and that hate and anger made Caleb feel worse inside. He'd trade places with his mother in an instant if he could, but all he could do now was to wait for her embrace when he truly met her again.

In what felt like the span of minutes turned into hours. Caleb awoke, the door behind him vibrating with the pounding of someone's fist. With the feeling in his foot and the trembling in his hands gone, Caleb stretched out and stood avoiding the mirror before he could dwell on his reflection. He knew he was starting to look better, but that was before. Now, things were going back to how they had been when he was simply waiting for death's grip and had no other hope.

"What?" he asked as the pounding grew louder. No one answered. The pounding continued, and for a moment, he thought maybe it was the buzzing sound returning in full force, but his mind was clear.

"What?" he yelled, swinging the door open and finding only darkness. Caleb poked his head out the door. "Dominic?" he called. The hallway was empty. The lights flickered as Caleb walked out of the bathroom to investigate. "Anyone here?" he called, again receiving no answer.

This wasn't funny. Who was pounding on the door? He continued to maze the hallways until he was at the stage entryway. The chairs were stacked and the piano sat in the middle waiting for him to complete his earlier work. The audience seating was dark, but the stage was lit. "Hello?" he yelled out into the darkness.

A movement across the stage caught his eye, and he took a step forward. "Why won't you answer me?" he asked. The figure stepped back into the darkness. "I can see you."

His words echoed throughout the hall. The figure remained shrouded in darkness and silence. Caleb didn't want to play games. If the stranger didn't want to be known, he wasn't going to pursue it. Caleb wanted to go home to his bed, to stop thinking and let his mind rest.

Turning to leave, a chill ran up his spine, and he turned quickly to see the dark figure float to the piano. His eyes went wide, and he froze in place, knowing immediately what he was looking at. The figure sat at the piano. A foreboding fog floated along the keys, hovering as Caleb's hands would when he prepared to begin a piece.

"Is it time?" Caleb asked. The figure didn't move. "I'm ready," he said breathlessly. He didn't want to cause any more trouble. The concert was ruined. Rylen had moved on, and Dominic needed to get his life back on track instead of worrying about him. It was time. "Please," he whimpered, "end it." He was ready to be at peace, to move on so others could move forward. He longed to see his mother and tell her that the ends justified the means, that he was truly sorry.

The figure moved toward him, the chill apparent now that it stood in front of him. It gripped his arms and leaned close. Caleb's energy waned, and his body lunged forward. The figure was ripping out his soul, if he even had one. Did murderers have souls?

"Sir?" a man from the audience called.

Caleb fell to his knees, and the darkness drifted away. The chill retreated. It shouldn't have gone away. It should have taken him, but it left him behind. He prayed for it to come back, to finish the job, but the figure was gone, and the janitor had no idea what he had just interrupted.

"I'm going to be shutting down," he said.

"Y-yes," Caleb stammered wiping the cold sweat from his face. They'd meet again.

~

After the concert and the revelation about Rylen, Caleb wanted nothing more than to lie in his bed. Rain was falling steadily now, and the air had a chill. The car pulled into the driveway, and Caleb got out before the driver could open his door. He may not be allowed to drive, but he could manage to open his own door.

Waving the driver away, Caleb ran toward the front door but was stopped short by the car in his driveway. The door opened to Rylen, waiting for him in his entryway. She smiled and stepped onto the porch, hesitating as she took in his countenance. He was unhappy to see her. She could tell.

"Hi," she said.

"How'd you get into the house?" he asked, ignoring her greeting.

"I have my ways of breaking and entering."

"Then you know the way out," he said, walking past her into the house.

"Did I strike a nerve or something?" she asked, following after him. "What happened today? I've never been a part of a performance that got shut down before the first —"

"I want to be alone," he interrupted, slipping out of his shoes. A wave of guilt swept over him, but he pushed it aside. No need to feel guilty. This time, he didn't do anything wrong.

For weeks he had been carrying around the song he wrote for her. The composition felt as though it was burning a hole in his back pocket. He intended to give it to her, but even though he wanted her to have it, he was scared. Even as he thought of it, an inner voice berated him for being vulnerable. He knew he must give her the composition if he was to have any peace. Otherwise, he'd always wonder.

He pulled the music sheets from his back pocket and held them out to her. "This...this is for you," he stammered. "Please don't open it until you get home." Arnie barked by the screen door. "Goodbye, Rylen," Caleb said, disappearing outside.

Letting out a shaky breath, Caleb walked through the yard, following after Arnie. "Do you think I did the right thing?" he asked his friend. Arnie glanced over his shoulder and kept walking. "Yeah, I know. Shut up while you find a spot."

They wandered around the yard. Arnie was taking his good old time tonight, and Caleb just wanted to go inside. The numerous trees helped to shield him from the rain so he could barely feel the chill. His body was a mass of confusion. He debated taking back the composition, snatching it from her as she had snatched his dreams. Had he made a mistake?

Arnie had finally decided on a spot when Caleb was stopped short by the sound of his piano. He was caught off guard by the drifting melody of his piano keys in motion. The notes eerily reminiscent of music he heard before, music he had written. He shouldn't have given it to her. He didn't want her to play while he was around. He was secretly afraid she wouldn't like it, that she'd find it sad and lonely. She would see through him and know his feelings. He chastised himself for giving her such a meaningful gift, but he knew if he was to leave her, he must leave her with a piece of himself.

He glided up the yard, hiding in the shadows so he could peer inside undetected. His chest heaved in fright as he wondered if he had made a fool of himself by giving her the music. He needed to see her face, to know what she thought and how it made her feel. Peeking inside he was able to see her head bent in concentration as she studied the keys.

It was beautiful. The music brought forth all the emotions he had felt as he composed the music. The memory of his mother is what drove him to play, but never before had any other woman, a woman so mesmerizing, so heartwarming, made him want to sit at that piano bench and drive his fingers into a frenzy to compose just so he could imagine the look on her face.

The shadows of the darkened living room and the obstruction of her hair made it difficult for Caleb to see her facial expression as she played the music. He so badly wanted to see the emotions play across her face that his hands trembled and fell to his sides. He wasn't sure if it was his body's reaction to all the emotions swirling around in him or a normal tremor that gripped him at inopportune moments such as this. Nuzzling Caleb's quaking hands, Arnie pressed his head into his master's palm in comfort.

"I'm okay," Caleb reassured him.

As silently as he could, he slid aside the screen door, stepping quietly into the room, trying to get a better look at her face as she played. He was stock still staring at her, taking in how truly beautiful she was. The song was affecting his judgment, making his blue eyes darken with desire.

She looked up, sensing she was not alone. When she saw him, her stomach dropped. Was he angry with her for staying? Would he ask her to leave again? She had been unable to resist sitting down at the piano. The man had written her a song, and she was compelled to play, to see if there was a hidden meaning underneath the notes. In need of answers.

She tilted her head forward, hiding behind the hair that touched her shoulders. His gaze made her feel naked and vulnerable. There was a soft, distinct intake of breath, as if he had finally come to a decision; yet he didn't move, or speak. The look in his eyes confused her. It was almost hard, unforgiving, as if he was closing her out.

Caleb's head clouded, dizzying his senses and making the room spin on its axis. Things felt foggy, and he was gripped with an unknown fear.

"I think," he said, "that it would be best if you left."

Doubt crept in and Caleb knew something terrible was going to happen, and she'd see him at his weakest. She would be afraid for him, and that was something he could not allow.

In that instant, she wanted to tear the music he had given her up and throw the pieces in the air. If he wanted to put up walls and make her feel awful, she would give him a reason to. But she also wanted the truth. She was tired of his games, tired of his mood swings. She grew weary of trying to read his mind.

"Coward."

He stared at her. For a moment, he couldn't seem to find words. His lips parted, but nothing escaped for what seemed like eternity. Looking back at his behavior, it all made sense. His responses to her, his actions, and his words were all those of a coward. If the shoe were on the other foot, he would think the same thing. It was all a defense mechanism.

"Do you know what you want?" she asked.

"Yes." No. He frowned, taking a few steps toward her. The piano stood between them. He laid his hands on the lid, needing to focus on something other than her intense blue eyes burning into his. His entire body shook, making him uncomfortable and fearful.

"You give me this beautiful song, and I see the way you look at me, but you always find a way to close me out," she bitterly cut off.

The statement made him silent and in that moment he knew she was right, but he was trying to break the hold she had on him. Her anger made his heart pound with uncertainty, and his stomach clenched in frustration.

She took a deep breath and straightened her shoulders. Pushing the bench back, she stood. "Now you go and pretend like I'm not even here." She exhaled a shaky breath. "Thank you for the composition, but I don't think I'll need it." At her parting comment, Caleb's head snapped up. Rylen saw the pain on his face, the hurt in his eyes, and she felt sick for having put it there.

Caleb tried to remain composed. Upon hearing that she didn't want the song hurt more than he could have ever imagined. He had written the piece specifically for her and for her to throw it back at him was an insult, professionally and personally. He needed to confront the situation, but all he wanted to do was lie in bed and hope that when he woke up the next morning it was all one of his crazy dreams.

She didn't wait for him to say anything more. Rylen was going to leave. She had put herself through the ringer for him, and he was still shying away.

"Play for me," he whispered, his voice so soft and emotionally drained that she could only nod her head. Why was she giving into him so easily?

Caleb watched her, unable to grasp how he had come to this moment. How had he managed to fight the good fight but lose to such a worthy opponent? He was helpless and lost.

To truly show her how he felt, he needed more than words. Instantly he was behind her, his mind now off and his emotions guiding his way. She paused, now knowing what to make of his nearness.

"It's okay. Play. Please." He placed his hands on her shoulders so carefully that she felt her resolve slowly cracking as it had that evening on the beach. Her fingers shakily started to play again, turning the sheet music to the next page. The song was truly beautiful, quiet and passionate. She could feel him lean up against her, his hands tracing the length of her collar bone, feeling the heat of her flesh.

He swung his legs around her, sitting behind her on the bench. He enveloped her body with his, hugging his legs to hers, pressing her back again his chest. She could feel his heart race, the hitch in his breath as he molded against her, her body fully in his embrace.

He ran his fingers down the length of her arms until his hands were resting atop hers, playing the notes of the song he had written for her together. He gently glided his fingers back up her arms sending a shiver down her spine. How gracefully his thin and nimble fingers inspire such reactions from her. He breathed deeply against her neck, his fingers now slipping down her back. He brushed the hair from her shoulder, giving him better access to her neck. There he bestowed a series of soft kisses.

She could focus no longer. Removing her hands from the keys, she circled them around her waist, holding Caleb's arms in hers. She turned her face as, helplessly, he bent his head down to her lips.

Rylen felt Caleb's lips meet hers. All questions were answered, all fears put to rest. She could hardly bear the sweetness of it. Passion rippled through them as they responded to each other.

Caleb stood, helping Rylen turn and face him. The keys rumbled underneath her weight. Caleb lifted her by her waist and sat her atop the piano. He spread kisses from her lips, trailing down her neck and settling his lips against her stomach. She ran her fingers through his hair, tracing the length of the scar on the back of his head.

"Are you still going to London?" he asked, needing to know the truth.

"Who told you that?" she asked, but he didn't answer.

"Does it matter? You didn't tell me," he remarked.

"I don't know," she said, pulling his head up to look at her. She sweetly kissed him on the lips, but what she said triggered a cold response.

"Haven't I given you a good enough reason not to?" he said, pulling back. He no longer cared that she was better off in a world without him.

"Caleb, it's not that –" Caleb took a step back, and she could see in his eyes that he was walling up, shutting down as he normally did. It had felt different for a moment, but they were right back at the beginning. "I won't waste my time explaining myself, because I know you won't listen," she said, sliding off the piano.

"How could you not tell me? I've –" he paused unable to continue.

"You've what, Caleb?" she asked. Their bodies lingered barely an inch apart. He had to stay strong. "What?" she whispered. "Just say it."

"I wish you luck in your endeavor." He swallowed hard, taking a step back.

There was no need to look at him. She could feel it was over by his hardened exterior. He was finally finished. Instead of fighting it, she left. It was the only thing could do that would get his attention.

Chapter Twenty

Standing in the doorway, Dominic listened to the sounds of the heart monitor and ventilator. The jacket that had sheltered him from the rain was now shedding water into a puddle at his feet.

He wiped the previous hours' grief and pain from his face and put on a reassuring smile, a smile that he hoped would strengthen his resolve. Maybe, just maybe, those blue eyes would open and he'd see that smile he was so desperately clinging to.

"Hey. Sorry I was gone so long. Miss me?" Dominic walked into the room, closing the door behind him.

He slipped off his jacket and walked into the bathroom to hang it in the shower so it wouldn't make a mess. He quietly closed the door for some privacy, aware of the irony. For all intents and purposes, he was alone in the room. He sat down on the edge of the tub and leaned his head against the wall. The pounding was agony, and every bone in his body ached. He wasn't sure how much longer he could go through this.

He rubbed his hands through his hair in an attempt to alleviate some of the pressure he was feeling. His tie was suffocating him. He loosened it and threw it against the bathroom door. The room was starting to spin, and Dominic fought to keep his bearings. He stood up, supporting himself on the sink, and stared down at the drain. Avoiding the mirror would allow him to avoid the reflection he dreaded. He knew what he would find staring back at him. The light was irritating his headache, and he turned it off. He wanted to sit in the darkened room and regain his composure, but instead, he started to cry. Sinking to the floor, Dominic curled up and leaned against the corner of the tub.

Dominic wished he could wake up in his bed at Caleb's house. He would awaken to the smell of coffee, and when he walked into the kitchen,

Caleb would be there, looking out the window into his yard. He felt like Dorothy just wishing to be home again. When he heard the knock on the bathroom door, he knew this was reality, and the comfort of his dreams would have to wait.

Dominic collected himself and moved to answer the door. Expecting the doctor urging him to make decisions he was unprepared to make, Dominic was surprised to find his father, James, waiting for him.

"I thought you'd gone to make sure everything was in order," Dominic muttered.

"Everything's fine, Dominic. You did a wonderful job," his father said, pulling him near. Dominic was too tired to control the tears. James stood, inviting his son into the comfort of his embrace. Dominic staggered forward, letting everything go. Father held son as the heartache overwhelmed them.

"Debbie and Joe took the baby home," he began, "I stayed back so I could be here with the both of you."

"What's the point?" Dominic asked, wiping his tears.

"If you don't see the point, Dominic, why are we here?"

"Because I can't do it. I can't be the one that gives the order."

"You know what the end result is going to be. You've given yourself months to grieve."

"Are you saying this is supposed to be easy by now?" he glared into his father's eyes.

"No. When you're a father, you'll know your children are not supposed to go into the ground before you. This is harder on me than you can realize, but I know this isn't what he would have wanted, putting us through this heartache, praying for a miracle when there's no chance."

"There's no way I can just move on from this."

"I can guarantee none of us will, but he needs to."

"I wanted to help him. He's my responsibility."

James shook her head. "No, he's not. He's a grown man. He can take care of himself. What you're doing, Dominic, is holding on to a memory of the man that is lying in this bed. He's not here anymore, son." James started to cry realizing he couldn't help either of his sons'. Couldn't switch places with him. "You forget. At one point, this is what he wanted."

"He has something to live for now."

"I wish he would have believed that sooner. I think we lost him after your mother's accident."

"It wasn't his fault."

"No," James paused, "but that didn't stop Caleb from believing it was. I'd hold him every night after one of his nightmares and rock him to sleep, telling him that he had nothing to do with the accident. Your mother knew the risks when she drove. I should have been there."

"Don't place the blame on yourself, dad."

"I know, and I understand why he thought it was his fault, but no matter how many times I told him the Huntington's Disease was the reason she got into the accident, he never believed me. And when he was diagnosed with it, I prayed to take his place. You never think it's going to happen to you," he whispered.

"She was feeling good that day. She told me so when I begged her not to go."

"And that's why he feels guilty. She took him because he didn't want to miss his lesson, and she was a sucker for music."

"I should have gone with her. I could have helped."

"Or you could have died right next to her. I wonder if he knows."

"Knows what?"

"That this accident wasn't his fault either," James said, pushing the hair off of Caleb's forehead to place a kiss. "We all make our own choices. She made one that day, and Caleb made his. The past is the past. You can't change it, and most of the time, you can't forget it."

"I should have seen the signs when they began," Dominic murmured. "I was with him every day. I knew something was wrong, but Caleb just keeps going. He doesn't stop. I should have done something, but I was in denial. I didn't want him to end up like mom."

Dominic had noticed Caleb losing weight and struggling with insomnia. He saw the involuntary movements that Caleb tried to mask-- -the personality changes and his constant need to be alone. Dominic had been positive Caleb suffered from a mild form of depression. The warning signs were there, but Dominic had attributed his brother's behavior to overwork. Whenever there was a break in his performance schedule, Caleb would complain that he wasn't working enough, and Dominic would book more performances. Eventually, Caleb's irritability, loss of appetite, and often-jerky movements became a part of everyday life. Then one day, Caleb gave into his brother's incessant prodding and went to see the doctor. It was only then after numerous blood tests, CT Scans, and psychiatric evaluations, that Caleb was informed he was in the early stages of Huntington's Disease.

Instead of talking treatment, Caleb had turned to Dominic and asked when his next concert was scheduled. Dominic couldn't believe his brother's audacity and utter lack of acknowledgment of the crisis before him. While Dominic sat in the doctor's office in stunned disbelief, Caleb got up and left.

Caleb told his brother that he felt all of the treatments necessary for a disease that would kill him would take away from his playing. He had concerts to perform, contracts to fulfill, and a need to play as compelling as his need for breath.

"What's next?" Dominic had asked the doctor. He needed to know the next steps in order to fight the disease. If it had been cancer, they might have been able to treat it, but according to the doctor, Huntington's Disease had no cure. Still, it was not the lack of treatment that concerned Dominic but the disease itself. It caused certain nerve cells in the brain to waste away, resulting in uncontrolled movements, emotional issues, and mental deterioration. Dominic could handle the mood swings, they were a part of Caleb's nature, but Caleb was a pianist. The aggressive deterioration of his motor functions would progress viciously since he contracted the disease so young. The fingers he lived by were going to take on a life of their own, twisting the melodies of the compositions he played with such ease and grace. His life wasn't only in jeopardy, but so was his livelihood.

As Caleb had declined, he had never acknowledged the suffering his illness was causing Dominic. Endless nights were spent awake, worrying, and researching ways to fight the disease.

"I'm going to take him home," Dominic informed his father. "They should be together."

"And when he's home, then what?"

"I don't know," Dominic shrugged.

Dominic's mind reeled as past and present collided in his thoughts. Every waking moment had been spent thinking about Caleb, and though people told him there was no hope, Dominic could not relinquish his responsibility.

"He needs me now." Dominic sunk into the chair, taking Caleb's hand in his.

"Dominic, your family needs you, and I know you need your brother, but you need to take into consideration what he needs." James turned the knob and disappeared, leaving Dominic alone again.

"You need to wake up," he said angrily to Caleb. "I'm trying to help you, and here you are throwing your life away."

I'm not throwing it away.

"It's survivor's guilt," he said with his back to Caleb, watching the traffic outside.

You can't understand, Dom. Not until you're put in that situation.

"You're right. I don't understand. Sometimes I feel invisible to you, and it makes me hate you. I hate you with every fiber of my being, because one day you stopped being my brother. You stopped, but the world around me kept going. You may not care about what I'm saying. You may have already thrown me to the wind, but I want you to know I don't think I can forgive you for this, for turning your back on me. You're taking this step without me when I've tried so hard to walk along side you. But now I'm walking ahead of you, and you're watching, watching until I come to the end and fall over the side while you stay put, content to let whatever you believe in carry you into a realm where I'm not willing to go just yet. You, Caleb, are willing to die, and I can't, for the life of me, figure out why."

I can't just live because you want me too.

"Why not?" he yelled. "You're selfish."

Maybe.

"I won't lie to you. I'm here at your disposal. The question is: can you trust me? And the answer is yes. It's up to you whether or not you choose to believe me." Dominic buried his face in his hands. "Do you know why you lose every time we play, Caleb?" he asked. "Because the light always defeats the dark. We have a duty to ourselves to never let the darkness prevail."

Then I'm never going to win.

"Don't succumb to defeat before you've had a chance to step on the battle ground. Have you ever thought you're just playing with the wrong pieces? I just want to help you," he said, staring at the chessboard. "You trust me, don't you?" Dominic wiped his tears and moved his bishop. "Check," he said, the game nearing its end. He was afraid what it would mean when he finally said Checkmate.

Chapter Twenty-One

Tonight was the last performance. Caleb had been dreading this moment for weeks, and now it was finally here. He took a few deep breaths as the orchestra players filed out onto the main stage to take their places.

Rylen walked by without acknowledging him. They hadn't spoken in over a month. He had kept his promise to ignore her this time. Tonight was her last performance with the Chicago Symphony, and by morning, she'd be a ghost.

"So, this is it?" Dominic asked, standing next to him.

"This is it," Caleb sighed deeply. "Do you think I've made the wrong choice?"

"It's your choice. I've wanted you to stop, to focus on your health, but you always said if you didn't play you'd," Dominic paused, "I just wish you'd take the time to go to treatments; keep the disease at bay a little while longer."

"That's not for you to decide."

"No, it isn't."

"I did something horrible long ago and this is the only way I can live with myself," Caleb admonished.

"Mom –"

"Please, let's not ruin this," Caleb pled turning to face Dominic.

"Right," Dominic said putting on a smile. "Lay off the high ones," he hugged Caleb closely resting his head on Caleb's shoulder.

"I like the high ones."

"Mule."

"Nag." Caleb pulled back and smirked, giving Dominic a wink before he gave him a smack on the ass and walked onto the stage.

Caleb tugged on his tuxedo, putting it back in place before following Riccardo out in front of the audience. He donned the biggest smile he could muster, ignoring Rylen's intense gaze, and walked stoically to the piano, greeted by applause as he took his seat.

The orchestra ran through the play list like clockwork. Caleb was sweating more than he normally did. The perspiration ran down his face and dripped onto the piano keys, making them slippery. His chest heaved with his labored breathing. Dominic could tell something was wrong, and the urge to help Caleb took over. He stepped forward but quickly regained his composure and forced himself to watch without interfering. Caleb looked up from the piano and stared directly at Dominic. A few moments passed as the brothers continued to watch one another, everything said and unsaid floating in the great chasm between them.

The conductor raised his wand once again, signaling the finale. The Rachmaninoff piece was going to take so much out of Caleb. His head hurt just thinking about it. He had practiced, but lately he had let himself indulge in the one thing he never indulged in, life.

Instead of positioning his fingers on the appropriate keys, he stood. The crowd murmured wondering what was going on. "It's hot in here," he joked. The crowd laughed as he took off his tuxedo jacket. "You're all welcome to disrobe if you like." The crowd broke into applause and questioning murmurs started up once more. He threw his jacket onto the bench and next started on his bow tie. "I'm sure you're all wondering what I'm doing." The bow tie was undone, and now he was working on his vest buttons. "Before we start the finale, I want to take a moment to inform you all of something, not only to share with you this performance but to tell you -." The vest was gone, and his nimble fingers now tore at the buttons of his shirt. The stage was set. It was now or never. Caleb knew if he ignored this moment he'd die on stage, and that wasn't how he wanted to go out. Not anymore. He wanted to go out his way, admirably and with the knowledge that he was finally in control. His throat constricted with his next words, and he wiped the tears that were stinging his eyes with his shirt before letting it fall to the ground. He stood before his audience in only his pants, under shirt, and suspenders. "To tell you that tonight you are bearing witness to my final performance. Ever." The crowd hushed. "I want you all to know I did not come to this decision lightly. For many years I have lived behind the piano, but I think now is as good a time as any to start living in front of it." For a moment he afforded a lingering look at Rylen, then back to the audience. "I want to thank everyone who has supported me and grown with me. And now, let's give you a piano concerto you'll never forget."

Caleb walked back to his bench, and before he could sit, the audience overwhelmed him with a standing ovation. It was time to leave it all on the floor.

Mere hours had passed since that final performance. Caleb sat at the piano in his home staring down at the keys, wondering what a life spent without the piano would be like.

"Do you regret it?" Dominic asked, sitting down next to Caleb.

"No, but I'm scared. Yesterday I knew what tomorrow was going to bring. Now – well, now I'm not so sure."

"Isn't that exciting? You can do whatever you want now," he replied.

"Couldn't I before?" Caleb implored. "And what if what I want to do is play the piano?" He ran his fingertips along the keys he had come to believe were his family, his home.

"Then you play."

"Voice of reason."

"And what if Rylen were still in the picture?" Dominic asked.

"She's not, so there's no point in thinking about it."

"But what if she were?"

"What are you getting at, Dominic?" he raised his voice, his finger slowly tapping the middle C key.

"I know you love her."

"You don't know anything."

"She's leaving tonight."

Caleb tensed but tried to play it off. "I'm happy for her."

"Would you stop being such a butthole."

"Seriously?" Caleb gaped. "Did you just call me a butthole?"

"Yes, because you're acting like one. I understand a lot of things, Caleb, but when it comes to you, I'm lost. You're a conundrum. You get sick, but you don't want to get better. You want to play the piano, but now you want to retire. You love Rylen, but you're willing to let her go. For what?

So you can just die in your bedroom alone? Do you know what all of that adds up to?"

"What?"

"You being a butthole. She's. Leaving. Tonight," he annunciated.

"I understand what you're saying."

"Do you? Because you're still sitting here. Don't you think that if I could get Ashley back, I would? If I could just say I'm sorry and she'd be back in my arms that I wouldn't do it?"

"I'm sorry, Dominic, but it's for the best. She deserves a good life and I can't give her that."

"You're full of it. You've given me a good life."

"You're my brother, that's different."

"And she's someone you love as well. You love her, and she loves you. I'm pretty sure in a lot of people's lives that's all that matters."

"How do you know she loves me?"

"Because I wouldn't know where she was if she didn't."

"I'm confused."

"If she wanted to leave, she would have left right after the concert. A friend of hers flies private jets. He has to go to London this evening, and he was going to leave earlier. She asked for a later flight."

"So?"

Dominic closed his eyes and clenched his fist before taking a deep breath. "If you don't get your ass off this bench and into the car that I have waiting for you, I will bust this piano."

"You'd threaten the life of this beautiful baby grand piano?"

"I think I just did."

Caleb thought for a moment before a smile crept up. "You're the best big brother anyone could ask for," he said.

"I'll believe that when you're on your way."

Caleb jumped off the bench and headed for the door.

"And Caleb." Caleb stopped and turned. "You're still a butthole."

~

It was all pointless. Caleb had gone out of his way to find her, had been stupid enough to fall for Dominic's words of encouragement, but it was too late. She had already gone. The jet was gone; the airstrip empty. It was all meaningless.

"If you could take me back home that'd be great. Thank you," Caleb informed the driver. Small droplets started to sprinkle down the window. His finger followed their tracks. The sky was weeping for him. He had no tears of his own left.

"Mr. Montgomery?" the driver called back to him.

"Hmm," Caleb grunted closing his eyes and leaning his head back against the seat. It had been a long evening, and he was ready for it to end.

"Is this the jet you're waiting for?" he asked pointing out the driver side window toward a private jet that taxied onto the strip.

Caleb's head flew up. Scooting across the seat, he squinted at the jet trying to get a clear view. There was no way of knowing if anyone was on it.

"I'm not sure," he said.

"Would you like me to go check with the pilot?"

"No. It's fine. I don't see anyone," Caleb responded, putting his seat belt on. "Let's call it a night." He glanced at his watch and realized he had put his broken one on. Why was he still wearing it? Thunder rang out drawing his attention for the last time, glancing out the window to see the storm's display which, only moments ago, was a few droplets of water. As the lightning flashed again, she appeared.

Caleb didn't think. He just reacted, launching out of the car and into the heart of the storm. He ran to the jet just as she was stepping onto the stairs to exit the aircraft.

"Rylen," he yelled into the wind. She froze on the stairs when she saw him but didn't respond. Gathering up her resolve, she ignored him and walked down the remainder of the stairs, pushing past him.

He could feel only pain: pain for what he lost; for what he was never going to have; and for letting her in where she did not belong. At that moment, Caleb realized he would never get his heart back. He had given it to her fully, and the passing of time was never going to make it hurt any less.

The past few months had been filled with decisions, and they just kept coming. He was on the verge of another major decision. It was time to go after her. She was the reason he was there, the reason he retired. He just couldn't picture his life without her, and he was willing to fall on his sword once and for all.

He rushed toward her uncertain of everything but his need to catch her. He had no pretty words to woo her, only the feelings that tortured his soul. "I'm terrified of you," he yelled, the rain freezing as it pelted down on him. She was standing just outside the hangar, but she stopped and turned to him, angered by his statement.

Whatever she'd expected, it wasn't this. "Who are you?"

"You know who I am!" he screamed.

"You don't allow anyone to know you." She stalked toward him and slapped him. "Who are you?" she bellowed into the storm, the downpour soaking her to the bone.

"I'm Caleb!" he answered.

"That's your name. It isn't who you are. I'm tired of trying, Caleb. It's not worth my time anymore." This time she didn't raise her hand. She took a step back and turned to retreat. Now, the daunting look of defeat was on her face. Tonight he wasn't who she wanted him to be or who she believed he was.

"I'm the man that's in love with you," he called out to her. His proclamation of love was enough to stop Rylen in her tracks. Though she didn't turn, she could feel his breath on her neck. The violent rain became all but nonexistent. "I'm someone that, when something bad happens, I retreat. I cut everyone off, and I try to take it on alone, but I'm scared. I'm the man that loses himself in music. I never thought I'd love anything more than music, and then..." He ran his fingers down her arm until her hand was in his, "...Then you." He spoke in a whisper, his voice gruff with emotion. "You appeared, and I was lost." Rylen turned to him to see if he truly meant the words he was speaking. "I was able to give up playing because I knew you'd be there. Life's too short. I don't want to go through it alone anymore. Believe me, I tried. I didn't want to, but how can I not love you?" He leaned his forehead on hers and closed his eyes. His hand caressed her cheek, and everything around them disappeared. The rain and thunder no longer mattered. Now all that lay before them were endless possibilities. "You seeped into my soul, and I don't know how to lose you without losing myself. I'm asking you, how can I not want to love you?"

His lips were barely a whisper away. "Can you answer that?" He paused, gazing at her.

"Rylen," he started but did not know how to continue.

All he could do was relay three simple words that meant much more than he ever imagined. "I love you."

He kissed her. How he'd missed her lips since they last touched, and yet, he felt like he had been kissing them for ages.

"I love you, too," she cried, throwing her arms around him.

It was impossible not to smile. His face was aglow as he picked her up and swung her around in a circle, their own little eye of the storm. She was his ending. Not a fairy tale, far from it, but she was his forever.

~

A low haze lingered just above the sand, obscuring the lake waves, but the lap of the waves onto shore assured Caleb the water was still there. He leaned against the gazebo, his heart and mind in a tug-o-war of emotion and reason. Was today the day? He debated whether or not to let the truth unfold between him and Rylen. He wanted to keep it a secret, to allow what they had be enough, but he couldn't look into her eyes knowing she didn't truly know who he was. Then again, he feared looking into her eyes once she was able to see the real Caleb. She would look at him like a stranger, and that rocked Caleb to his core, so much so that he was willing to let his secrets lie in their bed. She'd hate him for luring her in under false pretenses, making her love a monster.

Caleb closed his eyes and listened to the sound of the world coming awake around him. He loved dawn. It brought a peace to his mind, but today he was unable to find the solace he so desperately longed for. Deep down he knew today would be the day. Today would be the day his world crashed around him. His secrets would finally be uttered aloud, and the eyes he loved to lose himself in would turn against him. He was going to tell her, even if it killed him. He loved her that much.

Caleb felt like he was struggling to be someone else, to grab hold of a new life—a reinvention. One thing was for sure, he'd still be incomplete. For Rylen's sake, Caleb would like to become a new person.

She had already, in some ways, changed him. Caleb just didn't believe he had the confidence to overcome his guilt.

Rylen awoke to the chill of being alone in bed. She spread her arms out reaching for Caleb, but all that was left was the outline of his body among the sheets and his pillow. She sat up and saw that the sliding glass door was slightly ajar, the curtains swaying in the dawn breeze. She grabbed Caleb's dress shirt thrown over the chair and walked outside to greet him.

Lost in thought, staring out over the beach hidden beyond the foggy haze of the morning was how she found him. He was shaking, wearing only a pair of sweat pants in the damp morning air. She walked up behind him and slowly wrapped her arms around his waist. Resting her head against his back, she listened to his heart beat and his intake of breath at her touch. She smiled, loving the way each touch felt like the first. How they had managed to stay away from each other as long as they had was beyond her. It seemed they were meant for each other. Perhaps that's why they resisted for so long. They were scared of what a love like that meant.

"Hey," she murmured, kissing his back.

"Hi," he answered desolately, rubbing her arms and intertwining their fingers. He needed to feel her against him. He wondered if this would be the last time she'd touch him, the last time his body would feel safe and warm against hers. He reprimanded himself for the thought. He needed to be positive. They fit together well. Maybe that was enough. For some it was, but most didn't hold dark secrets like his.

"It's cold. Why don't you come back inside with me?" she asked, placing her lips against his shoulder.

"I'm warm now that you're here. Besides, it'd be reckless to let such a beautiful morning go unnoticed." He let out a deep breath. The words that were to come out next had him swallowing the lump in his throat. His stomach churned with uneasiness making him feel physically ill. "Rylen," he choked out.

Rylen could hear something different in his voice and circled around to face him, leaning against the railing of the gazebo. She could see the worry lines on his forehead. For the first time, she noticed circles under his eyes from lack of sleep. Face pale making him look sickly.

"Babe, are you okay?"

"I have something I need to tell you. It's important, and I'm not really sure how to say it out loud."

Rylen placed a hand under his chin, forcing him to look at her. Confusion clouded her face. "Caleb, what is it? You're scaring me."

He shook his head as tears started to well up in his eyes. "I'm not who you think I am," he said in a barely audible whisper. He collapsed on the bench, and Rylen knelt before him, their hands still clasped together as if in prayer.

"Just let it out, and we can figure it out from there. You need to tell me in order for us to fix it," she pleaded, trying to pry the truth from his lips.

"You can't fix something that's already been done."

"Look at me, Caleb," she prodded, "Look at me."

He lifted his head, taking a deep breath and averting his gaze. "I can't force myself to look at you while I tell you this. I'm afraid you'll hate me."

"Caleb, I could never hate you. I love you, remember. We said it last night."

Caleb let his emotions overflow. Her kindness was making his task so much harder, and he almost changed his mind. He wanted her to stay like this--kind, loving, and caring. As soon as he said it, she would leave. Rylen sat next to him, cradling Caleb in her arms. He tried to reign in his emotions but could only cry harder.

"I can't help you if you don't tell me," she whispered in his ear. "It'll be okay," she calmingly reassured him, soothing him from within. He laid his head on her lap for what seemed like hours before he was able to continue. Both of them were scared, their eyes rimmed red and their faces grim. "There are things that I can't explain out loud, but I rationalize them inside, and then everything seems as it should. If I start dwelling on the things I've done in the past, I'm afraid I won't be able to get back out. And if I do that, I'm afraid that what I set out to do today will be in vain, and you'll never trust me again." He wanted to explain, to give her a chance to walk away from it all now. Secretly, he wanted her to walk away so he wouldn't have to tell her; yet if she left, it would be the end of him. He wouldn't judge her. He couldn't. He waited for her to get up or talk, but she only watched him, waiting for him to shed his burden. "I killed my mother," he blurted out, not even trying to ease her into the knowledge, just trying to get it out before he changed his mind.

"No you didn't. I was told she died in a car accident."

"It was my fault. None of it would have happened if I hadn't been so selfish." He turned away from her as he submerged himself in the memory of that day. His voice steadied and he continued. "I was five and wanted to take piano lessons after having seen the orchestra play in Millennium Park one summer." He smiled, remembering how his mother loved the music.

When Caleb expressed interest in playing the piano, Kathryn Montgomery immediately called an old family friend and set up lessons. The next day, Kathryn's friend was available to begin lessons, but James was going to be out of town for work. Kathryn wasn't allowed to drive. The Huntington's Disease made it difficult for her to operate safely, but Caleb was relentless. He cried and begged until Kathryn gave in, deciding one trip would be harmless.

When they arrived, Kathryn watched Caleb sit behind the piano for the first time, in awe of the mythical instrument before him. He tentatively touched the keys, pressing down, their sound making him pull his hands away in uncertainty.

There wasn't a detail about that lesson he hadn't remembered: how to place his hands on the keys; where to position his fingers; to sit up straight; to be calm and not outplay the notes. He was able to play 'Twinkle, Twinkle', something he couldn't wait to show his mother when she came and picked him up. The hour flew by, and Caleb was already looking forward to the next lesson.

With Mrs. Marshall they waited on the porch of her duplex, anticipating showing his mother what he had learned. He couldn't know that, while he was learning his finger positions, his mother had been in a car accident. She had suffered a tremor and lost control of the car, driving into a telephone pole. If not for her young son's persistence, she would have been safe at home.

That was the day Caleb vowed to devote his life to music and making his mother proud. He saw the piano as the object that had taken away his happiness. Now his sworn enemy, he made sure he looked at the instrument every day as a reminder of what had ripped his mother from his world too soon. The piano would remain his reminder and his penitence.

"I sent her to her grave," he lamented. He took a deep breath, taking a break from his admission. Rylen remained silent next to him. He wasn't sure if that was a good or bad sign, but she was still beside him. "I hate the piano," he said through clenched teeth, his voice bitter and full of disdain. He looked into Rylen's eyes, the anger evident in his glare. "It stole my life." A tear streamed down his cheek. Rylen brushed it away with the back of her hand and kissed the moist trail it left.

"That's not true." She squeezed Caleb's hand. "Caleb, you were five years old. You wanted to learn to play the piano. The accident had nothing to do with you. No one's at fault. You couldn't have known," she put his face in her hands. "You did not kill your mother," she emphasized. Caleb huffed in her embrace. "And as for the piano, if you hated it, you wouldn't play it the way you do."

"I play because she loved the music." Caleb struggled to get the words out.

Rylen took a moment to think about her next words. "Caleb, if you could see what I see when you play the piano, you wouldn't think you play the way you do because you resent it. You play because you love the feeling you get when you sit at that bench, when your fingers touch those keys, or when you compose something that allows the audience to feel as you do. You play because when you sit down you can see your mother watching you, and she's not blaming you. She's praising what you've been able to accomplish in a short amount of time."

"I'm a horrible person, Rylen. Why don't you see that?"

"Caleb, if I were to describe you I'd use the words compassionate, honest, loyal, boundless, colorful, courageous, and beautiful. That's you." She placed her hand on his heart. "You're not a killer, Caleb. No five-year-old is."

"So you understand me better. Now what?"

"We go back to bed. You have nothing to be ashamed of." She kissed the palm of his hand.

"But —" Caleb was confused. She now knew his darkest secret. Why was she not taking all this seriously? "You just heard me, right?"

"Right."

"Why back to bed then?" he asked, confused at the suggestion.

"Because I want to wake up with you, and everything is better when you're in bed."

"Why are you not taking this seriously?"

She cupped his face, leaning in to kiss him on the tip of his nose. "I understand all of you now, and I'm not running away. You can try, but I'm not going anywhere. What's wrong with having one person in the world that understands you and still loves you?" she arched her brows. "Nothing." She stood and offered him her hand. "Now, let's go to bed and wake up together."

Caleb was exhausted. His resolve was draining, and his walls were melting away. The things she was saying were hitting home in a way that nothing he told himself ever could. He needed to wrap his head around the concept that he wasn't the result of his mother's demise. He loved her and she him, he knew that much. Rylen was telling him the truth. She would never lie to him like he recklessly did to her.

Caleb thought back to his diagnosis. The weight of it was deadly, but that was certainly a secret he would struggle with and take to his grave. He didn't want her thinking in terms of days. He wanted to live uninhibited and to spend as much time as he could with her. She could very well be his miracle.

However, Caleb reeled with the realization that this dream may come to an end. That Rylen would finally find out what he had been keeping from her for so long. He didn't even want to imagine the look on her face when he told her the news. He had allowed her to fall in love with him. He had taken advantage of her feelings. He was going to die, and it couldn't be helped. She would hate him for bringing her into his life when his life was to be cut short, but she had said it herself: Caleb would rather have the experience of love than the heartache of letting it pass him by without knowing what it felt like.

Caleb stared at her hand; there was nothing in the world that was going to stop him from taking it. A weight lifted and his mind felt a little less cluttered. His heart was full. So this was what it was like to be in love. He took her hand to start the day anew.

She flashed a smile. "I'm staying right here, Caleb. Remember that. I don't care what's wrong with you," she said, her eyes conveying more than her words. He searched them, his body freezing at the implication and suddenly he saw the truth. She knew what she was getting into. Knew about the disease that was taking his strongest articulation of expression. How did she know? Dominic would never have told her. Suddenly, it didn't matter. He didn't care how she knew. She just did. She pulled his face to hers and kissed him with the promise of many tomorrows. "You ready to go to bed now?" she asked breathlessly, biting his ear lobe.

Caleb felt the loneliness that once threatened to crush him retreat completely. Now all he saw was a life filled with unimaginable happiness and adventure. His arms reached around her body and pulled her close to him. The sun was peeking over the trees, and the flowers around the gazebo were getting visits from the butterflies. He reached his hand out as a monarch fluttered around them and landed on his index finger.

"Would you rather be a butterfly or a star?" Caleb asked, wondering if, when a person passed from this life, he came back to shine light down on the Earth or got to wisp through it on the breeze.

"Both are beautiful," she said as she stared at the butterfly hovering on Caleb's finger. "Long as you're next to me it doesn't matter." She smiled as the butterfly flew away.

"I'll remember how beautiful this day is till the day I die," he said, his eyes twinkling.

Doing as Rylen wished, Caleb finally took her back to bed. They lay down next to each other and just held hands, smiling. He rolled over atop her, supporting himself above her.

"What?" she asked in response to his odd look.

"Thank you for loving me," he said in all seriousness.

The look on his face pained her. He acted as if it were a surprise anyone could love him, but it was more difficult not to love this man. She knew. She had tried.

"You act as if I had a choice." She smiled, caressing his cheek, smoothing over his doubt. "It took you long enough to figure out you loved me. I was just waiting for you."

"I found that, if you try and rush it, it won't be worth remembering." He slowly lowered himself to her. "Marry me," he said.

"Are you serious?" she asked.

"I wouldn't ask if I weren't. Marry me, Rylen."

"What makes you think I even like you?" she grinned.

"Hmm," he paused, leaning down to kiss her neck. "Do you want me to stop?" he asked, his face buried in her neck.

"Yes," she murmured.

He laughed pulling back. "Really?"

"No. I mean yes."

"This whole scene went a little more smoothly and seemed more romantic when played out in my head," he said.

Rylen laughed and ran her fingers through his hair. "I'm answering you," she paused. "Yes."

"You know what marrying me is going to mean?" he asked, not waiting for her to respond. "It means you're going to have to love me forever."

"Only forever?"

"Does that not work for you?" he laughed.

"I'm going to let you in on a little secret," she pulled his head down to hers and whispered in his ear, "I started loving you a long time ago, and I haven't stopped yet."

"That makes two of us," he said.

He didn't need to say it. All was evident in the way he looked at her, the song he wrote for her, the way he kissed her, and how he made love to her. In everything he did, it was evident he loved her. And she loved him.

Chapter Twenty-Two

*T*he baby cried, and Dominic could feel Ashley begin to roll out of bed. "No," he said, popping up, "I'll get him. You go back to bed."

"Are you sure?"

"No," he answered truthfully and left the comfort of the bed. Trudging down the hall, Dominic opened the door to the shrieking baby and gathered him up to quiet his rambunctious lungs. Arnie pushed his head against Dominic's leg. Dominic absently patted the dog's head and took the baby downstairs to the kitchen to warm up some milk.

"Why are you being so loud at this time of night?" he asked, his voice an octave above normal. Baby talk was not as foreign to him as he thought it would be. Grabbing one of the numerous bottles from the refrigerator, Dominic set to warming up the milk and bouncing the baby in his arms. He leaned into the fragrant remnants of the coffee left in the cup to help keep his eyes open.

"Arnie go get the door," he instructed him.

The child was starting to calm down as the bottle got closer to his mouth, then, sweet silence. Dominic sighed with relief and cradled the baby in his arms as he continued down the hall. Arnie stood in the doorway waiting for them.

Everything had been set up for ease and accessibility, the machines on the left side, closest to the patio door; the right side, where Caleb slept, empty. It was odd how serene he looked, lying there while Dominic held the child.

"Do you mind if we sleep in here with you tonight?" he asked Arnie. Caleb's sidekick had not left his side since they transferred him back home from the hospital, machines in tow. Arnie whined and jumped on the bed, lying at Caleb's feet. "Thanks," Dominic said, sliding in bed next to them.

He was careful to place the baby in between their bodies so the tiny thing couldn't roll anywhere.

Leaning on his elbow, Dominic rubbed the baby's belly to help soothe him, coaxing him into sleep for another four hours until hunger would again awaken him. Cuddling up to the baby, Dominic moved them closer to Caleb and grabbed his hand, placing it on the baby's belly. Lying there, he watched the two as they slept.

Was this it? This was the main reason Dominic couldn't bring himself to pull the plug, to let his brother just disappear. A child was now involved, and he wanted Caleb to meet him. The baby whimpered as Dominic's hand tired and the bottle fell from his lips. Righting the bottle, the baby resumed eating, and Dominic lay his head down on the pillow, looking past the child at Caleb. He wanted a sign. Something to tell him it was okay to let go, to do the unthinkable, but all he heard was silence.

Just before drifting back off to sleep, he saw the chessboard with Caleb's black King surrounded by his own white pieces. There was only one thing left to do now.

Chapter Twenty-Three

For once it wasn't the sun streaming through the blinds that woke Caleb. He had slept through the night. In fact, since that night a month ago that he had professed his love to Rylen, he'd slept every night. His normally tired body was awakened and invigorated by her spirit. He was a fool to let her pass him by.

Caleb squinted, his face planted in the pillow. He wasn't ready for the day. He wanted a few more moments to let everything he had been feeling sink in, but his body wouldn't fall back into slumber. Waking up early didn't bother him so much anymore. Now was the time to delight in all the things he had previously cast aside; things he never thought he'd get a chance to do. The disease still clung to him, but the muddled voices had finally subsided. He had a new lease on life with the only person he wanted to share it with.

Caleb turned on his side, propping his head up on his hand. He smiled seeing her there by his side. He brushed her hair back from her face as he listened to her even breathing. Every morning he awoke and made sure she was there. He knew she would be, but he had this eerie feeling it was all a dream, and he would wake up without her. She'd be gone as if a figment of his imagination. He traced his finger down her cheek, leaning in to kiss her lips gently so as not to wake her. She stirred, and he lay back running his fingers down her arm to her stomach. She flinched at the feel of his soft palm making contact with her bare skin. As he was about to lean in and kiss her, his breath hitched and his head exploded with rancorous thunder, the buzzing drowning out her steady breath. He flew up in bed grabbing his head and crying out in pain. Rylen slept soundly while the pain gripped him as never before. Startled by the brutality of the attack, Caleb rolled off the bed onto all fours trying to crawl away from the noise, but there was nowhere he could hide.

"Checkmate."

The voice sounded familiar, but it was hard to decipher through the noise in his head. Caleb was soaked, his hair plastered to his head. The buzzing was unrelenting as it coursed through his body making him vomit.

"It's time."

"You're sure?"

"No, but I'm not going to put him through this any longer."

A pulse of electricity shot through his body. Images of past memories flashed across his mind and weighted him down. He fell, limply, against the ground able neither to move nor cry out for help.

He was driving. The back windows were down. The music blared, and Rylen giggled next to him. He grabbed her hand in his and smiled. Everything felt right, and they were happy. The glare of the ring on his left hand, a new addition, gave him pause. He glanced over at her hand, her matching ring glistening in the afternoon sunshine. They were married.

A song came on, and Caleb belted it out, his vocals subpar compared to his compositions. Rylen laughed harder, joining in. The rearview mirror reflected his eyes, happy and full of life.

It all happened so fast. The smiles disappeared, and his own horror was reflected in Rylen's face. There was no way around it. The car was barreling straight at them, and Caleb did the only thing he could. He turned the car so that his side would take the brunt of the damage. He reached out for her, but the force of the impact launched his head into the window. His head exploded in pain, and the airbags rushed toward him. Everything around him disappeared. Air was replaced with fast rushing water. Music was replaced by a horrific buzzing static sound. The blood rushed to his head. Upside down, he could feel the pain of the impact, but he couldn't see anything. Then, as the water slowly engulfed him, the pain seeped away.

"Wake up. Wake up. This is a dream. I'm lying in bed next to my fiancé, not drowning in a car. Wake up."

In accordance with his wishes, Caleb no longer gasped for air. He was now standing in his bedroom. The horrible scene vanished, and another played out in front of him. He was standing at the foot of a hospital bed, or at least he thought he was; yet not only was he standing there, but he was also lying in bed. Frantic, he looked around and saw that Rylen was in a hospital bed next to his. Their hands were intertwined, and both were breathing through machines.

"What is this?" he cried, looking around for anyone that could give him answers. Caleb stumbled up to the bed, reaching out for Rylen, but he couldn't grasp her.

"But -" Then the room changed.

He was still in bed, but now it was his own bedroom, and Dominic stood vigil at his side, holding his hand. Next to him stood Ashley, her hand in his, staring down at Caleb's body. The machines drew Caleb's attention as they continued to beep, the ventilator making his chest rise and fall. Most importantly, Rylen wasn't in the room with them.

"I know it's hard, Dominic, but there hasn't been any activity for months now. We both know he's not here anymore."

"I know," Dominic said. He lowered his head, staring down at Caleb's body. Tears ran down his face, falling on his hand. "I've made my decision," he took a deep breath. "It's time."

"Time for what, Dominic?" Caleb tried to ask. "Time for what?" He looked at Ashley for an answer, but she made no response.

"Do you want to be alone?" she asked.

"Yes, please," he turned and kissed her. Behind her, the door closed, and Dominic remained where he stood.

"What's happening here?" Caleb rushed over to the other side of the bed, peering into Dominic's eyes. "I'm right here, buddy. Look at me!"

Dominic slumped down into the chair next to Caleb, his elbows resting on the side of the bed. He clasped his hand tightly in Caleb's, lightly kissing the fingertips, never seeing or hearing Caleb's pleas for help.

"Just so you know, dad was here. He said his goodbyes yesterday, he didn't want to be here for this. He loves you. Just be aware of that." Dominic held back some tears as he continued, "Caleb, you have to know, I don't want to do this. You have to forgive me. Please, God...this is the hardest thing I've ever had to do."

The tears poured down his face more quickly now. A sob like Caleb had never heard before escaped from his brother. He had never seen Dominic like this and wished never to see it again. He wanted it all to stop.

Dominic leaned over and pressed a kiss to Caleb's cheek. He lingered there for a moment before he turned and whispered in his ear, "I love you, brother. Be at peace, but if you could do me one last thing. Please...wake up." Dominic rose to attention and took the black King between his thumb and index finger. "Checkmate," he said, laying it down on its side.

Caleb gasped for air and awoke in a puddle of his own perspiration. He cried out, flying forward out of bed. Rylen roused next to him and sat up alongside him as he tried to get his breath back.

"Caleb, are you okay?" she asked concerned.

She caressed the side of his face. He grabbed her hand and studied her, making sure she was real. "Just a nightmare is all," he said reassuring her.

They both lay back down, cuddling and facing each other, their fingers intertwined. "You're sure?" she asked.

"Yes," he smiled running his hand down her arm. "Have I told you that I love you yet this morning?" he asked.

"I love you, too," she grinned leaning in and kissing him sweetly on the lips. Caleb reached his arms around her and pulled her close, deepening the kiss, never wanting to let her go.

"We should stay in bed today," he said against her cheek.

"Maybe," she said, her mouth next to his ear, "but you need to wake up first."

"I thought I was," he laughed pulling back to see her beautiful face.

"Checkmate," she said, her blue eyes burning into his.

Chapter Twenty-Four

Caleb's body took one last breath, and then it was still. It had taken him awhile, but Dominic had finally given Caleb the peace he deserved. The tubes and machines were no longer in the room. A group of men had come and gathered them up. In his mind, Dominic could still hear the beep of the flat line as he watched Caleb's chest rise one last time. He flinched, knowing it was completely over. His best friend, his brother, was now dead, and he was all alone. His one and only fear had become reality. The room was eerily silent except for Dominic's strangled cries. When Caleb's heart had stopped, Dominic's stopped with it. He was cold from head to toe, and he wanted nothing more than to trade places with Caleb. Yet, he must go on. Dominic now had two families to care for—his own and Caleb's.

The baby monitor lit up with the shrill screams of an angry baby. Ashley wiped a few tears, took a deep breath, and grabbed the door handle. Arnie came to attention, but instead of going to Ashley's side, he jumped onto the bed and lay curled up along Caleb.

The screams got louder, and Arnie whined. Ashley's tears began to stream again as Dominic clutched Caleb's hand in his. His knuckles were turning white from holding on so tightly. Realizing he could be crushing Caleb's hand, he relieved the pressure and let go for the last time.

EEEEEEEEEEEEEEEEEEEEEEEEEEEEEEEEEEEEEEEEEEEEEEEEEE EEE!

The alarm clock went off, startling both Dominic and Ashley. Dominic reached out to quiet the alarm, when suddenly, Caleb's body shot up in bed like a missile, his eyes fluttering open as he gasped for breath.

Dominic jumped back from the bed, and Ashley screamed in astonishment. Dominic looked to Ashley who stood by the doorway, her hand over her mouth, unmoving. "Caleb?" Dominic exhaled, wondering if this was something bodies did postmortem. "Caleb, can you hear me?" Dominic choked out, falling into the chair beside the bed, crushing Caleb's hand with his strength.

Caleb didn't move he remained transfixed on the windows across from him. Slowly, he started to fall back against the bed, his body void of any strength to keep upright after months of being bedridden.

Caleb opened his mouth to speak, but his throat was raw. "Give him some water," Ashley said, rushing to their side to help. Dominic poured him a healthy glass of water and shakily brought it to Caleb's lips to help soothe his aching throat.

An overwhelming happiness spiraled through Dominic at seeing Caleb's eyes open. He could barely contain his tears. But, with the happiness came a sense of sadness. Dominic was going to have to tell Caleb about Rylen and the baby.

"Caleb, there's so much to tell you. I don't even know where to begin."

"Give him a minute, Dominic," Ashley urged.

Glass upon glass of water disappeared before Caleb was finally able to speak his first words in months. "The end," he choked out.

Dominic poured another glass, but Caleb pushed it away. Leaning back in his chair, the anticipation and the shock was just too much for Dominic to handle. The baby cried again, and Ashley went rushing out of the room. Arnie nuzzled closer to Caleb, licking the side of this face. Caleb barely reacted. Normally he would have laughed and pushed Arnie away. Now, he turned his head and looked at the faithful mutt.

"Hi," he said.

Arnie whined and placed his head on Caleb's chest. Dominic watched the rise and fall of Caleb's chest, making sure that what he was witnessing was real and not his imagination running wild.

"Dom," Caleb whispered. Dominic shook himself from his haze to see Caleb watching him. "What's going on?" Caleb asked, needing to know why he felt as though his body had been through the ringer.

"I don't even know how to say it out loud," Dominic replied.

Walking into the room with a bundle cradled in her arms, Ashley bounced the baby to keep him quiet. The baby stretched, making a little noise that grabbed Caleb's attention.

"Ashley," he said.

"It's nice to see you, Caleb," she smiled.

He squinted at her to make sure his eyes weren't deceiving him. "You're pregnant," he said, turning to Dominic to make sure he was correct.

"About to pop," Dominic laughed, leaning in and trying to gather the strength to tell his brother the news. "She has something for you," he said.

Ashley approached the side of the bed and sat on the edge. "Meet your son," she said.

"What?" Caleb asked, confused. Arnie moved from Caleb's chest down to Ashley. Caleb sat up, with Dominic's help, placing a few pillows behind his back. "I don't understand," he whispered, gazing at the child with dark brown hair and bright blue eyes.

"I told you. There's a lot to tell you," Dominic said, taking the baby from Ashley's arms and holding him out to Caleb. Caleb leaned back, afraid to touch the child, but Dominic insisted.

Without being given an answer, Dominic placed the baby in Caleb's arms. The weight was too much for his atrophied muscles, but Dominic sat on the bed to keep the baby positioned comfortably. In that moment, Caleb should have had Rylen with him, but Dominic had yet to drop the bomb. Watching Caleb with his child brought more tears to Dominic's eyes. What was before him was truly a miracle.

The baby felt heavy in Caleb's arms like a foreign object. He'd never held a baby before. "What's his name?"

"He's kind of nameless right now. We've just been calling him baby."

"Why haven't you named him?"

"Because he's not ours to name."

"I'll leave you two alone," Ashley said, getting up and closing the door behind her.

"Caleb," Dominic said, kneeling beside the bed, "didn't you know?"

Caleb glanced up at Dominic wide-eyed and awestruck. "I don't know. I think so."

He strained to remember, "Maybe," he swallowed hard. "Where's Rylen?"

This was the moment he had been dreading. Now he had to divulge the truth, and it was going to hurt more than letting his brother go, because now he had to see him in pain.

"She didn't make it, Caleb," he whispered.

"Make it home? What?"

"She didn't make it through the accident. I tried. I swear I did, but she had a DNR in place. The doctors kept her alive until the child was viable."

Caleb opened his mouth to speak but clamped it shut. Behind his eyes, his mind was reeling with the realization that Rylen wouldn't share their bed together. She wouldn't get to see their child grow up. She'd never play the cello again. She was gone.

"Was it the accident?"

"You remember the accident?" Dominic asked surprised.

"Just bits. Someone struck us. The inside of the car exploded, and I couldn't find her. Then everything was wet."

"Your car flipped several times until you wound up in the lake. The rescue workers got you both out in time, but neither of you woke up. There was no brain function," he said quietly. "Then, with Rylen pregnant, we all made the decision to keep her body on life support until the birth," he gulped. "She held him. I made sure of it."

"I couldn't protect her," Caleb mumbled, more to himself. "She's gone," he said, looking down at their creation.

"But you're still here and your son is healthy and beautiful."

A sad smile spread across Caleb's face. "He's your son. You've been able to know and love him longer than I have."

"He has you now," Dominic said scared.

"Sure," Caleb said.

~

The tension could have been sliced with a knife. Caleb stared out over the lake, petting Arnie who was relishing every minute of it. He looked battered and beaten up, but he was alive. Though Dominic wasn't sure if Caleb was present or trying to remember the past, his brother did seem more relaxed now that they were outside by the water and surrounded by Eden.

Inside, Ashley watched the baby, and Dominic wasn't sure how the rest of this was going to play out. Was Caleb going to take responsibility and try to get better, or was he going to fall back into old habits? It was hard to believe that Dominic's prayers had finally been answered. They sat on the beach, Eden blossoming behind them, but even though Dominic's prayers were answered, Caleb's weren't.

"You're going to have a baby." Caleb still couldn't believe the news. Dominic had filled Caleb in on Ashley's journey through pregnancy and their subsequent reunion. "You'll be a great father."

"You have a baby," Dominic reminded him. "Mine's not even here yet, and I'm scared as hell, Caleb. Who would have thought?"

"When you guys got married you planned on having a family. Why is it so astonishing to you now?" Caleb asked.

"Because she left me. I never imagined things panning out the way they have."

"Nothing goes according to plan. If it did, she'd -" Caleb choked up, not finishing his thought.

"I want you to be the Godfather." Caleb coughed and shivered under the blanket. Dominic wrapped his arm around him and drew him closer. "I'm serious," he said when Caleb didn't answer.

"I know you are, but Dominic –"

"There's no one else I would choose. You're it, Caleb."

Caleb started thinking about being a Godfather, about being a father, but he didn't have the heart to tell Dominic he didn't think he'd make it to see his new Godson, that he wouldn't be around to take care of his own son. His body had developed pneumonia, and Caleb knew better than to imagine a future he couldn't see. He wasn't necessarily falling into old habits of pessimism, but Caleb knew his body. It didn't feel right.

"Can I ask you a serious question?" Caleb pondered.

"Sure, shoot."

"I want you and Ashley to take care of him for me," he said.

"That wasn't a question."

"Alright, then it's an instruction. I need you two to take care of our baby."

"Caleb, he's your son, why wouldn't you want to –"

The look Caleb gave him was one of regret; regret that he'd never have the family he dreamt of, the woman he loved with him as their son grew to be a man; regret that he'd never play the piano again.

"I need to know that you'll take care of him, that Rylen's family will be a part of his life. That in every way he's your son."

"Can we talk about this later? I don't like where this is going. Besides, he needs a name," Dominic said, changing the subject.

Caleb paused for a long moment, recalling the memory of them lying in the Botanical Gardens discussing the number of children they'd have. "We never discussed it," he exhaled with a smile. "It's for you to decide. Tell him about his mother. How beautiful and caring she was. And that I loved her so much I couldn't breathe without her. Tell him every day how much we loved him and how much you and Ashley love him. Give him what we can't."

"I don't know what I could give him that you can't," Dominic questioned.

"A family. Give him a family."

Chapter Twenty-five

Caleb wanted to purge everything, to tell her what he had left unsaid. Possessed, words turned into sentences and sentences into tears. The tears spilled faster than he could wipe them away and fell upon the paper. When his hand finally came to a rest, Caleb gazed at his creations.

Dear Rylen -

I wake up, and the first thing I see is your smile, even when you're not next to me. Your breath caresses my ear as you whisper that you love me from the deepest crevice of your heart. The touch of your skin on mine makes me shiver with anticipation of your next touch and the thousand touches after that. Your eyes make me feel a warmth I never thought I could feel as the deep blue lets me lose myself in them and drowns me with the possibilities. Possibilities of what is to come next. How lucky am I that I found you? Is it even luck? Or was it God's will that led you to my heart and allowed you to plunder my soul? Even when you're not here, I dream of you, and it makes me weep. I weep knowing that we lost our time together, but then I wipe my tears and remind myself that we have forever. You are my forever.

Loving you was the easiest decision I have ever made and, yet, the hardest. And it wasn't really a decision but a moment in time where things fell into place. The planets must have aligned. I never knew my life wasn't complete until I saw you on that stage. My heart is still aching to seek and I may no longer breathe without breathing in you. E.E. Cummings wrote a poem that I think sums up everything I have to say.

> I carry your heart with me
> (I carry it in my heart)
> I am never without it
> (anywhere I go you go, my dear; and whatever is done
> by only me is your doing, my darling)

I love you, Rylen, and thank you for our son. I wish you could have met him, he's beautiful and has your smile. You will be with me forever, and forever isn't even long enough.

Sleep Sweet,
Caleb

Caleb kissed the letter, imagining it was Rylen he was kissing goodbye. He folded it up and stuffed it in the envelope Dominic had given him. The letter to Rylen was the easiest. He'd had time to get to know her, fall in love, and create a child together. Now, he had to write a letter to his son, and he had no idea where to begin.

Dominic and Ashley had left him alone with the baby. They sat on the bed together and, in a sense, composed the letter to Rylen together. His love for her was amplified while their child lay next to him. Putting the pen and paper down, Caleb gathered the child into his arms and cradled him against his chest. When he held their baby, he could feel her. He couldn't protect her, but by making sure their son was taken care of, he was securing the tiny child's future. Dominic and Ashley could give the baby the life Caleb and Rylen never would. Caleb knew all too well he could barely protect himself.

The blanket gathered up around the baby's face and Caleb pushed it down to see his son's beautiful face, a face eerily similar to Rylen's. The little guy was her child through and through. His blue eyes shone up at his father, and even though his mother and father both had blue eyes, Caleb could tell they were Rylen's. The only feature Caleb could take credit for was the baby's long, skinny fingers.

"I wish things could be different," Caleb said, "but the only thing I can tell you that will never waiver is my love for you. I love you and I know she loves you."

Looking down at the product of his love for Rylen, Caleb could have no true regrets about the life he had lived. The paths he ventured were of his own choosing. The paths he followed and paved allowed him to see new things, have new experiences, and meet new people who have forever changed him. He was not regretful. He was thankful. For he lived the life he imagined, though he had faltered more than once, he was proud of what he had done.

And then there was Rylen. He chose not to regret what he didn't have. If he decided to regret his decisions he would ultimately start to regret his life. He could not, and would not, regret it.

Caleb's journey was not about following a pre-ordained path but creating a path. Nothing made sense in this life or the next. What did make sense was the beat of the heart and the music that comes from it. It chose the path. He was finally able to stop resisting, and with that, his journey unfolded in a beautifully unique way. And it was still unfolding, giving him new avenues of expression without music.

Why live life afraid of the unseen? Focusing on the obstacles dishonored the life by ignoring its value. Caleb couldn't be afraid. He refused to be afraid, though it seemed to be the next logical step.

Caleb gazed down at his child, and even though he was feeling a range of emotions, he had no idea how to put them down on paper. He looked away before he could cry and saw the picture of himself with Rylen under the crabapple trees at the Botanical Gardens. Carefully, he put the baby down next to Arnie and took the picture out of the frame. On the back, he wrote "We will always love you" before shoving it in the envelope along with the sheet music to "Sleep Sweet." It was all he could give the child since he refused to give him a name. Without Rylen there, he simply couldn't preform such an intimate task.

The envelope sat on the end table next to the empty picture frame and Caleb decided it was time. Leaning down, he kissed his baby boy one last time. "You're my miracle, and if you can remember to do one thing for me, I'd appreciate it." He pressed his lips lightly against the boy's forehead, and inhaling the pure, unique smell associated with babies, he smiled. "Be like your mother," Caleb said before he sent Arnie to retrieve Dominic.

"What are you thinking about?" Dominic asked, carrying Caleb back out to the beach. "Just how happy I am for you."

Dominic looked as if he wanted to say something, but didn't know how to say it. Sitting Caleb back down on the blanket, Dominic sat next to him. Caleb knew that Dominic needed to know more, a desire to know the truth about what happened behind Caleb's closed eyes.

"You want to know more about my coma?" he took a deep breath. "I heard you. It was like a train going through a tunnel in my head, but I could hear you sometimes. I didn't necessarily know it was you, but there were voices."

"So you knew what was going on?"

"No, because I was too busy reliving the past. It began with the start of the concert series in Chicago. I was reliving all those memories, but sometimes I could hear the voices of the people around, then I'd just pick right back up where I left off."

"What would you have done in my shoes? Let me go?"

"Maybe." Caleb rubbed the sides of Arnie's body and kissed him on the top of the head. "I do know one thing," he paused, "I would have beaten you in chess." They laughed.

"Only in your dreams, buddy," his said, his laugh dwindling off.

"What I felt was real. It was all real. And then, in the middle of all that, this buzzing noise would interrupt, and I could hear your chess moves or what everyone in the room was talking about."

Moments passed before they spoke to each other again. Caleb let his mind wander caressing Arnie's slim body, remembering the feel of Arnie's soft coat of fur and foul odor of dog breath. He could feel his time left was short, and he wanted to enjoy the simple things.

"You wouldn't be able to beat me, even if I were in a coma," Dominic informed him.

"I suck at chess," Caleb sighed. "Teach him how to play," Caleb said. "Teach him how to live, not exist."

Dominic drew the blanket tighter around Caleb's shoulders. "It's getting cold. Do you want to go in?"

"Just a little while longer. I want to see the stars." Arnie licked his hand, moving closer to Caleb. He was going to miss this. "You know I love you, right?" Caleb asked, unsure if he'd told the people around him what they really meant to him enough.

Dominic glowed next to him. "I know. I never questioned that. I love you too, bro." He put his arm around Caleb's shoulder and sat idly, watching the calmness of the lake lap onto the shore.

"I wanted to make sure I said it out loud." Caleb looked down at Arnie. "Love you too, big fella." Arnie barked in response. Caleb sighed and leaned back on Dominic's shoulder, keeping the blanket close around him and the warmth from Arnie and Dominic at his side.

"When you leave, can you do me a favor?" Dominic asked.

"Hmm?"

"Please don't say goodbye. I don't want to know," he pleaded, afraid of being faced with knowing it was going to happen. He just wanted to sit there and not worry about it.

"I can do that. Since you asked so nicely." Tears shined in Dominic's eyes as Caleb snuggled into his shoulder.

"That almost feels like goodbye," Dominic whispered.

"Na, it's just me cuddling," he laughed. "Tell Ashley I'm sorry."

"You did nothing wrong. It was my decision."

"If I was a better brother, I wouldn't have allowed you to make it."

"I'm the oldest, I make up my mind," he said. "And you were the best brother anyone could have asked for. I got to see the world because of you, which lead me to Ashley. I have a family because of you. So don't say things like that, mule."

"Nag," Caleb chuckled.

As the sun neared oblivion for the day, Caleb thought about his life. He had been given a gift. He used it. People listened. For the longest time he breathed through his music, lived through it, even though he thought he hated the piano, he truly loved it. He forced himself to play because he felt obligated to mother, but during that time, he fell in love with it because his mother loved the music. No matter how many times he said he was never going to play again, that he hated the sight of it, he continued to play.

Then, like a breath of fresh air, she came into his life, and he was able to breathe and live on his own for once. He was uninhibited by the music that he allowed to be his only source of happiness. And even though it was short lived, he was able to open up and allow what he had denied himself for so long. His dreams were so powerful that they gripped his heart, his soul.

The Huntington's Disease didn't beat him. He beat it, even though it still ravaged his body. In the end, he didn't allow it to take anything away from him. What finally beat him? A broken heart, and this he chose not to fight, because now he knew where he belonged—at her side.

In this world Caleb was given many things to believe in. Most of the time he forgot to believe in the most important thing—himself. Caleb was given opportunities, whether they presented themselves or he was able to make them. Caleb wanted and needed to believe in. Anything that would push him to be better, stronger, smarter, kinder; to be who he has so many times dreamt he could be. The person he was meant to be. The person he was inside.

Rylen was brought into his life to help reawaken him so his mind and body could become one again, giving him a chance at love and peace, a chance at life. But Caleb had turned his back, afraid of how he might feel, believing what had been put in front of him was not for him to take. He did not put faith in the unseen. He sacrificed himself in believing what happened to his mother was his doing and, in effect, the disease was his punishment. In fact, it had been the first stage in his reawakening process.

Caleb found his way and changed his course, having finally found his way. He found the Eden he dreamt about with the woman he feared to love.

In the grand scheme of things life shouldn't be about what he hadn't done, but about what he had accomplished and the people he loved. Some days he needed to stop asking what comes next and just live the life he had. Caleb was lucky enough to touch his dreams, when others don't get that opportunity. The tragedy would be lying awake at night thinking what if. It was now time to look at what was in front of him and not dwell on what waited. Sometimes the ocean engulfs him, other times he engulfed the ocean.

The sun was now completely below the trees. Caleb's breathing and heart rate started to slow in rhythm with the lap of the waves. Mind and body were as one while he watched a wave race on shore toward his toes, touching them ever so gently and receding back to its home. The faint sound of seagulls departing for the night and Arnie's whines in his lap put him at peace. Then, he saw her.

"Checkmate," he mumbled.

Angelic, in a white flowing dress that kissed her ankles as she approached, her hair blew behind her, and her eyes still made him want to drift away. Caleb glanced up at her, wondering if she were a manifestation of his sadness or the indication it was finally his time. Dear God, let her be real. Rylen held her hand out to him, and when he worked his way up to her face, she smiled. Caleb couldn't help but reach out to take it. Her hand was as he remembered, soft and warm to the touch. And then she spoke, her voice like the sunrise.

"Do you hear that? It's our song."

He listened, and sure enough, "Sleep Sweet" was playing, rising from the waves on the night's breeze, gliding down from the wings of the seagulls. Caleb grasped her hand fully and was lifted from his body.

"You're real," he whispered, caressing her cheek.

Arnie whined as he watched Caleb walk away. He whined because he knew he couldn't follow. Caleb and Rylen walked down the beach hand-in-hand, as if they never parted, together as one. Arnie put his head back down in Caleb's lap and took sanctuary in the last remaining heat in Caleb's body. He listened as Caleb's remaining breath escaped, never to return.

Caleb and Rylen walked until they were suddenly surrounded and engulfed in a white light. The beach slowly disappeared behind him, the sounds quieting and his life fading away. Caleb turned to take one last look at Dominic and Arnie. Seeing them, he shed a tear. They were now his past, and his unknown future lay ahead of him.

"Caleb, now is the time to look ahead, not back." She wiped the tear from his cheek and kissed his lips, trying to make the transition easier on him.

It was because of Dominic and Arnie that Caleb was able to leave everyone behind. They made him into the man he was. They took care of him when he couldn't take care of himself, and they helped him to believe. If Caleb thought he was only leaving them for his own personal reasons, he would not have taken Rylen's hand, but he took her hand because, deep down inside, Caleb knew it was time. Dominic and Arnie had each other. They would never be alone. Dominic was starting a family, a family that Arnie would happily be included in as would Caleb and Rylen's beautiful son. With those thoughts, Caleb was able to face what lay ahead of him. Eden stood before them, and as the white light blotted out the world he knew, the warmth welcomed him into the world he was about to know. It's because everything must end that everything is so beautiful.

Chapter Twenty-Six

*T*he wind was picking up, and though it was chilly, it was refreshing. Just sitting on the beach, watching the sun disappear over the waves calmed his nerves as if there was nothing to fear. Dominic took a deep breath and could be satisfied that everything was going to be alright. It had to be. His partner in crime was once again at his side. How close Dominic had come to losing his most trusted ally in this world and being the one to make the final decision to let him go. The thought was a pain he'd never known and wished to never know, Caleb was here now and that was all he could ask for.

"It's so peaceful out," he murmured, stealing a glance at Caleb.

The wind ran its gentle fingers through Caleb's hair as the color in his cheeks slowly receded. His eyes were closed, and his smile relaxed. And Dominic knew. Caleb's hand lay next to his side, palm up as if reaching for something. Arnie's head rested in his master's lap, waiting for Caleb to open his eyes. Those eyes would never open again. He was gone. This time, forever.

Caleb passed without pain or complaint. He looked truly happy sitting there on his patch of sand, his loving companion near, and his brother at his side, and the unknown ahead of him.

Maybe it wasn't truly unknown. There was a peace about Caleb that Dominic didn't understand. Weren't those faced with the unknown scared? That's when it hit Dominic. Caleb was smiling because he was finally with Rylen, and the prospect of going over to the other side was just too good to pass up. He had found the Eden he so wistfully spoke of. Dominic smiled through the tears that welled up in his eyes and looked to the sky. Shakespeare's words sprang to mind as the perfect farewell to his friend.

"And when he shall die, take him, and cut him out into little stars and he will make the face of heaven so fine, that the entire world will be in love with night and pay no worship to the garish sun."

At that moment, Dominic's mind didn't know how to process what had happened, but his heart told him exactly what to do. Dominic scooted over to Caleb and wrapped his arms around his brother. He held Caleb close to him, keeping his friend warm and close as he wept. "Thank you," he whispered into Caleb's ear. "You have given me more than I could ever have hoped for, and I pray that I'll see you again someday." Then he tightened his grip around Caleb's waist and waited for the stars to come out of their hiding place and shine down upon them. Caleb always loved the stars, and now he was among them. Because of that, Dominic knew he'd never be alone.

Oliver Wendell Holmes once said: "Many people die with their music still in them. Too often it is because they are always getting ready to live. Before they know it, time runs out." *I agree with Holmes.*

Epilogue

Dawn was coming, Dominic could feel it. Glancing at the blinds he saw the dim beginnings of light. It was almost time. He loved the tribute, but he wished he didn't have to do it. The evening before he had lain on the dock, his hands behind his head and his face turned up to the sky, watching the stars reveal themselves. He did this whenever he could. Sometimes, in the earlier days following Caleb's death, he would wake up realizing he had fallen asleep waiting for Caleb's star to appear. Now he had the luxury of coming home to a warm bed, an incentive he relished.

He tiptoed to the blinds and parted them to look out at the trees and the lake just beyond the vast Garden of Eden. The upkeep was a pain, but Dominic determined he was never going to allow Eden to be over ridden with weeds. It would continue to grow and thrive. Caleb's memory was living on with every blossoming bud.

The floorboards creaked under his weight as he made his way into the kitchen. Dishes from the previous evening's dinner sat in the sink. Dog food littered the floor, and hand prints dirtied the front of the refrigerator.

The stove burner came to life, a pan for the eggs waiting at the ready, the toaster fed wheat toast that only needed some grape jelly to make it edible. Putting on a pot of coffee, Dominic got breakfast ready for the two for them. She'd need some tea since he'd kept her awake tossing and turning all night. He always slept uneasily on the eve of their tribute, the anniversary of Caleb and Rylen's union.

Footsteps crept across the floor overhead and quietly down the stairs.

"Morning," he mumbled gruffly.

"Hi, sweetie," she leaned in and kissed him grabbing the tea cup from behind his back.

"Sorry about last night." He smirked over his cup, taking her free hand in his as he ran his fingers over her smooth skin, looking down at the ring that housed two birthstones now and a wedding band.

"It's okay. I understand."

He pulled her close to him, her breath a morning mixture of tea and toothpaste. "That's why I love you so much, Ash," he said, swelling with pride.

"I love you, too." She kissed him, and Dominic couldn't help but feel life was as it should be in some respects. They were meant to be together, and he had once almost thrown it away. Even to this day he apologized for the poor decisions that had long been forgiven.

Dominic stretched the sleep from his body as the toast popped from the toaster and the eggs started to sizzle on the stove. Ashley grabbed two plates and readied their breakfast while Dominic opened the door to listen to the birds awakening their little ones. He glanced over his shoulder at the piano and cello in the corner of the room and was greeted by the soft clicking of Arnie's nails as he trotted across the tile.

"Hey boy," Dominic greeted him.

Arnie nuzzled Dominic's leg while Dominic's hand fell absently to his side and rubbed Arnie's head. Both were aware of what the day represented, and both knew what they were to do for their tribute.

Every year they ventured down to the beach and waited for the sun to rise. Gathering up a bundle of wildflowers from his Eden, a place he loved, and placing them on a raft that they, as a family, would push out onto the lake to celebrate their life. A lit candle would shine in the middle until the flame was extinguished by the waves of the lake or the swoop of an eagle diving towards the water.

To most it was just another day, but not for Dominic. Since Caleb's passing he had tried to learn the lesson that Caleb had so unknowingly taught: death is not the greatest loss. The greatest loss is what dies inside ourselves while we live. And because of that lesson Dominic has been able to make each day his own, to live like it was the last and to wake up every morning grateful.

Dominic stepped out into the dawn. The sun was barely noticeable. The blanket of night was slowly receding, and nature was starting to blossom for a new day. Before, he never took notice of his surroundings, and now he couldn't help but notice the leaves changing color, the wind tickling the grass, and the miracle of a baby bird taking its first step out of the nest.

"You think it's time?" he asked Arnie. Arnie whined, licked his palm, and barked in response. "Then round up the troops." He dispatched Arnie to wake the household for their yearly tribute to Caleb and Rylen.

Arms wrapped around his waist, and the comforting smell of cinnamon intoxicated his senses. Her touch brought about a sensation in his body that only she could elicit, and the patter of little feet bounding down the stairs always uplifted him.

"They love this," she muttered against his shoulder as he turned his body into hers and cupped her face in his hands. His lips gently caressed hers in greeting.

Caleb had given Ashley and Dominic the authority to name his son. For days after the funeral, Dominic fought internally, decision weighing heavily on him. Jumping out of bed, Dominic woke Ashley to share with her his inspiration. There was only one name that would truly suit the boy and honor his parents. Caylen was the perfect combination and befitting in the young child's circumstance.

"I love them for doing this with us," he said, wrapping his arms around her. They turned in unison to see Caylen and Dorian bouncing into the room and launching themselves on to the couch with their faithful guard, Arnie, close behind.

Ashley and Dominic laughed watching Caylen and Dorian play with Arnie. Their little giggles brought life to the house.

Gathering them up, Dominic clung to his young sons who had come to mean the world to him. He never thought he could care for anyone more than he cared about Caleb, but he was wrong. Caylen was a perfect mixture of Caleb and Rylen, his blue eyes gleaming, a smile always on his face, and a love for music in his heart. Dorian had black hair like Dominic and green eyes like Ashley. Looking at the two of them gave Dominic chills. They resembled Caleb and Dominic in every way, and Dominic could only hope they'd be as close as their fathers once were.

His little family gathered and headed out down to the beach where Dominic had devised a little makeshift raft with the wildflowers that inhabit the gardens flanking the house that Caleb so loved. His Eden. In the middle, as was customary, Dominic lit a small candle, and all four of them, with Arnie's help, pushed the raft out into the lake.

Taking a seat on the beach, they watched the raft float farther and farther away as the sun started to rise. Then, as was customary, they'd have a picnic on the beach, fly a kite for Arnie to chase and tumble on the beach. They would create memories that their children would remember and pass on.

Dominic kissed his wife and wrapped his arms around her watching their sons chase after Arnie. "I think we should have 4 more," Dominic said.

Ashley laughed. "We'll talk about that the day you start giving birth."

"But you're so good at it," he said, running his hand over her stomach.

"Maybe one more after this one," she said.

"The more the better. Just need to make room on that ring," he laughed.

"At least this one will be a girl. Too much testosterone in the house."

"You're right. Arnie is full of himself," he laughed, kissing her.

Arnie came running with Caylen and Dorian chasing after him.

"Better get out of the way," Dominic informed her jumping out from behind Ashley and playfully tackling the boys. Ashley stood to the side running a hand over her stomach, their new addition just a month away from partaking in the tribute and Eden.

About the Author

$\mathcal{C}$ourtney Imbery is a noted playwright and author whose writing career began during her time as a member of the Second City comedy writing program. Her dramatic works have been showcased in the sketch production "Mom, Close the Door," performed by Second City as well as the 2007 community theatre production of "The Soon-to-Be In-Laws." She has twice been invited to participate in the popular 8-Minute Madness Festival held by Turtle Shell Productions. Courtney credits her work under the instruction of the late acclaimed writer and director Mary Scruggs as a vital part of her literary development.

"Sleep Sweet" is Ms. Imbery's first novel, and she looks forward to continuing her novel-writing career with the publication of her future works. A native of Northwest Ohio, she spent several years studying and writing in Chicago, Illinois, before returning to her hometown of Genoa, Ohio, to be near family. She spends her time working on future projects and enjoying her family who inspires and encourages her literary endeavors.

Printed in the United States
By Bookmasters